Rubies and Revenge

JUNKIN' JEWELRY MYSTERIES: BOOK 2

ANGELA McRAE

Rubies and Revenge

Junkin' Jewelry Mysteries™: Book 2

Red Adept Publishing, LLC

104 Bugenfield Court

Garner, NC 27529

https://RedAdeptPublishing.com/

Cover Art by Streetlight Graphics[1]

This is a work of fiction. Names, characters, places, and incidents either are the product of the author's imagination or are used fictitiously, and any resemblance to locales, events, business establishments, or actual persons—living or dead—is entirely coincidental.

---

1.   http://StreetlightGraphics.com

In Loving Memory of

Ruby Webster Powell and Doris Lee Howell

Chapter One

Grandma might have gotten run over by a reindeer, but on that Saturday morning in November, Frosty the Snowman was about to get creamed by a lead-footed golf cart driver at the Rockin' Roseland Holiday Bazaar and Christmas Extravaganza. Frosty lunged for the sidewalk, trailed by a festive-looking Santa and three elves. Blasts of loud, shrill whistles ensued, and a gray-haired man in a red vest appeared ready to have a meltdown that had nothing to do with snow.

"Slow down!" the man in the vest yelled. Official North Pole Volunteer was lettered on it.

Unrepentant, the laughing driver—perhaps having sampled some of the bazaar's famous volunteers-only eggnog—sped off and did doughnuts in front of the school gymnasium.

I was privy to the prebazaar revelry after pulling into one of the coveted VIP parking spots in the Lawrence J. Ellis Middle School lot, where I unloaded hampers brimming with my latest Emma Madison Designs jewelry. I piled the black canvas totes onto my collapsible rolling cart. The bazaar, held on the first Saturday in November each year, was the most highly anticipated event of the preholiday shopping season in Roseland, Georgia, and I was thrilled to have a booth for the third year in a row. Barely eight o'clock in the morning, it was almost two full hours before the show opened to the public, and I was eager to get my space set up.

"Are you an exhibitor?" The eager-looking teenage girl who approached me was adorable in her emerald-green elf costume.

"I sure am." I smiled. "Are you the volunteer checking me in?" In years past, a registration table had been prominently placed by the front door, but I hadn't yet spotted one that morning.

The chipper blond elf shook her head and pointed her giant faux candy cane in the direction of the Ellis Middle School cafeteria. "It's supposed to be in the eighties today, so we've moved it indoors, where there's air-conditioning. You'll see the check-in as soon as you enter, but we're available if you need any help getting your stuff inside."

Despite the heavy tote in the crook of my arm, I could manage. "I'm good. Thanks for offering, though."

She nodded and skipped away, no doubt in search of a needier vendor. Thanks to our unusually warm November temperatures, she and three of the other elves sported emerald-green flip-flops instead of boots.

My wardrobe was just as confused as that of the elves. I'd worn a red knit T-shirt and a matching lightweight shrug with a flashy new statement necklace featuring vintage ruby-colored rhinestones. And despite all that silly "Southern gals don't sweat—they glisten" nonsense, I was already sweating profusely. Maybe I was simply suffering from the holiday overload I always experienced whenever Halloween, Thanksgiving, and Christmas started bumping into one another.

My purse contained a few leftover pieces of my favorite Halloween candy, Goetze's Caramel Creams, which I'd caught on clearance the week before. It also held an invitation to a Thanksgiving tea at my friend Carleen's house, and I'd promised to take my secret-family-recipe pumpkin pie. Yet I was all dolled up in a glorified T-shirt masquerading as a Christmas sweater simply so that I could sell my latest jewelry designs at a Christmas bazaar in early November. It was utter madness. Not for the first time, I wondered why my town insisted on kicking off Christmas so early. No wonder folks had taken to saying, "Merry Hallowthanksmas."

But a chipper "Merry Christmas!" rang out as I entered the school. Santa Claus and his helpers from the North Pole were in fine festive form. They found my name on the list, checked me in with a swift "You're good to go!" and handed me a goodie bag. Santa said it was courtesy of the Happy Ho-Ho-Hometown program. *Clever.*

I peeked inside and spotted pens, pencils, notepads, sticky notes, two bottles of water, some packets of instant cocoa mix, a glittery red travel mug with the Happy Hometown logo on it, and some protein bars. Bazaar organizers had certainly upgraded the swag, and as a brand-spanking-new member of the Happy Hometown board, I was glad to see its logo splashed all over the place. I hoped it would help us get our name out to the community.

Apparently oblivious that a high of eighty-two was predicted for the day, the velvet-clad Santa welcomed everyone into a middle school that had magically morphed into a winter wonderland. A glance around the foyer revealed mountains of "snow"—fluffy piles of batting courtesy of the local quilt shop—that surrounded a small forest of towering Christmas trees, each one decorated in a different brilliant color of the rainbow. Someone with a fine sense of color harmony had ensured that the purple tree flowed into the blue tree, the turquoise tree, the green tree, and so on, all of them leading to one gigantic red tree decorated entirely with iridescent red-and-white candy cane ornaments.

As I struggled to wheel my stack of jewelry totes into the cafeteria while propping open the heavy double doors, I grabbed one of the middle totes, which was threatening to trigger a jewelry landslide. A cute brunette in a bright-green elf costume raced to open the door, ushered me through with a flourish, and plopped an oversized candy cane into my topmost tote as she cheerfully wished me a "rockin' Roseland Christmas!"

With a nod and a "Thanks," I looked past Santa's helper and entered the cafeteria. No school lunches were needed on a Saturday, so I was one of a hundred twenty-five exhibitors who had packed the space for the annual fundraiser for the Roseland Foster Parent Association. Fifty percent of admission proceeds went to the charity each year. And to ensure that our latest event was another resounding success, Miranda Hargrove, a newcomer to Roseland and the first executive director of the Happy Hometown program, was marching through the lunchroom with the military precision of a general commanding his troops in Normandy.

"Miranda, hi," I said. "I believe my booth is supposed to be—"

Her eyes shot to her list. "Madison, Emma. Row four, space nine."

I guess being your newest board member doesn't earn me any special privileges, huh?

She pointed her fuzzy-white-pom-pom-topped pen at the spot where I would set up shop for the day. "The other exhibitors are already in place, so please hurry up so that it doesn't look like there are any vacant spots. I don't want our visitors to think we weren't able to fill the show, because we most certainly were." She tossed her head, and her lush auburn locks fell in perfect spirals down her back and onto the red velvet of her Mrs. Santa costume, which had fluttery white feathers trimming the sleeves and hem.

I looked at my glittering red-and-green-rhinestone Christmas watch. "But the show doesn't start for another—"

Miranda strutted off before I could finish.

"Hour and forty-five minutes," I whispered as my artist friend Savannah Rogers walked up.

"The drill sergeant blow you off too?" Savannah cut her eyes in Miranda's direction.

"She's probably just busy getting everyone in place before the show opens." I propped my overloaded tower of totes against the nearest empty table and set down the one I'd been carrying, giving my aching limb some momentary relief.

"She might be busy, but that's no excuse for being rude." Savannah planted her hands on her hips as she surveyed the cafeteria, tracking Miranda's path through the room. Savannah and I served on the local arts council together, and her watercolor prints and note cards were always hugely popular items at the bazaar.

"I got my application in by the deadline, but she claims I left some line blank on the form this year and said I really should have been disqualified. And out of the *goodness of her heart*, she's letting me share a spot with the crochet club." Savannah wrinkled her nose. "Nothing against the crocheters, of course."

I stared at her. "You're kidding me, right?"

Miranda Hargrove had moved to Roseland from Rochester, New York, in August after being hired to launch the local chapter of the national Happy Hometown program, which had generated a lot of buzz for helping downtowns all across the country flourish. City leaders had hoped she would bring some fresh ideas to the local Christmas bazaar as well. She'd been quoted in Roseland's *Daily Tribune* as saying that her inaugural event would have lots of surprises in store and promised to be the most memorable bazaar in Roseland history. I hoped she was right. If she was dissing one of the town's favorite artists, however, she was in for a rough ride.

"But enough of that." Savannah picked up one of my totes. "Let's get you set up. My display sure didn't take long this time." Her wry laugh told me she wasn't thrilled about that.

We headed to the open spot on row four—it had a great view of the stage—and sure enough, Savannah had only a tiny display area near mine. All she had room for were her note cards and a small placard that read Signed Prints Available. In the past, Savannah had always displayed her prints on a large table. The new setup couldn't be good for her.

I pointed at her sign. "Why don't you give me two of your prints, and I'll use them on the table behind my jewelry. When customers ask about them, I'll send them your way."

Savannah's eyes lit up. "You'd do that? Oh, Emma, you're the best!" Savannah plopped the tote down in front of my booth and headed off to gather some prints. I usually displayed a small placard advertising my custom designs, but I was already up to my eyeballs in special orders and wouldn't have time to design many more custom pieces before Christmas. Showing Savannah's prints would solve a dilemma for both of us.

As I worked on my jewelry displays, Nat King Cole's Christmas tunes streamed through the sound system, and I caught a whiff of the decadent burnt-sugar smell from the Kiwanis Club's kettle corn. I'd heard a rumor that an elaborate make-your-own-hot-chocolate station was set up for the exhibitors. And warm November or not, I intended to sample some of that hot chocolate before the day ended.

The PA system screeched with an eardrum-splitting "One, two, three, testing! Merry Christmas!"

I jumped and blew out a breath, longing for some of that hot chocolate or at least a strong cup of coffee.

But before I could contemplate indulging in a hot beverage, I needed to double-check the to-do list on my cell phone. I whipped out the totes packed with cute display pieces I used when selling my jewelry. The Christmas shopping season was the perfect time to offer glittering jewelry sets for gifts as well as impulse purchases. Few women could resist some cheerful new Christmas jewelry, so I offered it in every color and style imaginable. Lately, I'd experimented with broken china jewelry and created charms with pieces of Spode's famous Christmas Tree pattern. The pieces closest to my heart, though, were my new Ruby & Doris line, necklaces and bracelets constructed entirely of vintage elements and named in honor of two of my great-grandmothers.

Christmas pieces were some of my best-selling jewelry of the whole year, and I was eager to see if my new designs would do well at the bazaar. As I looked up from a rack of Ruby & Doris bracelets I had just set out, Savannah approached with a small stack of water-color prints, and Miranda was fast on her heels.

Some tiny white faux feathers from the trim on Miranda's outfit arrived before she did, and I quickly brushed them off the black velvet jewelry display where they landed.

"I told you, Savannah, only one seller per space. You *cannot* sell prints at both your space and Emma's. That's a violation of the rules."

From the set of her mouth, Savannah's normally gracious manners were strained.

I piped up, "Actually, I needed something that represented Roseland as a backdrop for my Christmas pieces, so Savannah's letting me decorate with a few of her Christmas prints. You don't have a problem with me filling out my display, do you?"

Miranda humphed. "As long as you don't mind, I guess I don't have a problem with it." She fluffed one of her white cuffs. "We really must kick things up a notch if Roseland wants to increase attendance at this bazaar. I'm trying to elevate the event so that it doesn't seem so small-town."

"But Roseland *is* a small town." It popped out before I could think.

"Yes"—Miranda narrowed her eyes at me—"but it doesn't have to act like it." She marched off.

Savannah and I shared conspiratorial grins, and I hoped we'd banished the drill sergeant for a while.

I was all for supporting Miranda in her new role leading the Happy Hometown program, but she had already ruffled a few feathers by implying we weren't as sophisticated as the good people back home in New York.

"Here, let me have that print." I reached for Savannah's watercolor of a historic Roseland home with Christmas topiaries on the veranda and placed it on a display easel behind some bangle bracelets. "Can you set the matching one over there?"

While Savannah arranged her prints, I pulled my bins of bagged jewelry sets from their totes and snapped into businesswoman mode. After graduating with my degree in journalism, I'd worked as a reporter at Roseland's *Daily Tribune*. Seven years in, I realized the news biz had changed so much that I didn't enjoy it anymore. Meanwhile, the part-time jewelry business I'd started as a side gig had turned into something bigger and more lucrative than I'd ever dreamed. Making and selling jewelry was how I'd earned my living for the past few years. For the Christmas bazaar, I had outdone myself, designing some of my best and boldest pieces ever.

"Ooh, what is that?" Shareta Gibson, my basket-weaving friend from the arts council, dropped off some of her miniature woven baskets at the table across the aisle from mine. Her eyes sparkled as I set out a linen-covered torso modeling one of my latest creations.

I pushed the display toward her. "Do you like it?"

Shareta stared at the hunter-green necklace on its plush black-velvet choker. With its lush green marbleized beads wired to resemble the petals of a flower, the pendant could certainly be considered Christmas-like if worn with red and green during the holidays, but it didn't scream jingle bells and candy canes either, so a woman could get a lot of mileage out of it.

Bob Mathis, another friend from the arts council, bolted over to my table in a huff, red-faced and waving his hands. "Did you hear what she's done now?"

Shareta and I looked up.

"What who's done?" I asked.

"That Miranda! She said my wooden bowls weren't 'festive' enough to be on the first row, so she decided to move me to the very last row, in outer Siberia." Bob jabbed a pudgy finger toward the far reaches of the cafeteria. "Way back there."

"Didn't you sign up for your old spot like always?" Shareta looked puzzled.

Bob had been one of the founders of the bazaar thirty-three years ago and, by tradition, always got a spot near the entrance.

"I sure did." Bob whipped out a handkerchief and wiped his glistening brow. "And I told Miss Rochester that I want it back pronto. She said there's nothing to be done about it this year and we'll talk about it for next year."

I'd never seen Bob so mad. I didn't blame him for being disappointed about losing his old spot, and I had a feeling Miranda didn't realize who she was messing with.

Bob's eyes widened as if he'd had a flash of insight. "I know. I'm calling the mayor." Roseland Mayor Jim Mathis was Bob's younger brother. "Jimmy'll put a stop to that woman's foolishness. He told me he was already sick and tired of her thinking she runs this town anyway. Wait till he hears about this!"

Then Bob darted off again.

I looked at Shareta. "Sounds like Miranda needs to read that book about how to win friends and influence people." I bit my lip. "I mean, I know she's new and all, but this show is important to a lot of people in town. I hope she understands that."

"I don't think she gives a rip about what the exhibitors want." Shareta wore a sour expression.

"And you say that because?"

She glanced at the entrance to the cafeteria, where the auburn-haired woman in the Mrs. Claus getup was jabbing her clipboard in the face of yet another exhibitor who had apparently shown up for the bazaar and received some unsavory news. The man had a cart full of pink and red Christmas cactuses beside him, and Miranda picked at their leaves with a look of disdain.

"She said that my traditional African baskets weren't as colorful as she'd thought they would be and asked if I could make them in cherry red and grass green next year."

"Seriously?"

Shareta nodded. "That woman is not going to last long in this town if she doesn't climb down off her high horse and stop telling everyone how they used to do it in Rochester. I'm not from here, and even I'm tired of her criticizing everything and everyone in Roseland. One more of those comments, and you know what I'm going to tell her, don't you?"

I laughed and nodded. "Delta is ready when you are."

The saying was a favorite among Southerners when they got aggravated with those who moved to the South and wanted to change the old-fashioned charm that had drawn them in the first place. The comment was even funnier coming from Shareta, who had lived in Roseland for the past ten years but was originally from New Hampshire. She considered us family now.

"Emmaaa."

I would have known that screech anywhere. Turning around, I spotted the smiling face of Harriet Harris, owner of the Making Memories Antique Mall—and the woman who happened to be my number one competitor when it came to scooping up the vintage and junk jewelry so essential to my livelihood.

"Gotta run." Shareta winked at me. Locals knew that any conversation with Harriet was likely to be a long one, and Shareta probably needed to get back to her booth. *Smart woman.*

I had a love-hate relationship with Harriet. I loved her antique mall and had found quite a few deals there since I'd started "upcycling" jewelry using old and orphaned baubles. But I also sold vintage costume jewelry online, and I hated—or at least was extremely jealous of—the way she always beat me to the local garage sales and flea markets. As she made a beeline for my booth, Harriet tucked a wayward wisp of her gray pixie cut behind one ear and peered at me over her black reading glasses.

"Looking forward to a big day of sales?" Harriet cast an appraising eye over my display.

I followed her gaze and admitted, "Fingers crossed."

Harriet motioned toward the front of the cafeteria. "Holly's a little late checking in, so I'm here to help her set up her new jewelry display. She's started making her own line of jewelry, too, you know. But don't worry. Her sales shouldn't affect yours at all."

Holly Harris Burke was Harriet's twentysomething daughter and the mother of young twins. Occasionally, Holly filled in for her mom behind the front counter at the antique mall. Inwardly, I bristled at the news that Holly was designing jewelry, but I knew I was being ridiculous. Lots of women tried their hand at jewelry making, and Roseland was certainly big enough to support two jewelry artisans.

"That's great." I pasted a smile onto my face and determined to remain upbeat. "Where's her booth? I'll be sure to tell the jewelry lovers who visit me to check out Holly's jewelry too."

"Actually, they'll see her booth before yours." Harriet's eyes crinkled. "When she applied, Holly told them she had to have a spot near the entrance where the light would best reflect off her glass beads." She pointed at the space where Holly appeared to be looking around as if she wasn't sure what to do. To my chagrin, her space was one of the first ones visitors would see when they walked in. Those booths were usually reserved for the local nonprofits and a few veteran sellers—like Bob Mathis. Even if she'd put in a request, I wondered how Holly had finagled that spot. I didn't at all like the jealousy that had come over me and tried to shake it off.

Harriet wore a look of motherly pride.

"Good for Holly, then." I tipped my head toward Harriet's daughter. "Listen, I really need to finish setting up my booth, so..."

"I understand, dear." Harriet peered at me again over her reading glasses. "And good luck. I know how hard you work on your little jewelry line."

I nodded and tried not to let her set my teeth on edge. *My "little jewelry line" is making me a comfortable living these days.* But all I said was "Thanks."

Having survived yet another encounter with Harriet, who had a knack for getting under my skin, I knew my day had nowhere to go but up, and I couldn't wait for the bazaar to open.

Chapter Two

"Hey, lady, you got anything I'd like in there?"
The tap on my back startled me, and when I turned around, I laughed at the woman with curly red hair.

Augusta "Gus" Townsend, another of my fellow arts council members—and Savannah's younger sister—had walked up just as I finished emptying all the totes and tucking them under the red skirt of my table. Roseland's resident bohemian, Gus was a vision in blue that morning. She wore a denim jacket over a Wedgwood-blue floral blouse, a lace-trimmed denim prairie skirt, and embroidered denim ankle boots with chunky heels. Despite her frilly exterior, Gus was a serious artist who had received regional and national awards for her socially conscious collages—large-format pieces she made with "found objects." Incorporating everything from plastic grocery sacks to used coffee filters and tea bags, her art was unlike any I'd seen before. Whether she was making a statement about the #MeToo movement or promoting environmental awareness, Gus admitted she always worked with a social issue in mind. She definitely wasn't just a small-town artist anymore, so I was surprised to see her at the bazaar. Gus had long said she was no fan of "cattle call" crafts shows, as she called them, and I couldn't remember ever having seen her at a Christmas bazaar before.

"Before you ask, no, I'm not here selling my artwork today." Gus gave a mock shudder. "I'm volunteering at the Humane Society's booth. That is, if we still get to have it in here."

I was puzzled. The Humane Society was one of the bazaar's original nonprofit exhibitors and had been involved since day one. Of course they would always have a booth. "What do you mean, 'if'?"

"Atilla the Hun over there"—Gus motioned to Miranda—"said she thinks some of the pets don't smell 'clean enough' to be inside this year and ordered us outdoors. She even suggested we keep them caged while they're outside. But it's kind of hard to encourage prospective pet owners to pet the animals and get to know them if they're in a cage. Plus, it's going to be awfully warm outside, and I don't know how many people will want to stay out there when they could be inside with the air-conditioning. "

That made sense, and Miranda wasn't too smart if she banished one of the most popular attractions at the show. The puppies and kittens from the Humane Society were always a huge draw for the kids who came—kids whose parents spent money on admission, refreshments, games... and Christmas gifts like my jewelry. Miranda sure seemed to be stirring up a lot of bad blood.

"Do you think maybe she's just worried about the success of the show this year?" I tried to think of any possible reason Miranda might be keeping such a tight rein on the Christmas bazaar, definitely more than we'd ever seen from leaders in the past.

Gerald Adams, the balding thirtysomething president of the Humane Society, walked up and nodded at me before addressing Gus. "Could you help us transport some of our four-legged friends? Some of them finally passed muster with Miranda."

"I'll be glad to." Gus whirled around, clearly about to rush off with Gerald, then looked back at me. "Catch you later."

I reminded her, "Don't forget to stop back by if you get a chance. I made a lot of those dangling charm bracelets you like with special Christmas charms, just for this show."

"Oh, save me one." Gus bounced up and down. "Any one. I trust your judgment." Then Gerald whisked her off for pet duty.

What a morning. I glanced at my watch. The show wouldn't open for another hour, yet already there had been more drama than I could recall at any show in recent history. Sure, there was the year Santa's elves had imbibed too much of the secret stash of eggnog and fell into the children's face-painting tables, spewing eggnog onto the faces of surprised children and angry parents, but that was an aberration. Most years, the Christmas bazaar was the same old beloved town festival it had always been. It seemed like Miranda was doing her best to change that.

I gazed around for a flash of bright-red velvet but didn't see it anywhere, and that probably wasn't a bad thing.

Before I forgot, I set aside a Christmas charm bracelet for Gus. I'd had her in mind when I made the romantic charm-packed bracelet, so I went ahead and pulled it and two others.

The noise level in the cafeteria was rising, and almost all the exhibitors appeared set up and ready to roll. Jimmy Buffett's "Run Rudolph Run" was being piped through the cafeteria's speakers, and I bobbed up and down to the catchy tune.

"Full of the Christmas spirit, are we?" Trish Delgado, the president of our local arts council, had a twinkle in her eyes.

"There's nothing wrong with that." I stepped up my shimmying. "If you'd get out of your studio more, you could catch some of this Christmas spirit yourself. And hey, I thought you were supposed to be out in Colorado at a tile workshop this week."

"Got canceled at the last minute," my tall, slim friend said. "And I couldn't see sitting at home when I could be here." Trish paused and pointed at one of Savannah's prints before frowning at me. "But why is Savannah's artwork on the table with your jewelry?"

"It's a favor for her." I lowered my voice. "Her space wasn't as big this year, and I told her I didn't mind using these as part of my decor."

Before I could show Trish some of my new designs, a commotion near the entrance had a few of us looking that way. Harriet Harris was jabbing her finger in Miranda's face, and Miranda looked unfazed.

"Furthermore"—Harriet's finger was getting closer and closer to Miranda's nose—"everyone here is disgusted with the way you've tried to take over this Christmas bazaar, and I can promise you that you'll never do it again!"

With Holly lagging behind her, Harriet stomped out of the cafeteria.

"Sheesh." Trish grimaced. "Wonder what that was all about."

"No idea, but I'm sure we'll find out."

Sure enough, Savannah came up a few minutes later and asked if we'd seen the fracas between Harriet and Miranda.

"How could we miss it?" I straightened a row of costume jewelry rings in a black-velvet-lined box. "That was a pretty public dispute, whatever it was about."

Savannah's eyebrows shot up. "I got the scoop. Harriet had just learned that Holly's registration was never approved. Miranda said it didn't arrive at the office in time. It was apparently slipped under her office door after five o'clock the day registration closed. Miranda said the bazaar's website clearly stated that applications had to be in her office by five p.m., and the website also stated that only officially approved exhibitors would be permitted to set up."

"How were we supposed to know we were 'officially approved'?" I frowned. "When my credit card payment was processed, I assumed that was as official as it got."

Savannah shrugged. "I guess Holly never followed up and assumed she would get the spot she requested, and when they got here, Harriet thought she could bulldoze her daughter's way in—kind of like she's always done with everything else in town." She glanced toward the stage. "Looks like we're about to start. I'm gonna scoot."

The bad feelings were piling up, and I hardly registered that Johnny Mathis's "The Christmas Song," one of my favorites, was playing in the background. Suddenly, my Christmas spirit evaporated. I hoped Miranda's shenanigans weren't having that effect on everyone.

A blare sounded over the loudspeaker.

"Ladies and gentlemen—"

The piercing wail of an overactive PA system caused hands to fly over ears, and heads snapped toward the stage.

"Excuse me, ladies and gentlemen, but the bazaar is about to open to the public." Caitlyn Hill, Miranda's fresh-faced assistant with a stylish asymmetrical blond bob, was all smiles. "We're just waiting on a few words from our fearless leader, and we'll be all set. So without further ado, I'm delighted to present... Miranda Hargrove."

The music crescendoed, and Santa's wooden sleigh glided onto the stage, pulled by two costumed reindeer. Only these muscular "reindeer" wore red bow ties over their tight white T-shirts and looked more like overdressed Chippendales dancers.

Savannah's hand flew to her mouth. "Good heavens."

Biting my lip, I fought the urge to chortle, then I realized the dancers were reaching into Santa's sack of toys. Out popped Miranda, who flung aside the cape to her Mrs. Claus costume, and the spotlight shone right in the center of the strapless bodice of her tight red-velvet dress. "Have a Holly Jolly Christmas" was booming through the loudspeakers. In a moment of spectacular timing, the line about having a cup of cheer came just as Miranda's more-than-ample cleavage was ogled by the beefcake boys lifting her down to the stage.

Irrationally, perhaps, I recalled the scene in *Gone With the Wind* in which Scarlett O'Hara swanned into Ashley Wilkes's birthday party while wearing a thoroughly inappropriate—and similarly low-cut—ruby-red gown. I had a feeling the musical number might just be Miranda's Scarlett-at-the-birthday-party moment.

"Seriously?" Gus had returned, and she and Savannah traded looks of disapproval. "This is her idea of how a 'professional' emcees an event?" Gus turned to me. "Why do women like her think they have to exploit their bodies in order to be successful?"

"Shh." Savannah twirled a strand of her sleek dark hair. "We don't want to miss whatever comes next."

Miranda took the microphone and turned on the charm. With a dazzling smile that was totally at odds with her everyday persona, she welcomed everyone to the bazaar. "And now, ladies and gentlemen"—she gave a coquettish smile—"it is my great privilege to announce that the advance ticket sales have already hit an all-time high, and with that, let's get this ball rolling."

Two hunky reindeer lifted Miranda by the elbows and whisked her into the wings as she tossed a peppermint-design beach ball off the stage and into the lunchroom.

"Can you believe that?" Savannah's eyes were the size of saucers.

"I can't even." Gus slowly shook her head.

I couldn't help snickering. "I'm not convinced Miranda has the greatest stage presence, but I would have paid my entrance fee all over again just to see the expressions on your faces when she popped out of that sleigh."

"So she nitpicks my display this year but then decides to turn our family-friendly event into a PG-rated affair?"

Savannah was truly scandalized, which I found amusing. And the show was just getting started.

Promptly at ten o'clock, the doors opened. Eager shoppers bustled through, their red plastic tote bags—compliments of the Happy Hometown program—flapping at their sides and ready to be filled with Christmas crafts, gifts, and decor.

My first customers arrived within minutes, and soon I was packaging jewelry sets, answering questions about my designs, and whipping credit cards in and out of my iPad's card reader. *On Dasher! On Dancer! On Visa! On Mastercard!*

"You made all of this yourself?" A pretty redhead clasped an eight-inch Ruby & Doris bracelet over a plump hand that already sported rings on four fingers.

"Yes, ma'am. Except for the vintage Christmas tree pins in the case to your left"—I pointed at the display—"every piece here is personally handmade by me."

The woman tenderly fingered the "charms" on the bracelet—the jeweled remnants of vintage clip-on earrings—and looked as if she might cry. "This shiny crystal one here?" She pointed. "My sweet mother, God rest her soul, wore earrings just like this to church every Sunday." She wiped away a tear and handed me the bracelet. "I must have this one. And"—she sniffed—"thank you for the trip down memory lane."

I told the woman to let me know if I could help her with anything else. She must have liked my jewelry, because she bought that bracelet and seven others—for her coworkers at the bank, she said. As she was about to walk away, she whipped out her credit card again and said she wanted two of my vintage Christmas tree pins, both Eisenberg Ice models, for her sister. She was positively giddy by the time I handed her a bright-red shopping bag with my Emma Madison Designs sticker on the front and red polka-dotted tissue paper spilling out.

Some of my regular customers from the arts council gallery stopped by, and later in the afternoon, so did Evelyn Wilson, the longtime receptionist at the Roseland Police Department. Evelyn adored handmade jewelry, and I wasn't surprised when she began amassing a pile of dangly earrings for her granddaughters. I had gotten to know Evelyn when I was a reporter for the *Daily Tribune*, and we stayed in touch. I always tucked a little something extra in Evelyn's bag when she purchased jewelry from me. Since Christmas was coming, I slipped in a silver-soldered charm with a Christmas tree design.

Caitlyn and her band of Christmas elves came around and asked whether I needed a restroom break, but I was fine. During one rare five-minute lull in the action, I pulled out a bottle of water and a protein bar. Just as I finished scarfing down the last peanut-butter-flavored bite, I discovered it was already five o'clock, and the predinner crowd was coming through.

Michele Fairchild, owner of the Feathered Nest gift shop in downtown Roseland, had apparently made a dash for my booth the minute she got there after her shop closed at five.

"Naturally, since I was hoping to slip out early, the shop was busy all afternoon." Michele rolled her eyes good-naturedly. "Murphy's Law, I guess. Thank goodness one of my part-time girls was able to close for me today."

Michele flipped through a stack of silver wire bangle bracelets with semiprecious stones. "You made these too?"

I nodded, pleased that the new pieces had captured her attention.

"I wish I had half your talent, Emma."

"And I wish I knew how to style a display that looked half as good as those in your shop." Michele was the undisputed merchandising queen of Main Street in Roseland, a shop owner whose windows literally stopped traffic—foot traffic anyway—along the street. The Roseland High School football team had recently won the state championship, and to celebrate their big win, Michele decorated her windows with mannequins decked out in football gear. They appeared to be rushing for gifts in the window, all in team colors of purple and gold.

Michele held up a bracelet. "You know I'll be happy to take any of these you have left over for the shop, right?"

I was busy replenishing my quickly dwindling stock, but I paused long enough to dip my head in her direction. "Yes, and I appreciate it. I plan to have some things to you by the first of the week, one way or another."

Michele dedicated a small area of her shop to the work of local artists and crafters. She didn't charge the hefty commission some stores did, so those of us lucky enough to sell at the Feathered Nest were grateful for the exposure as well as the generous sales policy.

"Okay, I'm ready for you to ring me up." Michele had her hands full of jewelry. "I've got three sterling-silver charms, two of these chunky bead necklaces, and a half dozen wire bangles, I think."

I wondered if they were for her or for gifts, but I'd learned the hard way never to question how a woman planned to use the jewelry she purchased from me. Early in my jewelry-making career, I'd asked a woman if she was buying all that jewelry for herself, and she'd immediately grown self-conscious and put half the items back. "You're right. I don't need to buy all this for me. That's overdoing things, isn't it?" she'd said. It paid—literally—to keep my mouth shut.

Michele hustled down the row to shop with the other exhibitors just as some women who worked in administration at the hospital showed up together, and I sold them set after set of matching Christmas beads and earrings. I had a feeling Roseland Medical Center was going to be a sparkly place to work come December.

Savannah fought the five thirty crowds to come over to my table and retrieve her watercolor prints. She'd sold all her others and had promised the last two to a librarian from Atlanta. The woman said she'd come to the Christmas bazaar after reading about it in a post her cousin shared on Facebook.

As Savannah left, she stopped to hug and chat with a handsome dark-haired guy whose denim vest sported a mishmash of dried-paint splotches. He wore stylish jeans and tennis shoes, so it looked like the vest was simply his artist uniform. He was probably some artsy friend of hers, and if he was any good, maybe she could get him to join the arts council. We were almost completely female, and we'd talked about getting more men to serve on our board.

As I tidied up my displays, I was grateful that I'd worn flats. The closer we got to the seven o'clock closing, the more the wear and tear of the day were getting to me. Sales had been brisk, so I was thrilled, but my feet were begging for relief. Those tiled floors in the school cafeteria hadn't exactly been designed with foot comfort in mind.

Even though I was ready to go home, the show wouldn't end until the last shopper had checked out. Or at least, that was the way things had always been. Show organizers had never turned a shopper away, even if a few of them always straggled in right at closing time. With Miranda's newfound insistence on following every jot and tittle of the show's rules, however, I wouldn't be surprised if she demanded the doors be hermetically sealed at seven o'clock on the dot.

And where is Miranda anyway? I didn't remember seeing much of her since the unforgettable opening number that morning. Maybe she'd been behind the scenes, probably scouring registration forms for any discrepancies.

My booth looked as if it had been ransacked, and in a way, it had. As usual, I'd brought far more jewelry than I thought I could sell in a single day, and to my delight, the vast majority of it had disappeared. I wouldn't be taking much of it home with me, and any leftover Christmas pieces could go to the Feathered Nest. I typed a note on my cell phone, reminding myself to take a small gift to Michele as a thank-you for always giving my jewelry a prominent spot in her shop.

As I finished typing the note, Caitlyn drifted by, craning her neck as she looked up and down the aisle.

I tapped her on the arm. "Looking for someone?"

"Yes, Miranda." Caitlyn looked puzzled. "No one's seen her for the last hour or so, and that's not like her. She's supposed to announce this year's best-decorated booth—Judges' Choice or whatever they call it—as well as the donation to the foster parent association. She was excited about doing that, so I can't understand why she's not here already."

A glance at my watch showed it was almost time for the show to close. "Maybe the judges had a hard time deciding on the winner and she's waiting for their decision before she comes back to the cafeteria," I suggested.

"You're probably right." Caitlyn twisted a strand of hair as if working off nervous energy. "I think I'll go check with the volunteer committee just to make sure they haven't heard from her. I don't know about you, but I'm ready to call it a night and get out of this joint."

I was surprised by her attitude, but I was tired, too, and Caitlyn had no doubt been there much longer than I had.

As the last of the late shoppers pawed through what was left of my jewelry, I began to pull the totes from beneath the tables and pack up. Several boxes and baskets were totally empty. For anyone in jewelry sales, leaving a show with an empty box and a wide-open expanse of black velvet was ideal. I needed to start making more jewelry as soon as possible.

I checked for phone messages and found one from Jen Davis, editor of the *Daily Tribune* and, more importantly, my best friend. *Todd's out of town tonight. Want to have dinner at Sombrero at 8?*

I texted my reply. *Sounds great. Whoever gets there first can claim a table.*

As I tucked my phone into my purse, Gus came by with an adorable Yorkie in her arms. "Say Merry Christmas to the nice lady." Gus waved his little paw for him.

"Merry Christmas to you." I shook his paw and stroked his soft golden fur. "This little guy is adorable. Is he up for adoption?"

She shook her head. "Mason is actually Gerald's new puppy, but he brought him to the show after that dustup with Miranda earlier. Frankly, I think it may be a good thing Gerald had to go home and get him. The kids loved him, and we even sold a few Humane Society memberships to parents who were standing around at our booth while their kids petted him."

"Way to go, boy." I gently high-fived the little pooch. "I've known several guys named Mason, but I don't know that I've ever met a dog named that."

"It's because he likes to drink out of Mason jars. At least, that's what Gerald said."

"Isn't that dangerous? I mean, couldn't he get his head stuck in there?"

"Not with Gerald. He said he holds the jar while Mason sips out of it."

I chuckled and gave the little fellow a final pat before he snuggled back into Gus's waiting arms.

"I'd better get Gerald's fur baby back to him. Ciao."

The screech of the PA system once again had everyone covering their ears and groaning. Somebody really needed to learn how to operate that thing.

"Ladies and gentlemen"—Caitlyn tapped the microphone and got everyone's attention— "I'm happy to announce that this is our most successful Christmas bazaar ever! We topped the number of visitors from last year by nearly twenty-five percent, and with a sell-out on exhibitor registrations *and* our record-setting attendance—" She paused dramatically. "That means our donation to the foster parent association will be the biggest one ever, more than seven thousand dollars!"

I stopped in the middle of packing up charms to join in the applause. That was fantastic news, and the foster parent group was going to be thrilled with the money, which was arriving just in time to buy Christmas gifts for all the children. How strange, though, that Miranda wasn't there to revel in yet another moment in the spotlight. But the way the day had gone, we were probably better off the less she was around.

Caitlyn cleared her throat. "As much as we all hate to leave, it's time to say goodbye, and in an annual tradition that everyone adores, the holiday elves of the Rockin' Roseland Christmas Bazaar would like to thank you with a musical number fit for the happiest hometown in Georgia! Let's give them a warm welcome."

Hmm. Caitlyn's sure changed her tune from just thirty minutes ago when she was ready to get out of here.

She stepped away from the microphone, and Mariah Carey's upbeat "All I Want for Christmas Is You" was piped through the loudspeakers. Ten little girls from one of the local dance academies whirled across the stage in sparkling red-and-green costumes, their tulle skirts dotted with sequins and crystals. For small-town Roseland, it was a pretty sophisticated dance number, with the girls smiling at the crowd and clearly enjoying their moment of fame.

It wasn't *The Nutcracker*, but the whole auditorium began humming, swaying, and clapping along as the dancers moved to one side while the bazaar's longtime Santa, Mayor Jim Mathis, slid along the stage next to his sleigh, which had just glided in from stage left behind them.

"Pretty cute, huh?" Savannah whispered. She had sidled up next to me, broken off a piece of candy cane, and popped it into her mouth.

I nodded. "I'm impressed. You've got to give Miranda credit for doing what she set out to do. Looks like she's really pulled it off."

As the song headed toward its rousing finish, the sleigh came to a halt, and Santa reached inside for his gigantic sack of toys. But Santa huffed as he struggled to lift the lumpy sack over his shoulder, and some in the crowd laughed. The bag was bulky, sure, but I imagined that the wrapped packages were empty boxes and didn't weigh all that much.

Within seconds, though, it was clear that something was horribly wrong. An ashen-faced Santa quickly lowered his bag to the ground, and it landed with a thud. Santa cried, "Someone call 911!"

A scream came from the wings, and a clearly panic-stricken Caitlyn ran forward and yelled, "Everyone off the stage!"

The dance moms rushed to collect their children while Caitlyn shooed everyone away from the sleigh. "I said everyone off the stage *now!*"

The screeching loudspeaker abruptly put a halt to Mariah Carey's tune, and the confused and disappointed-looking children were herded away while Santa knelt by his bag.

Spilling out of it was an arm clad in red velvet with white fur trim around the sleeve. Caitlyn stood near Santa and tried to shield him from the audience with a wooden Christmas tree prop but not before those of us closest to the stage got a glimpse of the lifeless face of Miranda Hargrove.

Santa tossed aside his white gloves before pressing both sides of her neck, no doubt feeling for a pulse. What appeared to be a dark-red cord dangled from her neck, and her glassy eyes stared upward in a grotesque mockery of her usual perfection. Gasps erupted from the crowd, then an eerie silence fell as the same two off-duty policemen who'd been patrolling the parking lot charged into the cafeteria, guns drawn, and ordered everyone to remain in place. Within minutes, two more officers had arrived and were posted at the cafeteria doors. They announced that none of us were to leave the premises.

Miranda had promised us a Christmas bazaar we would never forget. Tragically, she had just delivered it.

Chapter Three

For the past two hours, I'd been dreaming of getting off my feet after the long day at the bazaar. That dream wouldn't be coming true anytime soon.

The scuttlebutt said Mayor Mathis was backstage, trading his Santa outfit for civilian clothes so that he could hand over his costume to investigators. The dancers who'd just been on stage had been quieted with leftover hot chocolate and cookies. A volunteer elf came by, offering cocoa to the exhibitors, but I thanked her for the offer and waved her—and the sugary aroma—away. Sick to my stomach, I wanted nothing stronger than a sip of water.

Savannah and I watched as Caitlyn sobbed loudly on the cafeteria stage. The two police officers on parking lot duty had shown up almost instantly. I texted Jen to say I wouldn't make it to Sombrero by eight o'clock as planned, and I ended with a news alert. *Police want to interview us about Miranda Hargrove's death.*

As I could have predicted, Jen was tapping on the cafeteria doors less than ten minutes later, although the police insisted she keep out. Soon, her nose was pressed to the glass of a windowpane a few doors down. Whether or not she gained access was really a moot point. A photog from the *Trib* had been there for the past hour to snap photos of the closing ceremonies, and I noted—with the pride of a former journalist—that he kept doing his job, snapping away discreetly, even after police had arrived.

I was breaking down my jewelry displays when a racket on the stage made me jerk my head up. Caitlyn turned red in the face as she talked with a blue-suited fellow who had just shown up. *Is that...?* Oh yes, it was.

Detective Alan Shelton. *Ugh.* He might have been considered one of Roseland's finest, but the detective and I had tangled over another murder investigation not too long ago. I avoided being at events when he was around, but there was no escaping the current one.

Caitlyn was clearly a wreck following the death of her boss. I strained to listen as Detective Shelton questioned her.

"We can do this here, or we can head down to the station for the interview if you're more comfortable with that." Anyone within earshot could hear him trying to calm her down, but she wasn't having it.

"My boss has just been killed, and you're standing here asking me who was on the official registration list? Have you lost your mind?"

Even though I had gotten crossways with the detective in the past, I'd also respected his position. Caitlyn needed to watch her mouth.

The detective lowered his voice, and I couldn't tell whether he was being friendly or forceful. Whatever he'd said, Caitlyn stopped crying, and she nodded and followed him out into the hallway.

"I still can't believe this." Savannah put a hand to her mouth.

A stretcher was wheeled into the cafeteria, and my stomach clenched at what was coming next. Back in my reporter days, I'd been at crime scenes when a few bodies were removed, but it was still a sobering moment when the man in the coroner jacket came through the cafeteria and headed to the stage. Police officers and some volunteers held up blankets and shielded the area of the stage where Miranda's body lay, but all of us watching knew what was going on.

An uneasy but respectful silence settled over the room as the stretcher rolled past with the sheet-covered body. Savannah had tears in her eyes, and I blinked back a few too.

Sure, Miranda had ruffled more than a few feathers that day, but I didn't think any of those episodes had been enough to provoke a murder.

"So, who do you think killed her?" Savannah took in the entire cafeteria as she whispered. "Half of us here were ticked off at her for one reason or another. Me. Bob. Harriet. Gerald and the Humane Society. And I found out today that one of the show's founding artists got excluded when his application supposedly didn't arrive in time."

"Oh?"

She nodded. "Do you know Tyler Montgomery? You might have seen him around earlier. Wears this crazy-looking vest with dried paint all over it as his artist uniform."

I shook my head. "Never met him, but you were talking to him at your booth this afternoon, weren't you?"

"Yes, but don't tell Gus. She's had a thing for him for years, so I was doing a little intel, and I don't think he's got a girlfriend."

I couldn't help grinning. He was nice-looking, and a fellow artist sounded like just the sort of guy who might appeal to Gus.

One of the officers on stage tapped a microphone and captured everyone's attention. "Excuse me, ladies and gentlemen, but as you probably know by now, we've had a tragedy here tonight. I'm sorry to inform you that Miranda Hargrove has passed away. I apologize for the inconvenience when I know you're all ready to leave, but I'm sure you understand the importance of our gathering information while events are fresh in everyone's minds."

I was exhausted, both physically and emotionally, but I couldn't begrudge the police some time to complete their work. Someone in the room might have seen or heard something that would help the officers discover who'd killed Miranda.

Gus walked up and joined Savannah and me, and the three of us sat behind my stripped table and speculated about the killer while we waited to give our statements. When it was my turn, Detective Shelton motioned me over to the table where he and three other officers had an assembly line of interviews underway.

"Good evening, Emma. I'm sure you're ready to get out of here, but thanks for giving us some of your time," the officer said.

"No problem. What can I tell you?"

"I've heard that Miranda had some altercations with a few of the exhibitors today. Did you witness any of those?"

I paused, considering.

"Emma?" He raised an eyebrow, looking impatient.

"I'm thinking. I'm thinking." I sighed as I tried to figure out how many of the day's dustups to share. "And yes, I saw a few words exchanged but nothing that would have led to murder."

"We'll draw our own conclusions, if you don't mind." His lips thinned, and when I cocked my head at him, he seemed to chill. "Just tell me what you saw." He looked exasperated, and that annoyed me. The evening wasn't exactly a picnic for me either.

"I overheard a heated conversation between Miranda and Harriet Harris," I said. "Harriet was angry that Miranda was denying an exhibitor spot to Holly Harris Burke, Harriet's daughter."

"So Holly was registered like everyone else?" His pen paused in midair.

"That's what Harriet said." I nodded. "But you might want to confirm that with Caitlyn Hill, Miranda's assistant. I imagine she'd be able to tell you the particulars of who submitted registrations on time and who didn't. If anyone was unhappy about their assignment, she would know about it."

"Were they the only ones you saw today who seemed upset with Miranda?"

"I'm not sure whether 'upset' is exactly the right word," I admitted, "but Savannah Rogers, the watercolor artist, and Gerald Adams and Gus Townsend from the Humane Society all had some rearranging to do after they got their assignments. I wouldn't say those con-versations got as heated as the one with Harriet, though."

"I see. Anyone else?"

"Bob Mathis. He was irate that Miranda hadn't given him his old location. And Shareta Gibson had her artwork criticized, but that was a minor thing." *Sheesh, Emma. Ratting out half your friends to-day, aren't you?*

Detective Shelton wrote a few more notes in his small blue spi-ral-bound notebook. He seemed to be writing down much more than I'd actually said, so I took advantage of the break in the inter-view to pose a few questions of my own.

"I assume from the cord I saw dangling from her neck that she was strangled." I looked him in the eye and waited for confirmation.

Shelton simply stared at me, and I stared right back. The ques-tion was probably pointless, but I had to ask. "Have you gotten any leads about who might have killed her?"

"Emma." He looked at me and sighed. "We were called out here just about forty-five minutes ago and have been interviewing every-body we can since that time. Trust me. We'll do our best to find out who did this."

"I was just asking." He didn't have to be so touchy.

"And of course we'll try to solve this as fast as we can."

"I know that." Well, I didn't *know* that at all, but it was the right thing to say.

"You're free to go." He motioned toward the door. "We appreci-ate your time."

"Thanks." After tipping my head in his direction, I couldn't get out of there fast enough and wheeled my bulky, if largely empty, jewelry totes to my car. I tossed the final tote onto the back seat, climbed behind the wheel, and wondered whether my aching foot would make it to the gas pedal.

Thinking about dinner with Jen gave me the second wind I needed, though. I wondered what she'd heard about the murder, and I couldn't wait to bounce a few thoughts off her.

Chapter Four

The North Pole apparently had a thing for Mexican food, because the waitstaff at Sombrero was busy taking elf orders when I arrived to meet Jen for dinner. I recognized many of the girls as volunteers from the bazaar. It was almost nine o'clock when I slipped into a booth seat across from Jen.

She said her assistant news editor had offered to write the story about Miranda's untimely demise, and I was glad my best friend could be there to help me process my day. We quickly placed our orders—shrimp tacos for Jen and chicken quesadillas for me—and got down to business.

Jen scooped up some queso with a chip and scarfed it down. "Okay, I'm sorry she got killed and all, but according to one of our reporters, she was a real diva to all the downtown merchants. You know that, right?"

"That doesn't surprise me." I poured some salsa into a small bowl, sloshed a chip around in it, and took a bite. "So yeah, she had a reputation for being difficult, but she also had a reputation for being very good at her job. And I'm not just saying this because she's gone now, but she spearheaded the most successful Christmas bazaar in our history."

"Most successful money-wise, maybe." Jen twirled another chip in the bowl of queso.

"Huh?"

"I'm not sure having Santa open his bag of toys and pull out a dead body is the sort of advance publicity you want for next year's show, if you get my drift."

Jen had a point, but the raucous laughter coming from a neighboring booth interrupted our conversation. I looked over, and the elf girls were whooping it up.

One of them pointed at her cell phone as her friends gawked. "This was the *exact* moment it happened," she crowed.

"Ooh, gross." One of her blond friends pretended to gag.

"That's really the dead lady's arm?" A brunette with French-braided hair squeezed in for a better look at the screen.

I couldn't stand it another minute. "Excuse me." I raised my eyebrows at Jen. "I used to babysit some of those girls when I first moved to town, and I think they need to learn what's appropriate for public discussion."

I walked over to their booth and leaned in. "Hi, girls." I plastered a smile on my face. "I saw some of you at the Christmas bazaar today, didn't I?"

Clearly, I'd put a damper on things. Cell phone screens went dark, and the voices were noticeably quieter.

"Erin, you help out with that dance school that performed tonight, right?" I knew she did because her mom, Trish Delgado, occasionally left our arts council meetings early to pick up Erin from the dance studio three doors down from the library.

"Yes, Miss Emma."

"And Kaley, you're the new student council president at Roseland High this fall, I believe?" Her aunt, Carleen Wood, was a close friend and forever telling me how proud she was of her niece's latest achievement. "Now, if I could just sit here for a moment"—I shoved my way onto the vinyl-covered banquette, causing the girls to pack in—"I wondered if I could see that cell phone photo you had up a minute ago, the one of Miranda's arm."

Erin, who'd been brandishing the photo, sheepishly held out her phone, and I winced as I relived the moment I'd seen the fur-trimmed sleeve spilling out of Santa's bag.

"You know, it must have been disturbing for you to be around something like that this evening, but I think you may actually have photos that the police would like to see."

Erin looked alarmed. I'd heard that Trish ran a tight ship at home, and Erin probably assumed I wanted to get her in trouble.

"Yeah, the police could use everyone's help, and if you don't mind, I'd like for you to send these photos to a detective I know at the Roseland PD. You may have some clue there that we're not even noticing."

"You think so?" Erin perked up, perhaps relieved that I was more interested in police work than in her inappropriate behavior.

I nodded. "I sure do. I think they'd be grateful. And I know you *all* want to do the right thing and not just sit around laughing over some poor woman's tragic death. Right?" I made eye contact with each girl at the table.

"Right," Erin agreed then gazed into her plate of nachos.

"Yeah, right." Kaley and the others joined the chorus of "Rights" as well.

"Super." I stretched my hand out for her phone, and Erin reluctantly handed it over. "Let me just get these on their way to a friend of mine at the police department, and I'll leave you girls to your tacos and burritos."

Erin looked nervous as I tapped a few keys and forwarded the images to Evelyn. She would see to it that the photos got to the proper person.

"There." I clicked off the photos folder on Erin's cell phone and returned it to her. "All done. Thanks. And now I'd better get back to my meal."

When I returned to our table, Jen rolled her eyes. "You know they're gonna love you for that, right?"

"Yeah, well, they'll get over it." I waved away her comment. "It's not right for them to be passing around photos of a woman who's just died, for Pete's sake." I perked up when I saw that our entrees had arrived. "Shoot. Now my quesadillas are probably cold." I took a bite and was pleasantly surprised to find it still piping hot. Good—I was ravenous.

"So." Jen steepled her fingers and leaned across the table. "Who killed Miranda?"

I shrugged. "How much time have you got? 'Cause she offended a lot of people today. I don't think all those who were upset with her wanted to kill her, mind you, but I imagine the police are going to have their work cut out for them."

"What about that Caitlyn Hill?" Jen raised an eyebrow. "Maybe she's ambitious. Next in line for the job and all that."

I shook my head. "I can't see it. Besides, I saw her all over the place this afternoon, so when would she have had time to do it?"

Jen gave me a wry smile. "Doesn't take that long to choke somebody to death."

I widened my eyes. "And you know this how?"

"Morbid curiosity. I read two true-crime novels in a row in which the victim was strangled to death with a pair of nylons. The old newspaper stories I looked up about the cases said death can occur within minutes."

"Humph. Guess I've never thought much about how long it takes to choke someone to death."

Jen chuckled. "Most normal people haven't. So, who wanted her dead?"

I swallowed my last bite of chicken. "The people I saw getting into it with her this morning were angry, but I don't think any of them were angry enough to commit murder."

"Well, somebody sure was. And I'll bet that if Caitlyn didn't do it, she might have some thoughts on who did."

Jen's cell phone rang, and she picked it up and accepted the call. I heard a lot of "Yeah?" and "Uh-huh, that's fine" before she said, "Okay. Uh-huh. Bye."

"The office?" I asked.

"Yeah. The new guy they hired to be the assistant news editor can't make a decision without running it by me. Afraid he's gonna upset someone."

"Understandable."

"But he was calling to tell me he decided to run a 'tasteful' photo of Miranda's body being carried out on the stretcher. That one was a no-brainer, don't you think?" She grabbed another chip and scraped the last of the queso from the bowl.

I grimaced. "I definitely don't miss having to make those decisions anymore." I didn't miss the job pressure or the constant deadlines either.

"Now that you mention it, do you need any help making jewelry?"

"Yes, actually, I do." I laughed. "But I don't think you've got the patience to assemble beads and baubles all day or prowl thrift stores for things to sell online."

A commotion came from behind us as the elves from the Christmas bazaar left tips on the table and said their goodbyes. I tried to make eye contact with Erin, but she appeared to be avoiding my gaze and dashed off. Another girl gave me the stink eye as she left, but I could live with that. I wondered what Trish would think if Erin revealed that she'd forwarded some of her cell phone photos to the police. I hoped Trish wouldn't mind, but I knew I'd done the right thing.

After a glance at my glittery Christmas watch—now missing a rhinestone ruby, I noted—I was surprised that it was nearly ten. Jen and I settled up with the cashier and left the restaurant together before agreeing to meet for a walk the following afternoon. As I drove home, I idly wondered what else Jen's reporter had heard about Miranda's dealings with the downtown merchants. I wished I'd asked for details. But as I pulled into the driveway of my cozy bungalow on Buchanan Street, I wanted nothing more in the world than a good night's sleep. Then perhaps I would wake up ready to think clearly about that bizarre Christmas bazaar.

Chapter Five

The furry paw on my face told me it was time to get up. I opened one eye, reached for my cell phone, and checked the time—7:17 a.m. I might have slept till noon were it not for the intervention of my Siamese cat, Miriam Haskell, who was named after one of my favorite costume jewelry designers. Miriam's breakfast was late, and she didn't hesitate to let me know she found that unacceptable.

After slipping on my favorite old bathrobe, a pilled and ragged number I couldn't bear to part with, I padded into the kitchen, opened a can of Kitty Feast, and spooned some into Miriam's bowl. I refreshed her water then yawned as I turned the coffeemaker on. Caffeine was always a good idea.

I was curious to see what the *Trib* had written about the murder at the Christmas bazaar, so I stepped onto the porch and looked for my Sunday newspaper. It had landed on the front steps, so I didn't have to walk very far in my kitty cat pajamas.

Back inside, I sat at my kitchen table with a large mug of Colombian roast, added a splash of pumpkin spice creamer, and scanned the front-page article on the murder. It said officers had remained on scene until nearly midnight and noted that the mayor had declined to comment on his role in finding the body. That seemed odd.

Before I could read further, my cell phone rang. I fished it out of my bathrobe's floppy pocket, wondering who was calling so early on a Sunday, but I recognized the number as the Roseland Police Department. Maybe Evelyn had a question about the photos I'd forwarded to her. "Hello."

"Good morning, Emma. Detective Shelton here."

My stomach sank. "What can I do for you?"

He cleared his throat. "Evelyn passed along those photos from the young woman who was at the Christmas bazaar. She said you were behind that. Is that correct?"

"Yes. Was I wrong in thinking you would want to see those?"

"Uh, well..." He paused as if measuring his words. "No, but I wanted to ask how you happened to know of the existence of those photos."

He thinks I've been nosing around in his business again.

I rolled my eyes and aimed for a firm but pleasant tone. "I was in a restaurant with a friend last night when the girl passed around her phone with the photos on it. Frankly, it bothered me to see her showing those off in public. When I approached her and took a closer look, I realized it might be something your office should see."

"We've received a lot of cell phone photos from yesterday." He cleared his throat again. "But I'm sure it's better to have too much info than not enough."

"I agree."

"And I just wanted to assure you that we'll do everything we can to find out who killed Miranda."

Something about his tone struck me as not quite right. "Yes. And?"

"And I wanted to remind you that this case is serious and best left to the professionals, so it's good to remember that we don't need amateurs trying to help us investigate."

"I see." And I did see. He was telling me thanks for passing along the photos but to stay out of his investigation.

"I can assure you, Detective, that I have absolutely no interest whatsoever in burdening myself and my already overfull schedule by taking on information-gathering duties that are best left to those of you in our town's fine police department."

Shoot. I was doing it again. When I got mad or upset, I tended to adopt an overly formal tone that sounded like something out of the Regency romances I loved to read. But I didn't sound quite like anyone living in the twenty-first century.

"Okay, then," he said.

"I take it that's all you need from me this day?" *This day?* I was ready for my inner Jane Austen to zip it.

"Yes, and thanks for your time."

I stared at my phone screen until it turned dark, and I couldn't believe he was already warning me to stay out of his investigation.

That called for another cup of coffee. Sure, I was nosy about the murder, but I had zero intention of getting seriously involved in another homicide investigation. Upon leaving the *Daily Tribune*, I had happily said goodbye to keeping up with the town's cops-and-robbers news—what little there was of it in Roseland. I had a successful, growing jewelry-design business, and no way was I going to spend my precious pre-Christmas days playing Nancy Drew.

The clock on my coffeemaker told me it was time to get ready for church. I'd signed up to make a dessert for the choir lunch following the morning service. Thanks to the unexpected events of the prior evening, I hadn't had time to make anything after all. I would have to stop by a store, since—like most of the businesses in downtown Roseland—my favorite bakery, the Cupcake Café, wasn't open on Sunday. Our new choir director had suggested we have a potluck lunch so that he could get to know us better, and he also wanted to introduce new music for our Christmas cantata.

After a quick shower, I zipped myself into a maple-leaf-patterned shift with a lightweight gold sweater and cute metallic gold flats. I grabbed a vintage moonglow bracelet-and-earring set from Napier, some recent thrift store finds, and clasped them on as I headed out the door on my way to the car. Jewelry always pulled an outfit together and added the perfect bit of polish.

I pulled out of the driveway and in minutes was at my closest su-permarket, where I popped in long enough to grab an iced butter-cream cake from the small bakery—store-bought would have to do.

One minute past eleven, I hit the church parking lot and man-aged to grab a back-row seat before the first song ended.

"As you all have heard by now," Pastor Steve said, "our commu-nity experienced a tragedy yesterday. Some of you might even have been familiar with Miranda Hargrove of Roseland's Happy Home-town program, but sadly, she passed away at the bazaar last night."

The elderly woman in front of me snapped her head to the left and poked her daughter. "Passed away at *a fire* last night?"

The daughter whispered into her mother's ear, "Shh, Mom. Not a fire. The ba-zaar."

"Oh."

Pastor Steve asked us all to join him in praying for Miranda's family and friends. *Did Miranda have friends?* As we bowed our heads, I prayed that the killer would be found and brought to justice before he—or she—harmed anyone else. The pastor then kicked off his new sermon series on preparing our hearts for the holidays.

As soon as the offertory hymn began, I slipped out and made a beeline for the fellowship hall. Michele Fairchild and I would get all the salads, casseroles, and desserts laid out and lined up on tables. Her husband was picking up the meat.

"Ready to work?" she asked as soon as I stuck my head into the room.

"You bet."

She nodded at several stacks of red Solo cups. "Would you help me take these to the kitchen and fill them with ice?"

I followed her lead, and in no time, we were good to go.

"Whew!" Michele blew a strand of long strawberry-blond hair off her face.

Once everything was ready, Michele poured sweet tea from a gallon jug into one of the cups. "I'm still not used to it feeling like spring in the middle of fall." She fanned herself with a paper plate.

"Ditto." I held out an arm and asked her to help me out of my sweater since I was about to melt.

Michele's eyes widened. "Ooh, check out that bracelet!"

I smiled. "You like?"

"That's one of the most gorgeous bracelets I've ever seen." She fingered the charms. "Did you make it?"

I shook my head. "I wish, but no. This is an old Napier piece." I continued to hold out my arm as Michele examined the bracelet's chunky textured links, tiny gold leaves, and multicolored charms that practically glowed. "I was lucky to come across it, too, because these old moonglow pieces are getting harder to find."

"I can see why, since—" Michele's head jerked up, and I followed her gaze as she looked through the kitchen's pass-through window and into the fellowship hall. "Hey, honey, can you crank that air up while you're in there?"

Michele's husband, Wells Fairchild, had arrived in the fellowship hall with a box containing buckets of fried chicken. He checked his wristwatch. "Precisely twelve fifteen." He looked pleased with himself. "Mm, this smells heavenly," he said in his crisp English accent.

I was amused to note that her husband, an English businessman she'd met on a buying trip overseas, apparently liked KFC. He set the containers on the food tables, tucked the empty box under an arm, and headed for the thermostat.

Christopher Linley, the new Roseland Community Church choir director, stuck his head inside the kitchen door. "Are we good to go, ladies?"

"Yes, sir!" Michele gave him a thumbs-up, and I stood as I realized someone was with Chris.

"I've recruited a new soprano to join us"—he stepped aside—"and I believe it's someone you two might know."

"Shareta!" Michele gave her a big hug, and I did too.

Michele grabbed Shareta's hand. "I didn't realize you sang. If I'd known, I'd have recruited you long before now. And since you're here, how about helping us get all this sweet tea ready before the stampede arrives. Would you mind?"

"Sure thing." Shareta seemed eager to get to work. Michele and I handed over the cups, and Shareta filled them with tea. Within minutes, we were done.

Michele held out the last filled cup to Shareta. "This one's yours if you want it." She paused. "But wait a minute. You're from New Hampshire, as I recall. Do you even drink sweet tea?"

"Both my grandmothers are from Alabama, and yes, I drink sweet tea." Shareta reached for the cup and gulped half of it down. "Ah. That is some seriously good stuff. Sweet but not too sweet."

Michele pointed at her. "I knew I liked you. And by the way, Austin's pre-K teachers are going to love those baskets I got from you at the bazaar last night. Those pieces were such a great price too. If you ever have any extras you want to sell in my shop, just let me know."

Shareta bit her lip, and Michele apparently noticed too. "Did I say something wrong?"

"No." Shareta had a faraway look in her eyes. "I was just thinking back to the murder last night. That's all. What a horrible end to everything. In fact, I wanted to see if you two thought—"

"Showtime, ladies," Chris called.

What was Shareta about to say? I needed to follow up on that.

Michele hopped to it, placing cups of both sweet and unsweet tea in the pass-through window between the kitchen and the fellowship hall, and Shareta and I joined in. Soon, Chris welcomed the choir members and offered the blessing before everyone lined up to fill their plates.

Michele, Shareta, and I found seats at a table near the back of the room.

"Austin says 'Mr. Chris' is great with the children's choir, but I think Chris is just figuring out that he has his work cut out for him with our group." Michele jiggled the ice in her cup.

"Hey, what we lack in talent, we make up for in enthusiasm," I joked.

Shareta looked around the room and lowered her voice. "Now, as I was about to ask earlier, who do you ladies think might've killed Miranda Hargrove? Who wanted her dead?"

I tsked. "A better question might be 'Who didn't want her dead?'"

Michele raised an eyebrow. "We *are* in church, Emma."

"Look, I'm not being mean, I'm just..."

Shareta spoke up. "Keeping it real? She did tick off a lot of people yesterday." She drummed her fingers on the table and cocked her head. "I can't get over her telling me I needed to change the colors of my baskets. And that woman was supposed to help us promote the arts in Roseland? I still can't believe they hired her after—"

She quickly reached for her cup of tea and took a long drink.

"After what?" I peered at her.

"After all the other great applicants they must have had. I mean, who thought she was right for the job to begin with?"

Michele fidgeted in her seat and was uncharacteristically quiet. She chewed her lip then glanced toward the dessert table. "Oh, shoot, I forgot to slice the cakes and pies. Let me go do that before everyone makes a mess."

"Need some help?" Shareta wadded up her napkin and dropped it onto her paper plate.

"No, you two have done enough." Michele patted us both on the back. "This will only take a minute." She smiled and left the table, but something about her behavior seemed off.

Shareta's gaze followed Michele. "Was she friends with Miranda or something?"

"If she was, I didn't know about it. I wasn't well acquainted with Miranda, but it sounds like maybe you were."

"Nah." She swatted the air. "Just enough to have her feel comfortable criticizing my art. Of course, I'm still sorry she died. Nobody deserves that. It sure makes me edgy to think we've got a killer in our midst. And here when we're getting ready for Christmas..." She shook her head.

Just then, Chris got everyone's attention and said we had ten minutes to finish dessert before practice started. Shareta and I helped ourselves to generous slices of pie, Michele soon joined us, and after scarfing down dessert, we all threw away our plates and headed to the sanctuary. We ran through two new songs and were dismissed promptly at two o'clock, just as Chris had promised.

I'd agreed to meet Michele in the kitchen after practice to help her tidy up from lunch. She was rinsing pans when I walked in.

"Hey." I pointed at the sink. "Can I help?"

She tossed a dish towel my way. "I wash. You dry."

Before long, we'd cleaned a small mountain of pans, platters, and serving utensils, which we tucked into cabinets and drawers. A half pitcher of sweet tea remained from lunch, and she poured us each a cup.

Michele claimed one of two chairs near a small table that barely fit in a tiny corner of the kitchen. "Where'd you get this great purse?"

She fingered the new hobo bag I'd been carrying. Its lush crushed-velvet fabric and leather-and-gold-chain strap made it the perfect fall accessory.

"Picked it up from one of the sellers at a jewelry show last year." I stroked the fabric. "Aren't the fall colors great?"

Michele nodded admiringly as she traced the outlines of orange and topaz leaves on the body of the bag. "I know the calendar says fall is here, but it sure doesn't feel like we ought to be getting ready for Christmas already, does it?"

After taking the other seat, I shook my head and fanned myself with a stray church bulletin. "It certainly doesn't."

"And speaking of Christmas"—she looked me straight in the eye—"I don't want to have to get ugly here, but if you don't bring me some more of your Christmas jewelry soon..."

"I'll be there first thing Tuesday morning. You have my word." I knew better than to get on Michele's bad side.

She narrowed her eyes. "I'm holding you to that." Then she grinned. "Seriously, though, I've got a customer from Atlanta coming on Tuesday afternoon to pick up a special order, and if you have some necklaces for her to see, I have a feeling she'll be bowled over. She loves jewelry, and she loves handmade things, so..."

"So I need to get my act together and have some designs for her to see."

"Bingo. By the way, I adore that charm you snuck into my bag at the Christmas bazaar, and—"

The ding of a notification on my cell phone came through, and I fished the phone out of my purse and tapped the message. It was from the Happy Hometown office. *Reminder: Special called meeting, 3 p.m. today. Board to vote on Caitlyn Hill as acting director. Please respond if unable to attend.*

"Hmm." I set down the phone and grimaced.

"Bad news?" Michele looked concerned.

"Not bad. Just strange." I brought up the text again and let her read it.

"Wow, they don't waste time, do they?"

"Guess not." I glanced at the text again. "Looks like they emailed everyone earlier this morning while we were in church. This reminder came about five minutes ago, though. We've been so busy that I didn't even look at my phone till practice was over." The phone's clock read 2:53 p.m. "Good grief. I've got to run."

Michele reached for my cup. "Here, I'll toss that and lock up. If you leave right now, you'll make it."

Collecting my sweater and purse, I told Michele goodbye and promised to see her early in the week. I zipped out to the parking lot, and since the church was just two blocks from downtown, I pulled up outside the Happy Hometown office at 2:59 p.m. *Whew.*

I got out of the car and dashed into the building. When I got upstairs to the program's office, the door was open, and chatter filled the room.

Caitlyn, who appeared to be making the rounds of all the board members, looked up when I walked in. "Hey, Emma. I'm glad you could make it."

"Me too. I didn't see the message until about five minutes ago, but yeah, I'm here, so it's cool."

I glanced around the room. Mayor Jim Mathis was there along with Gerald Adams, Mavis Eastwood from the Cupcake Café, and a few other people I recognized but didn't know that well, like a local bank president and the director of the Roseland Public Library.

The mayor tipped his head at me, and as soon as I took a seat at the small conference table in the back of the room, he stood up.

"Good afternoon. First, I'd like to say thank you for dropping everything and coming out on a Sunday to tend to the business of the Happy Hometown program. You're probably all wondering why this couldn't wait until tomorrow."

The mayor reached for a stack of papers sitting before him and passed them around the table. "As you'll see from these handouts, because of Miranda's murder and the subsequent investigation into her tragic death, we're at a standstill following the bazaar. We've got out-side vendors to pay, prizes to award, and a donation to the foster parent group that is very much needed right now. Every day that passes is going to make it harder for us to wrap this thing up, so I talked to Caitlyn and asked if she'd be willing to serve as executive director on an interim basis, and—"

"Wait a minute." The library director raised her hand. "Can we vote on this outside of a public meeting? Legally, I mean?"

I'd forgotten that the city budget provided part of Happy Hometown's funding, so the group's work needed to be conducted in the open.

The mayor nodded. "We didn't have time to advertise this meeting, and this is a personnel matter, which would be exempted, anyway, so I think we're fine. The executive committee met right after lunch, and we'd like for Caitlyn to at least get us through the holidays. After that, we can put out a call for a new ED and get going on that without having to act so quickly to fill a permanent position. Does anyone have any questions? For me or for Caitlyn?"

All eyes turned to her, and she looked hopeful that she would get the nod.

"In that case"—the mayor turned to Caitlyn—"if you'll just step out of the room for a moment, we'll have a vote."

Caitlyn smiled and left. The minute the door closed behind her, Gerald's hand shot up.

"Yes, Gerald." The mayor's tone implied he was wary of what was coming.

Gerald waved his sheaf of papers. "While it's unfortunate that Miranda Hargrove got killed and that so many things are left undone, she caused a lot of friction in town, and Caitlyn worked right there with her all that time. We should look for someone new and start with a clean slate."

The mayor sighed. "And where do you propose we find this new person, Gerald? Keep in mind that we only want them to serve for two or three months and at a modest salary. They'll basically be doing damage control following the death of their predecessor. Got any recommendations?"

Gerald shook his head, and an uncomfortable silence filled the room.

The mayor's jaw clenched. "Then since we don't have any other nominations for the job, I suggest we take a vote. That suit everyone?"

He looked around the table, and most of us nodded. Gerald, however, didn't move.

"All in favor of naming Caitlyn Hill the acting director of Roseland's Happy Hometown program, please raise your hand."

My hand went up, and so did those of all the others—except Gerald.

The mayor looked at him with something like exasperation. "So, Caitlyn, it is. Emma, would you mind asking her to come back in?"

"Sure." I rose from my seat, and when I opened the door, Caitlyn was pacing the hallway. "Hey! We've got some news for you." I smiled but didn't relay the vote, since I thought the mayor should be the one to tell her.

Caitlyn reentered the room, and Mayor Mathis started clapping. "Everyone, let's give Caitlyn a hand and thank her for agreeing to serve with us on a temporary basis."

Surprisingly, Caitlyn teared up. "I appreciate that so much. I know it's a rough time for us right now, but I promise to do my best to see us through, and I'm going to be calling on all of you for help. If there's anything I can do for any of you, please let me know."

The mayor adjourned the meeting and said he had a few items to get squared away with Caitlyn before he left. I exited the room behind Mavis, who was scolding Gerald.

She thumped him on the arm. "Why do you have it in for that poor girl? Hasn't she had a rough-enough time without you piling on?"

Gerald was unfazed. "If you'd seen how she and Miranda treated the Humane Society before, during, and after the bazaar, you wouldn't be saying that."

I interrupted. "I know about the before and the during, but what happened after?"

Gerald's eyes grew wide. "When we were finally allowed to leave for the night, Caitlyn made a big production of pointing out a scrap of dog food and a few drops of water that had spilled out of a cage and onto the lunchroom floor. She said Miranda might have had a point about how pets never should have been in the bazaar in the first place. So"—he looked between Mavis and me—"is it too much for me to want a new Happy Hometown director who actually believes that *pets* make some people happy?"

Mavis grimaced. "Maybe she was just upset after what happened to Miranda."

Gerald seemed to consider that. "Maybe."

That debate wouldn't be resolved anytime soon. After my busy morning and afternoon, all I wanted was to get back to my own pet. I told the others goodbye and drove home.

The moment I walked in the door, Miriam greeted me with insistent meows. "Yes, I know. You're overdue for your afternoon treat." I reached into a kitchen cabinet, pulled out a big plastic jar of cat treats, and handed her one. Miriam practically attacked it, so whatever she'd been doing while I was away, she'd obviously worked up an appetite.

I usually liked a treat of my own in the afternoon, but after consuming that hearty potluck lunch then rushing off to the Happy Hometown meeting, I wasn't hungry. Instead, I turned on my electric teakettle to boil water for a cup of Earl Grey. Once it was ready, I poured the steaming water over the tea bag. Then my phone dinged to let me know I had a text.

My purse was still on the table, so I reached in and grabbed my phone. It was Jen. *We're still walking this afternoon, right?*

I glanced at my vintage Pyrex tea mug and sighed. I'd forgotten that I was supposed to meet her at the park at four, and it was already three forty-five. I texted a reply. *Heading out shortly. See you soon.*

I could always make another cup of tea. I couldn't always enjoy a walk in the fresh air with my best friend.

After swapping church clothes for jeans, a T-shirt, and tennis shoes, I drove to the city park several miles away. If I hadn't had such a jam-packed day, I could have walked there and asked Jen to drive me home.

As I pulled into the parking lot, I noticed a couple sitting on a bench at the far end of the park. The gal was leaning against the guy as they looked at something on a cell phone. The sight made me miss my boyfriend, Justin Hayes. An up-and-coming fine artist who was getting rave reviews for his oil paintings, he was on the road a lot lately, exhibiting at shows all over the country.

A movement in the center of the park caught my attention—Jen doing her stretching exercises against the brick rim of the fountain.

"Hey!" She stood and waved. "I was afraid you'd forgotten."

I hustled over. "Actually, I did. It's been a crazy afternoon, but I don't like to pass up an opportunity to exercise. Especially with you."

Jen pumped a fist. "You ready to roll?"

I waggled my favorite water bottle, a gaudy rhinestone-embellished model. "Yes, ma'am."

We took off along the half-mile walking trail around the park.

"So, why was your afternoon so crazy? Didn't you have some potluck thing at your church?"

I nodded. "We had a choir luncheon, where I helped with setup and cleanup, then I got a text about a special called meeting of the Happy Hometown program."

Jen halted. "They met on a Sunday afternoon?"

I gulped. As a board member, I probably wasn't supposed to mention that. *Why can't I keep my mouth shut?* "Yeah."

"So why wasn't the press notified?"

I recognized that tone and immediately regretted mentioning the meeting. Jen was a stickler about making sure local officials followed the open-meetings laws, and she wouldn't let it go.

"Look, I know what you're thinking, but from what I understand, no one was trying to hide anything." I paused, wondering how much I should tell her. How much I *could* tell her. "Basically, we voted to name Caitlyn Hill as acting director, just on a temporary basis, to see us through the holidays. This wasn't anything official, really—"

Jen's hand was on her hip. "But you took a vote, right?"

I chewed my lip. "Yeah."

She cocked her head. "And you didn't have a problem with doing this in secret?"

Ouch. My relaxing afternoon walk was turning out to be anything but. "Look, we're only trying to keep things running so that the foster parent association can get its donation and so our vendors can get paid. I can't believe you'd want to get us in trouble for not dotting every i and crossing every t."

Jen stopped and put her hand on my arm. "Hey, that's not what I meant."

"Then what did you mean?"

She huffed, and her conflicted expression told me something was on her mind. She looked around the park, and I followed her gaze—it was trained on the couple I'd seen when I came in.

Jen spoke softly. "They probably can't hear us over there, but let's wait till we get to our cars. I need to tell you about a rumor I heard.

Now"—she looked at the Apple watch strapped to her wrist—"I still need to get in a few more steps. Race you."

Jen sprinted off, and I ran to catch up with her. But I was grateful for the break in the conversation. She and I rarely disagreed on anything, and it was odd for us to be out of sorts. Still, I didn't like her implying that I'd been part of some shady vote at the Happy Hometown meeting, especially considering the circumstances.

When I got to our cars, Jen was already seated in her blue Honda Civic, and she opened the passenger door and waved me over. "In here."

I plopped into the seat, and she reached into a small cooler in the back then handed me a bottle of water. "I brought an extra, and it's got to be colder than yours. Want it?"

"Thanks." That sprint had me winded, and I was grateful for the drink. I twisted off the top, took a big gulp, and looked at Jen. "So tell me what's going on."

"You can't breathe a word of this to anyone, okay?"

I nodded.

"Here's the deal. When Miranda arrived in town and immediately started rubbing people the wrong way, I got phone calls from a few sources who suggested we check her out. Her résumé looked good, and she came highly recommended, they said, but something just wasn't right. And I did wonder why they'd tapped somebody from Rochester, New York. Nothing against Rochester—or New York, for that matter—but small Southern towns like to hire people from small Southern towns, right? It's not a requirement or anything, but for Roseland, that struck me as odd."

I shrugged. "Not necessarily. Sometimes they want fresh blood and somebody who's not from the South and will have new ideas. Nothing wrong with that."

Jen finished the last of her water and screwed the cap back into place. "Agreed. But one of my sources told me Miranda wasn't who she claimed to be and said we ought to check her out."

The plot thickens. "Did you?"

"Everything I learned about her on the internet was about her getting this job, so I've got a reporter looking into her background."

"So, this source of yours"—I cut my eyes at Jen, because I knew she would never disclose her source's identity—"does he or she know why Miranda would have lied about her background? Surely it wasn't just to help her get a job in a place like Roseland."

"That person doesn't know, and I don't know either." Jen rested her chin on her fist. "But of course I can't help wondering whether this supposedly fake background had something to do with her death. I mean, isn't it possible that she thought Roseland was a place where she could make a new life for herself and maybe have a fresh start?"

My mind raced. "Wow. I don't know where I thought the investigation into Miranda's death was headed, but it certainly wasn't in this direction." I shook my head then had a flash of insight. "So, that's probably another reason you wanted to keep eyes on the Happy Hometown program at its meeting today."

"You got it." She grinned. "I'm not just trying to make life miserable for you and the rest of the board. You know me better than that. But now that I know there was a special meeting without the press being notified, how am I supposed to handle that? You know I can't let that slide."

She was right. "First thing tomorrow, I'll call the mayor and offer to help him with a press release about Caitlyn's hiring so that he can send it to the newspaper. I'll tell him that I'm volunteering since he probably hasn't had time to see about it himself."

Jen looked pensive. "If you'll keep me posted, I'm okay with that. But considering that a local public figure was found murdered at the

Christmas bazaar, of all things, our readers are going to want any scrap of news that comes out of that Happy Hometown office. And I gather you'd prefer that I not go ahead and call the mayor myself."

I shook my head. "Please don't. Give me till tomorrow, and I promise, I'll make sure you get something on it."

After telling Jen goodbye, I got in my car and headed home—again. As soon as I walked in, I went to the living room and turned on a cable news channel. The political bickering wasn't the restful background noise I'd hoped for, so I clicked off the TV, walked to my bookshelf, and reached for the latest issue of *Jewelry Design Today*.

I took the magazine to the couch, and once I'd prepared a cup of chamomile tea, I snuggled in and tried to shut out all the things clamoring for attention in my head. With Miriam Haskell curled up beside me and pretty new jewelry designs to peruse, I'd found the perfect way to relax after a busy weekend. I would think about all the good things that had happened—successful jewelry sales, a fun Christmas cantata rehearsal, and an afternoon walk with my best friend.

Yet it somehow seemed wrong to focus on holidays and fun while Roseland still had a murderer at large. I wondered what Miranda's family must be going through.

Does Miranda even have a family in Roseland? If she'd brought any family members with her, I'd never heard them mentioned.

I went to the bookshelf for my laptop then returned to the couch and did a search on Miranda Hargrove and Roseland. All that came up were newspaper articles linked to stories about our Happy Hometown program, and the initial press release about her new job didn't say anything at all about her personal life. Newcomers usually mentioned a spouse or children or hobbies—Miranda didn't appear to have any of those.

Then I did a search for the Happy Hometown program in Rochester. Their director had just received an award thanking her for ten years of service, so I wondered where we'd gotten the idea that Miranda had been the head there. Their website hadn't been updated recently, so I looked for a Facebook page. I scrolled back through a year of posts and didn't spot Miranda in any of the photos. Then I kept going through another year. I searched on Facebook using her name along with Happy Hometown and Rochester, but nothing came up.

Miranda, who were you?

I closed my laptop, watched a home improvement show, and called it a night. And as I said my evening prayers, I hoped that the person who'd killed Miranda—whoever she really was—would be found soon.

Chapter Six

At nine o'clock Monday morning, the Cupcake Café was abuzz. I had stopped by for a caramel macchiato and a Danish on the way to work the morning shift at the Foothills Gallery. Lots of folks who worked downtown stopped by the bakery to fuel their morning, so it wasn't unusual to encounter a crowd there.

As I inhaled the pleasant scents of freshly baked bread and cinnamon, Mavis hustled behind her spick-and-span yellow counter, which was always a bright contrast against the old black-and-white tile floor. She looked harried as she refilled an empty doughnut tray with fresh crullers and rang up customers. I was early for my shift and not on a tight schedule, so I took a seat at one of the small round tables, pulled out my phone, and gave a final proofread to the press release I'd drafted for Mayor Mathis. I'd already taken the liberty of writing the piece about Caitlyn being named acting executive director of the Happy Hometown program. When I'd called the mayor that morning, I explained that since we'd all "forgotten" to notify the media of Sunday's meeting, I thought it might help us avoid any criticism by getting ahead of the issue. He agreed and asked whether I had time to draft something for him. I sent the draft before I left the house, and he'd already written back with his approval. After reading it over a final time, I sent the press release to Jen's work email at the *Trib*.

Just as I was about to check my Facebook feed, Mavis sat down across from me, brushed her cheek, and smeared what I guessed was flour on it. "So, have you learned anything yet?"

I tucked my phone into my purse. "About what?"

"Miranda's murder. What else? That's all anyone's talking about this morning. And to be honest, it doesn't surprise me one bit that she ended up the way she did." She fingered the ribbon ties at the front of her cheerful yellow bib apron, which had the Cupcake Café logo embroidered on it.

I leaned in. "And why's that? Did you know Miranda personally?"

"Didn't know 'er well"—Mavis raised her eyebrows—"but well enough. She came in here a couple of times to buy breakfast pastries for the Happy Hometown board meetings back before I joined the board. The first time, she tried to get me to give 'em to her for free. Said it would be 'good publicity' for my shop."

I grinned. People were always jonesing for free food and merchandise from the shop owners. "Can I assume you made her pay?"

"Shoot yeah." Mavis's brow furrowed. "How was it supposed to help me if the head of some committee, who'd been eating here for ten years, got a free doughnut? Anyway, she acted like it killed her to have to come by here and pay for things, but she did. She was one of those women who stayed on her phone all the time. To be honest with you, I got tired of listening to her private conversations."

"Nothing work related?"

"Oh, sometimes. She was always in a tussle with somebody in town. I heard her fuss about the mayor, the city council, and even Caitlyn, which is kind of ironic, considering that's who's replacing her."

"Caitlyn Hill tangled with Miranda?"

"Oh yeah." Mavis looked at me over her silver-rimmed bifocals. "I'm surprised she and Miranda worked together as long as they did."

One of the shop's employees came by and asked for help with a cake recipe, so Mavis excused herself for a few minutes. While she was away, I pulled out my phone and checked an eBay listing I was following. The seller was offering a huge bag of orphaned vintage earrings, exactly the kind of pieces I needed for my Ruby & Doris line. And I still had the high bid—$7.95 for forty-something clip-ons. My fingers were crossed.

Mavis returned to the table with a cup of coffee, and I put my phone away, eager to follow up on our earlier conversation. "You were saying that Miranda had gotten crossways with Caitlyn. What was the problem?"

She shrugged. "Not sure. But Miranda was always hateful to her on the phone, ordering her around and having her run personal errands. One time, Miranda told her to go pick up her dry cleaning, and she wanted Caitlyn to dicker with the owners about a stain they couldn't get out. That stuck with me, that Miranda wanted Caitlyn to take care of her dirty work like that. No pun intended."

I frowned. "I wonder if Caitlyn minded. Maybe that arrangement was okay with her."

Mavis finished her coffee and plopped her mug onto the table. "I can't speak to that, but I do know that Caitlyn came in here one day and—" She looked around the café as if making sure we wouldn't be overheard. "Told some friend she was with that Miranda was the evilest woman she'd ever met. She said she couldn't wait till something blew up so that Miranda would have to leave and move to another town."

My eyes widened. "Was she serious?"

"Yes, ma'am. She was as serious as a heart attack." Mavis peered at me over her glasses and straightened her bib-style apron. "And she also said something like 'She wouldn't want everyone in town to know about her little problem, would she?'"

"Any idea what that was about?"

"No, but I wish I did."

"But you didn't mention anything about that at the board meeting yesterday, so..."

Mavis grimaced. "After my dealings with Miranda, I kind of understood where Caitlyn was coming from. Caitlyn's been just fine to me, and I think she knows her stuff, so I figure the personal goings-on between Miranda and her don't matter anymore."

I glanced at my watch and confirmed that I needed to get going. I thanked Mavis for the tasty breakfast and headed down the sidewalk to the Foothills Gallery. Caitlyn had seemed so upset when Miranda's body was discovered at the bazaar. *What if that was an act? What if she had something to do with Miranda's death?*

Shaking off the questions that bubbled up, I told myself not to rent any space in my head to a murder investigation. *Not my circus, not my monkeys.* Besides, Roseland's downtown was swiftly transforming into its annual winter wonderland of twinkling lights and magical window displays, and I didn't want to spoil the upcoming holidays by worrying about something that wasn't my responsibility anyway.

Trying to shut the unpleasantness out of my mind, I admired the festive windows ahead. Skinner's Bike Shop had a buff, super-fit Santa in red Spandex sitting atop one of the latest bicycle models. The shop's display skipped Thanksgiving entirely, but that was the trend lately. Next door, Lamberson Jewelry Company had decided to have it both ways, giving nods to Thanksgiving as well as Christmas. Customers who entered downtown's oldest jewelry store were greeted by themed display windows on the left and the right. At the left, a whimsical stuffed turkey presided over a display of gold chains and bracelets and chunky topaz rings that sparkled in the morning light. The windows on the right-hand side of the store were home to a glittering display of the latest in fine jewelry, featuring ruby and emerald fashion rings showcased in red and green velvet boxes amid a sea of colorful glass ornaments. The vintage pink speckled tile at the store entrance was such a fifties throwback, but it made me smile. I loved every drop of Roseland's historic charm.

I headed on and hoped the gallery would have a busy morning with lots of customers. I unlocked the shop, turned on the overhead pendant lamps, and inhaled the comforting scent of the lemon wax used on the antique wooden countertop and tables.

Just as I stored my belongings behind the counter, the bell on the front door jangled, and who was there to shop so bright and early but Detective Shelton. I wondered what he wanted.

"Good morning." He tipped his head.

"Morning." I aimed for pleasant but had my guard up after his huffy manner during our conversations Saturday night and Sunday morning. "Are you looking for something in particular, or did you just want to look around?"

"Actually"—he nodded toward the door—"I saw you enter the store a few minutes ago, and since I had a couple of questions for you, I hoped you wouldn't mind answering them... unless some customers come in, of course."

"Sure. What can I help you with?"

He pulled his small blue spiral-bound notebook out of his pocket and flipped through a few pages. "What can you tell me about Caitlyn Hill, Miranda's assistant there at the Happy Hometown program?"

Caitlyn's name again. Interesting.

"Not much. I talked to her when I filled out my application for an exhibitor space in the show, and I've seen her at a few meetings since I recently joined the Happy Hometown board. I can't say I know her all that well."

"Have you ever witnessed Miranda and her having a confrontation?"

"No, I can't say that I've ever personally witnessed anything like that."

I wasn't about to feel guilty for not telling him what Mavis had disclosed earlier that morning. I was in no mood for the lecture that would surely follow: "Emma, we don't need to know what sort of hearsay you're picking up around town." *No, thanks.*

"Since you've been on the board, no bad blood between those two?"

"Not that I've ever seen."

"That's all I wanted to ask you, then." He closed his notebook and looked around the shop. He hesitated as if he wanted to ask something more.

I cleared my throat. "Is there anything else I can do for you before I get back to work?"

"Yeah, I wondered if you had any more of those beaded necklace-and-earring sets like the ones I bought earlier this year for my mom and sister. They really liked them, and with Christmas coming up..."

He wants to buy more of my jewelry? Would wonders never cease.

I gave him my best shopkeeper smile. "Here"—I waved at a plaid-skirted table—"are some of my newest Christmas designs. I have sets in Christmas colors as well as the more popular fashion colors. Green and blue are always good choices, and turquoise is still going strong this season. I'll leave you to look through these, and if I can help, just let me know."

What a hypocrite you are, Emma. The man turned from officer to potential customer, and suddenly my opinion of him did a complete one-eighty.

He looked me in the eye. "Thanks. I always like to shop local, and I know they'd like to have something else you've made."

Sheesh. I wasn't expecting this.

Actually, he was a nice-looking man and around my age, but I wasn't about to fall for a police officer. I'd covered too many of them early in my reporting career and knew the pitfalls of getting involved with someone in law enforcement, however much I might admire them. Officers had a dangerous career, worked late hours, and were often married to the job. Besides, I was still waiting to see where things went with Justin. So nopety-nope-nope to thinking about the detective in that way.

While he made his selections, I tidied up a display of scarves and gloves knitted by a Roseland woman whose pieces we carried on consignment. Her lacy, elegant designs never stayed in the shop long.

A gray-haired couple came in and said they wanted to check out Bob Mathis's bowls and lamps. While they browsed, Detective Shelton made his way to the front to check out. I rang up his purchases—a green set and a turquoise set, just as I'd recommended—and was packaging them in Christmas bags with tissue paper when Jen rushed through the door and up to the counter.

"Oh, hi there, Alan. You can hear this too." With a glance at the couple studying the lamps, she lowered her voice and looked at me. "We just got an anonymous tip that Gerald Adams was overheard looking for his misplaced lanyard on Saturday evening about an hour before Miranda's body was discovered. Did you hear anything about that when you were there?"

Detective Shelton cut his eyes at me before he turned to Jen. "If you've got something that involves our investigation, I'd really prefer it if you didn't publish it in the newspaper until you talk to us first."

Jen narrowed her eyes. "Look, we don't print gossip in the newspaper. If someone wants to go on the record with something, sure, but we don't do unsubstantiated rumors. You know that."

"Then why are you here talking to Emma?"

"Because"—Jen crossed her arms—"she happens to be my best friend *and* she was at the bazaar during the time in question."

He held up a hand. "Fine. I just don't want"—he looked at me—"some people in town to get the wrong idea and think they need to help us investigate. We sure don't need anyone getting in our way."

"Understood, Detective." Jen, whose husband, Todd, was friends with the detective, obviously didn't have the same strained relationship with him that I had. Once Jen excused herself to get back to the office, the officer clammed up.

He accepted the two festive-looking gift bags I handed over, I thanked him, and he left without saying another word.

Chapter Seven

Midmorning, a bus from Gatlinburg dropped off a group of tourists, and a dozen of them decided to make the Foothills Gallery their first stop.

"Is gift wrapping free?"

"Can I get this bowl shipped to my sister in Albuquerque?"

"Does the knitter who makes these scarves take special orders?"

They were questions I'd answered plenty of times before—yes, yes, and yes.

"Hey, I wanted that one."

I glanced up from the register, and two women were reaching for the last package of Savannah's watercolor note cards featuring Thanksgiving cornucopias. The empty-handed woman got a little testy with the other one, and the victorious shopper looked smug.

The tourists weren't the only ones who'd decided to make a dent in their Christmas shopping. The gallery was packed for the rest of the morning. Before I knew it, the lunch hour had passed, and Shareta walked through the door. She was scheduled to work the afternoon shift.

I grinned when I saw her. "Take a look at the table where your baskets are usually displayed."

Shareta glanced at the table near the front of the shop then held out her hands. "But there aren't any. Where are they?"

"On their way to Gatlinburg. A tour group this morning nearly wiped out the shop. They adored your baskets and said they were the perfect size to take home on a bus."

"Hmm." She looked pensive. "I never considered marketing them to tourists because of their size, but that's not a bad idea." Then her eyes widened. "Unlike Miranda Hargrove, the customers didn't have an issue with my color choices for the baskets, eh?"

"Clearly not," I agreed. *But how interesting that this is still on your mind.* "And by the way, a big order of gift bags should be arriving this afternoon, since we're running low. I'll be over at A Likely Story if you need a hand with anything."

After grabbing my purse, which I'd stashed behind the counter, I told Shareta goodbye and headed to Roseland's new bookstore and café. When I entered, I inhaled deeply, since I'd always loved the scent of books.

A Likely Story was Roseland's latest retail success. While other independent bookstores were closing, Nichole Silver had gone against the tide by opening one with a mix of used and new stock, a tiny eight-seat café, and a book club that was generating a lot of buzz. The two of us had even talked about offering a beginner jewelry-making workshop, with Nichole, a former nurse, offering jewelry books for those eager to make their own designs.

It was still humid outside, and I appreciated the store's air-conditioning. If there was one refrain I'd heard around town over the past week, it was how hard it was to get in the holiday spirit when the weather was still warm.

"You might as well stick these Christmas books in the back until Mother Nature decides to cool off." I recognized that voice—Martha Barnes, the oldest and most veteran member of the arts council.

I walked over to her. "Not you, too, Martha. I thought you didn't like to be cold."

Martha gave me a world-weary look. "I don't like the freezing cold in the middle of winter, but I would prefer that we actually have a fall this year. Instead, this is just one endless summer." She had a hand on her hip and seemed unusually cranky. I sensed that something besides the weather had her nose out of joint.

"Everything else going okay?"

She waved off my question. "Oh, things are fine. I just had an aggravating morning over at the Humane Society. That's all."

"Why's that?" Most of the people in that group were easy to get along with.

"It's Gerald again." She returned a quilting book to the shelf. "You know we've got a lot of animal lovers in this town, but Gerald acts like we're all monsters for not fostering a dozen kittens and puppies apiece."

I found that hard to believe. "Come on. He knows the volunteers can't foster them all. The whole idea is to get more pets into forever homes, right?" Maybe Gerald was starting to get anxious about the holidays approaching. I'd heard that in November, people started thinking about buying pets as Christmas gifts, and shelter groups tried to emphasize the virtues of "shopping" the shelter first.

"You'd think so." Martha waved a wrinkled hand in the air. "But he told us this morning that if we don't get every one of these animals adopted by Christmas, he may resign and leave us with them, because that'll mean we simply don't care. He was already livid about how the Humane Society was treated at the bazaar, and if Miranda weren't already dead, he'd still be on her case too. Did you know he'd started a petition calling for her removal as director? He's so angry about everything and everyone lately. I can't figure out what's gotten into him. He's—"

"Hi there, Gerald." Nichole's pleasant voice rang out from the front of the shop.

Martha jabbed an elbow into my side. "Speak of the devil."

I looked past the bookshelf I was browsing just in time to see Gerald approaching the register.

"Morning, Nichole. Just wanted to see if that book I ordered came in."

"The one about puppy mills?"

"Yeah, that one."

"I think it may be in a shipment that just arrived this morning. Give me a minute to check."

"I don't know if our state legislators can do anything about it, but those breeders responsible for all these inhumane puppy mills have to be stopped."

Martha tapped me on the shoulder. "He was grumbling about that this morning too," she muttered.

I leaned closer. "It *is* a problem, though. Right?"

Her tight little blue-gray curls bobbed up and down. "Absolutely, but I don't see a way to shut them down just yet. We're going to have to educate the public first."

She probably had a point. I whispered back, "Listen, I need to go meet a friend at the café, so I'll see you later."

"Okay, dear. See you at tonight's meeting."

I headed to the checkout counter as Nichole finished ringing up Gerald and his puppy mill book.

"It's a shame we even have a need for a book like this, isn't it?"

She held up the title, and I grimaced. It featured images of sad-faced puppies and kittens in cages, and I couldn't bear to think of my sweet Miriam having to live that way—or any other pet, for that matter.

"Good morning," I greeted Gerald. "Didn't I hear that you had a few dozen pets adopted over the weekend?"

He stuck a hand into his pocket. "Despite Miranda Hargrove's best efforts to sabotage the Humane Society, we did indeed manage to have a good number of adoptions. In fact, I think we're on track to have a record number this year, no thanks to some pretty lackluster volunteers. But that's a story for another day, isn't it?"

Gerald paid for his book and hustled out of the store.

"Miranda wanted to 'sabotage' the Humane Society, huh?" Nichole grimaced.

Martha came out from her spot behind the shelves. "Whatever you thought of the woman, she's as dead as a doornail now."

I couldn't wait until I was eighty and could say whatever was on my mind.

"Still..." Nichole shook her head. "Oh, Emma"—she turned to me—"that jewelry book you wanted came in today. It was in the shipment with Gerald's." She pulled out a book on Hattie Carnegie, the clothing designer whose costume jewelry was still prized, and handed over the large, glossy paperback, which I fingered reverently.

"Thanks again for tracking down a new copy for me. I've wanted to learn more about Hattie Carnegie for a while now. Sometimes I come across her name on vintage earrings, but I don't know much about her other jewelry." I flipped through the pages and spied lots of gorgeous pieces.

Nichole smiled. "I thought of all your pretty jewelry as soon as I saw those beautiful pearls on the cover. Let me know what you think about the book. I like to be able to tell my customers what others are reading."

After I paid for my book, I headed to the café area to wait for Jen, who had texted and asked me to meet her for coffee that afternoon. She'd said it was important.

I was thumbing through my new book and sipping from a cup of piping-hot chai when Jen arrived at two o'clock on the dot. She went to the counter and, after hearing the day's special from the college guy working there, placed an order for a large mocha before settling into her seat.

She stared at my book's cover. "Hattie Carnegie. So what kind of jewelry did she design?"

"None, actually." I tipped my head. "Hattie just licensed her name for some great costume jewelry that others designed."

"Was she related to Andrew Carnegie?"

I shook my head. "She just liked the sound of his name, since he was the richest man in the country back then, so she used that name instead of remaining..." I flipped back a few pages. "Henrietta Kanengeiser."

Jen laughed. "Good move."

"She was quite a businesswoman." I perked up, as eager as always to sing the praises of the women entrepreneurs I was so fascinated with. "Ran five companies at one time. Made clothes for the Duchess of Windsor. Even designed the suit Mamie Eisenhower wore to her husband's inauguration."

Jen's eyes glazed over.

"But enough of that." I quickly shoved my book back into its paper sack and set it on the table. "You said you had something important to talk about."

Jen took a deep breath. "Yeah." She looked tired.

I squinted. "Is everything okay?"

"I'm fine."

"Liar." I wasn't sure of too many things in life, but I knew when something was wrong with my best friend. "Spill it."

Jen leaned back and folded her hands in her lap. "Todd thinks I should consider moving on and looking for work at a bigger newspaper."

My heart skipped a beat as I thought of losing my best friend. "Seriously? In today's publishing world, why would you even think about that? Hasn't he been paying attention?"

"I know, right?"

Newspapers were struggling, and journalism jobs weren't as plentiful as they used to be. I'd left the *Daily Tribune* when I had the seven-year itch and was eager to launch my jewelry-design biz, which had turned out to be a good career move. But Jen had never wanted to scratch that itch. All her life, she'd wanted nothing more than to be a reporter and editor, and she couldn't have cared less about owning her own business. Moving to a bigger newspaper, though, and at a time when so many of them were downsizing and giving staffers the ax—that seemed awfully risky.

"What prompted Todd to say that? Especially now?"

"There's a lot going on I haven't filled you in on." She rolled her eyes. "The new owners are businesspeople who've never even set foot in a newsroom before, so they don't care about anything but the bottom line. They want us to do more 'special projects' and things that bring in new ad revenue, whether or not it's anything that benefits the community. They want us to host events and sell advertising sections that don't have a thing to do with the news."

I grimaced. That was an argument the editorial side of the operation was never going to win. "But, Jen, it *is* a business, not a nonprofit. Or at least it's not supposed to be a nonprofit."

She frowned. "I understand that. Believe me. But I wish that for once, I would hear management talk about readers and the community and not just revenue, you know?"

I nodded, because I did know. "So do you agree with Todd? Are you ready to move on?"

Jen tapped out a rhythm on the table. "I don't know. Until lately, I was pretty content. But now, I'm just not sure. I don't have to decide today, but I do have to figure out what I want to do with the rest of my life. And there are still a few dailies around Atlanta that I might enjoy working at. Where I could work in *news*."

I reached for her hand. "Whatever you decide, you know I'm here for you, right?"

"Yeah." She gave me a half-hearted smile.

"Just as long as you don't move away from Roseland."

That got a chuckle.

"So enough of that." I rubbed my hands together. "You always have the scoop on what's going on in town. Got any news to share?"

Jen shook her head. "I wish I did. The reporters are hard at work, trying to cover the Miranda Hargrove investigation, but no one seems to know where to start on that, since half the town had it out for her. She sure had a lot of enemies, didn't she?"

I was all ears. "What are you hearing?"

"We've had at least a dozen calls from people telling us who they think killed her. Our poor intern has had to sit there moderating Facebook comments all afternoon because of all the nasty things people are saying."

"So who are the top suspects?"

"How much time have you got?" Jen rolled her eyes, but I gathered she wasn't joking. "Pretty much everyone at the Christmas bazaar has been named as a suspect by someone, but the most creative suggestion is the entire Humane Society. One conspiracy theorist says the murder was a hit coordinated by the group."

"Why the whole group?"

"Well"—Jen leaned back in her seat—"there was some brouhaha over the pet display, right?"

I nodded, remembering that Gus had come by my booth when it was unclear whether they would get to participate in the show.

"It seems that Gerald Adams took to Facebook and had this big, long thread urging everyone to show up for the bazaar and refuse to pay admission if the pet adoption booth wasn't inside. Said something about making sure that Miranda would 'pay,' and people are shooting us screen grabs of his posts, which, of course, have mysteriously disappeared in the past few hours."

Somehow, I'd missed the social media kerfuffle, but it had been a busy afternoon, and I'd been preoccupied with my booth. "Anyone else interesting on the suspect list?"

"Yeah." Jen's eyes widened. "You."

"Me?" I nearly spit out my chai. "Why on earth?"

"No idea." She shrugged. "But one of our Facebook commenters said the gal with the big jewelry display was seen talking to Miranda during setup at the bazaar and looked unhappy."

I couldn't believe someone would mention that in a public forum. *Wait a minute. Yes, I can.*

Jen swallowed a sip of her mocha. "One of the reporters is still interviewing some of the vendors about their dealings with Miranda at the bazaar. So far, though, I'm not seeing anything worth making a big ruckus about, especially now that she's gone. You weren't on the board yet when they hired her, were you?"

I sighed. "No."

"Oh well. I had to ask. Somebody in town must have voted for her to get the job." After polishing off her mocha, Jen stole a glance at her watch, which probably meant she was ready to get back to the office and see what else the *Daily Tribune* reporters had learned. I needed to talk fast to get a few more questions in.

"Have the police given you a statement? The incident report?"

"Of course not." Jen wadded up her napkin and brushed a crumb off the front of her navy-blue blazer. "We're supposed to get the report before the day is over, though. I'm going to the office now to see if it's come in."

"So you'll let me know if you find out anything new?"

She nodded. "But you'll still read the article in tomorrow's paper, won't you?"

"You know I will." Declining circulation was a concern at the *Daily Trib*, just as it was at all newspapers, and Jen zealously guarded each of the *Trib*'s remaining subscribers.

She leaned forward and clasped her hands on the table. "I can tell you've been giving this case some thought. Let's hear your theories about who killed her."

I shrugged. "All I've got is theories, none of them very good."

She motioned for me to continue.

"Okay. Maybe she couldn't cut the mustard back home in Rochester and was trying to make a name for herself in a small town where no one knew her. Maybe she was escaping a bad relationship or something. And maybe this was going to propel her to her next job, you know? She could have been using Roseland as a launchpad."

"Sounds like a juicy mystery," Jen teased. "Have you invented a deep, dark past for her as well?"

I swallowed the last of my chai. "Nope. I didn't have to invent a thing. I googled her last night and found out her history isn't exactly what everyone here was led to believe."

Jen looked intrigued. "Sounds like you've learned more than my reporters. So was she or wasn't she the head of some Happy Hometown program in New York?"

"That was the local scuttlebutt, but when I looked on their Facebook page and scrolled through the past few years of posts, I found no mention of her at all."

Jen's brow furrowed. "I thought they hired her because of her great résumé. No?"

"That was what I thought, too, and maybe they did, but I can't prove it from the internet. She's not in any of their photos or mentioned in the newsletters. It's just odd that such a mover and shaker wouldn't have shown up there or on social media, you know?"

Jen crossed her arms and lifted an eyebrow. "You wouldn't mind if I shared that news with the office, would you?"

"Be my guest. In fact, maybe I missed something obvious. I'd feel better about it if someone proved me wrong."

Jen's phone rang. "Okay, then." She glanced at the screen and stood. "It's the boss, so I'd better take this and head on back."

"Gotcha."

Once Jen left, I shook off thoughts about the murder, said good-bye to Nichole, and drove home, determined to get going on jewelry designs.

After I got home and petted Miriam, I sorted the latest bag of junk jewelry rescued from a local thrift store so that I could use it to create more Christmas jewelry. Not ten minutes after I'd walked in the door, my kitchen table looked like a 1950s jewelry factory had exploded all over it. But when a chunk of my yearly budget depended on selling a significant amount of Christmas jewelry, I made Christmas jewelry.

When I heard steps on the front porch, I left the kitchen to go peek out the front door. Brad, the UPS guy, had just left a package in the rocking chair by the entrance. I stuck my head out the door. "Hey, Brad."

He turned around, and I waved. With a check of the return address, I smiled. "Ooh, I've been waiting for this."

"More supplies for the jewelry empire?" Brad called.

"Yes, sir. Have a good one."

Back in the kitchen, I tore into the package. The latest junk jewelry batch that I'd won online included claspless pins and earrings that I hoped would work for my Ruby & Doris designs. I couldn't wait to make new jewelry with them. *But what is that in the bottom?*

I fished out a pointy piece—the tip of a Christmas tree pin.

Seriously? Is this what I think it is?

The dangling pearlized "ornaments" meant that it could only be a Hattie Carnegie pin. I didn't know too much about other Hattie Carnegie jewelry yet, but I sure knew her Christmas tree pins when I saw them. The pin was in mint condition. I turned it over, and there was the famous designer's name on a tiny gold cartouche. Considering that I'd paid just pennies apiece for the jewelry parts, the Christmas tree pin was a fabulous gift-with-purchase that would likely fetch at least a hundred fifty dollars when I listed it online. *If* I listed it online.

While I sorted the rest of the vintage pieces and snipped off backs and filed them down—a task that didn't require great concentration—I made a catch-up phone call to my friend Carleen Wood. Carleen owned the Silver Squirrel, an upscale antique store in downtown Roseland. She picked up in two rings, so I set my phone on Speaker and placed it near my workspace.

"Emma, it's great to hear from you. I haven't seen you in what? More than two weeks now? You doing okay?" Carleen sounded concerned.

"Don't worry. All is well." I shoved the phone a little closer. "I've been working late every night on my Christmas jewelry, so I haven't been out and about much."

"I'm assuming you were at the Christmas bazaar on Saturday."

"Oh yes." I gave a wry laugh. "Although now, I kind of wish I hadn't been."

"It sounded perfectly ghastly. And now everyone's wondering what will become of the bazaar and the donation to the foster children."

"What do you mean? It may take us a little while to sort this out, but—"

"That's not what I heard." Carleen cleared her throat. "I don't mean to stick my nose in your business, but the rumor is that this murder investigation means all the funds will be frozen, and there won't be a Christmas donation this year."

"What?" I could feel my blood pressure rising. "That's ridiculous! One of the main reasons we had a called meeting of the Happy Hometown board yesterday, according to the mayor, was so that the vendors can get paid and the foster parents can get their donation to buy gifts for the kids."

Carleen was silent for a moment. "If that's what he said, then I'm sure Harriet Harris just got her wires crossed."

"Harriet?" I blew a wisp of stray hair out of my eyes and lined up the now-backless vintage earrings. "I can't imagine she'll ever have anything nice to say about Miranda or the bazaar this year. Is she the one spreading this rumor?"

"Yes." Carleen chuckled. "Harriet was coming out of the Cupcake Café when I stopped by this morning, and I heard her tell someone she was surprised Miranda hadn't run into trouble before Saturday. I had a hunch she'd done something to upset Harriet."

"Did she ever." I quietly snipped excess metal from the backs of some pins and shuffled the newly filed-off pieces to the side. "Harriet's youngest daughter, Holly, has started making her own line of jewelry. Seems Harriet was irate that Holly didn't get a booth at the bazaar like they'd assumed she would."

"That daughter who just sits around behind the counter at the antique mall all the time?" Carleen tsked. "I haven't been there in a while, but back when I was going regularly, all she did was read novels and eat snacks. Are you telling me *that* daughter is a jewelry designer now?"

"That's what Harriet said. But I never actually saw any of Holly's jewelry, since she never got to set up."

"Listen, a customer just walked in the front door, so I'd better—"

"Say no more. Let's catch up over lunch soon."

"I'll call you."

I put my phone away and finished prepping the rest of the vintage earrings. What a pity that so many were orphans. The makers were a Who's Who of vintage costume jewelry designers—Schiaparelli, Weiss, Eisenberg. I picked up one of the prettier unsigned pieces and studied the color variations of the beads and rhinestones. One deep, rich red bead triggered a disturbing memory of the dark-red cord dangling from Miranda's neck at the bazaar. And from what Jen had said, someone was claiming that Gerald had lost his lanyard late that afternoon. I distinctly remembered seeing him wearing it that morning, but the afternoon was a blur, and I couldn't recall when I'd last seen Gerald—or Miranda, for that matter.

Miranda had roamed the exhibit floor until four o'clock or so. I tried to remember precisely when I'd last seen her. Maybe it was when she'd sampled kettle corn at the Kiwanis booth. When the show was about to close around seven o'clock, Caitlyn had made it clear she hadn't seen Miranda in a while either. I wondered when she had last spoken to her boss. There was one way to find out.

I reached for my cell phone, but before I could tap the number for the Happy Hometown office, the doorbell rang. The only package I was looking for had already come, and I wasn't expecting anyone, but I got to the door and saw a tall figure with dark hair—Savannah.

The door was hardly open before she thrust a small paper bag into my hands. "Cleaned out my jewelry box and thought you might be able to use some stray beads and broken earrings."

I peered inside and saw some great loot. "You know I'll put these to good use."

"So, am I interrupting your work?"

I grinned. "Yeah, but that's okay. We can chat while I make jewelry. What's on your mind?"

Savannah followed me to the kitchen, and I pointed at my electric teakettle, offering her a cup of tea, but she shook her head.

"You haven't heard anything about them finding Miranda's killer, have you?" She looked intense.

"No, not yet. But it's only been two days since the murder. Why?"

"I mean, this may not be anything at all. Maybe I shouldn't even bring it up, but..."

"Yes?" If I could have literally pulled it out of her, I would have.

"I overheard something Saturday that's been bothering me ever since we saw her body on that stage." Savannah leaned in. "Right after Miranda fussed at me about having you display my prints, she got a phone call. All I heard was her end of the conversation, but she sounded angry with whoever was on the other end of the call. Just before she hung up, she said, 'You don't want to go there with me. Not after last week.'"

"Any idea who she was talking to?"

"Unfortunately, no. But I do remember thinking it was rather inappropriate for her to have that conversation in front of me—or anyone else, for that matter. Maybe it was no big deal and drama was just a way of life for her."

"You can't remember anything else about the call?"

Savannah sighed. "I've racked my brain, and I wish I could, but that's all. I remember the 'you don't want to go there' and the 'not after last week' parts but nothing more."

"So if she was on a phone call to the person, whoever it was wouldn't have been there at the bazaar, I guess." I would have to rethink the suspects on my mental list.

Neither of us had any idea who Miranda might have been speaking to, but we agreed that it would be helpful to learn that person's identity.

Savannah scooted her chair back and stood. "I really just stopped by to drop off the junk jewelry. Didn't mean to stay long, because I hope to get a little painting in before the arts council meeting tonight."

"I hear you. I definitely need to make some more jewelry so I'll meet my quota for the day." I walked her out and waved goodbye, wondering who had been on the other end of that testy phone call. The only person who could possibly know what Miranda had been up to in recent days was Caitlyn.

The mystery surrounding Miranda's murder was taking up too much of my mental real estate, and maybe I could help speed up the investigation. It wouldn't hurt to ask Caitlyn a few questions. If I learned anything useful, I could pass it on to the police. And whether or not we cracked the case soon, I wanted to make sure things were on track for the foster parent association to get that Christmas donation.

Since I'd completed a dozen new bracelets, further jewelry work could wait until the evening. I needed a chat with Caitlyn, and with any luck, I would still have time to run an errand or two before the arts council meeting.

Chapter Eight

The Happy Hometown program had the good fortune to have
been assigned some coveted office space on the second floor of
a historic brick building downtown. Those upper-story locations had
become trendy and highly sought after by loft apartment lovers who
liked living within walking distance of the shops and restaurants. Ten
minutes after leaving the house, I walked upstairs to the office and
stood at its bright-red door, which was standing open. I rapped on
the doorframe and peered in to find Caitlyn alone. Considering that
the bazaar had wrapped up just two days before, I'd expected a flurry
of activity.

"Emma, hi. Come in." She motioned me inside and pointed at
her guest chair. "It's kind of quiet around here this afternoon. I'm
trying to figure out where to start with all of Miranda's plans. We
still have the Holiday Gallery Stroll coming up right after Thanksgiving, then early next month, we'll have Santa Claus on the Square and
the Shop Roseland First promotion. I'm not sure I can get all of this
done by myself." She bit her lip, and her eyes looked glassy.

Caitlyn sounded like she was in over her head. Apparently, she
was used to taking orders but not giving them. "Can I help? If there's
anything you want to delegate, I'll be glad to give it a shot."

"Would you?" Her shoulders sagged. "Miranda never thought I
was up to being in charge of any of our signature events, and maybe
she was right."

From what I'd seen, Caitlyn was more than capable of leading
those affairs. I hated to learn that Miranda had made Caitlyn doubt
herself.

"That's nonsense." I humphed. "Look how you pulled off the finale of the Christmas bazaar on Saturday when no one could find Miranda there at the end."

Caitlyn grimaced.

Oops. Bad example.

"I mean, obviously the murder cast a shadow over everything, but prior to that, the exhibitors were happy, and I had my most successful sales ever at a Christmas bazaar. If you hadn't helped plan the event and publicize it so well that half of Georgia came through, it wouldn't have been a success."

Caitlyn offered a tepid smile. "Thanks, but the fact remains that the leader of our Happy Hometown program is gone, and with her are all those plans she had. Many of them existed only in her head."

I couldn't imagine that was true. "Didn't you guys have a calendar somewhere? Something on your computer, maybe?"

Caitlyn nodded and reached into a file drawer. "Right here." She pulled out a bulky folder. "Miranda always printed out an exhaustive to-do list for us each Monday and included follow-up tasks from the week before. You're welcome to check it out." She handed over the folder.

I scanned the latest list, and the current week was indeed a busy one. In addition to a follow-up meeting about the bazaar, Miranda had scheduled committee meetings, meetings with city leaders, meetings with some new volunteers, and the monthly Happy Hometown board meeting. That last one, not surprisingly, had already been rescheduled.

Then I looked at the follow-up list from the week before and found a curious handwritten notation: *Check on possible lawsuit.*

"I don't mean to be too nosy here," I said, which was a complete lie, "but what is this 'possible lawsuit' referenced in the follow-up list?"

"Oh that." Caitlyn waved a hand dismissively. "Gerald Adams threatened to sue us if the Humane Society didn't get to have a booth in this year's bazaar. It was a moot point, since she decided to let them stay in, but Miranda was thinking ahead to next year and wanted to see if the city attorney thought the society had a valid complaint."

Caitlyn's desk phone rang, and she stopped to take the call. "I'm sorry, but Miranda's not here." After telling the caller that Miranda had passed away unexpectedly over the weekend, Caitlyn choked up and explained that she was the acting executive director.

As she finished her call, I checked my watch. I had planned to make a grocery run before heading to the post office, but that could wait. She hung up and let out a deep sigh. Caitlyn looked so forlorn that I couldn't help feeling sorry for her.

"Guess your dance card's pretty full this week, huh?"

Caitlyn rolled her eyes. "You have no idea. I feel like I've talked to half the town already. People who liked Miranda want to say how sorry they are that she's gone. People who didn't like her want to tell me stories about her, as if it's supposed to make me feel better about her being gone."

I grimaced. "That's weird."

"Tell me about it." Caitlyn pulled a file folder from a stack on her desk. "And you won't believe this, but I've even had a few people call up to schmooze, since they think I'm going to be in charge of vendor registrations for next year's bazaar."

"Gee, why'd they let so much time go by?"

"Exactly, and—"

Another phone call interrupted us, and while Caitlyn fielded questions about the holiday open house, I stood and wandered over to a wall displaying some of Miranda's diplomas and awards.

When Caitlyn finished her call, I walked over and asked, "Were you and Miranda close?"

"Like friends?"

I nodded.

"No. I was definitely just her underling."

"The two of you never socialized?"

"Not unless we had to, like at a lunch with city officials or something. I don't think she liked me very much."

I pondered that. "Why do you think that was? The two of you just didn't gel or what?"

Caitlyn shrugged. "I couldn't tell you. I tried to get to know her, but Miranda had so many walls up that I knew she didn't want us to become friends, so I kept everything strictly professional."

"Did she have any friends here in town?"

Caitlyn looked up, as if giving that some consideration. "Honestly, I can't think of ever seeing her with any. I know she was tight with the mayor and some people at city hall, but I never saw her going to lunch or dinner with anyone, and no friends came by the office to see her, if that's what you mean. Every meeting she ever had and everything I heard her discuss on the phone had to do with getting Happy Hometown up and running."

"So you have no idea what she did in her free time?"

She pursed her lips before speaking. "She sure liked to keep up with the news back in Rochester."

"Why's that?"

"She was always looking on the town's website or Facebook page or something. Honestly, she seemed to love that town so much that I once asked her why she moved here."

"And her answer?"

"She was kind of snippy about it, actually. Said it wasn't my business but that it was a good career opportunity and she thought she could help Roseland make headlines."

I bit my lip. "She certainly succeeded in that, huh?"

Caitlyn's eyes widened. "Yeah, I guess she did." But then her eyes turned glassy again, and she stared off into the distance. "I don't know how I'm supposed to keep all the plates spinning with her gone. And I hate to think I might let everyone down right when this program was getting launched. Do you think the city will shut us down because of what happened at the bazaar?"

"Look, this Christmas show has been going on for decades now, right? So it was going strong long before Miranda came to town, and it will still be going strong next year. We'll make sure of it."

I hoped I sounded more enthusiastic than I felt. Next year's attendees would likely have heard about the current year's disaster, and the tragedy would be on people's minds. Then again, with the current level of interest in the macabre, Miranda's murder might actually boost attendance next year, although I felt guilty for even thinking that.

Then I had another thought. "Do you know anything about Miranda's family? I would think that funeral arrangements are underway by now."

"The only thing I know about that is the mayor asked me to start boxing up her personal possessions. Said his understanding is that her body will be flown back home, and she'll be buried there."

I looked at my watch again and was about to head out when Caitlyn reached for my hand.

"Can I ask you something personal?"

"Sure." I sat up straighter. "Shoot."

"You used to work for the newspaper, right?"

Oh no. I hoped she didn't want me to ask the *Daily Tribune* for a favor. I'd been approached about that more times than I could count, and I was never comfortable doing it.

"I was a reporter there several years ago. Why?"

"One of their reporters is supposed to come by to get a statement from me about the bazaar, and I'm thinking he'll ask me about Miranda."

I nodded. "That's probably a safe bet."

"So should I go ahead and talk about the murder up front, or do I wait and see what he asks?"

"Personally, I'd rather bring up the topic myself. That way, you won't be playing defense, and the reporter won't think you're trying to cover up anything."

"What if I said something like 'I want to start by saying how very shocked and saddened we were by the untimely death of our executive director, Miranda Hargrove.' Would that work?"

Caitlyn looked relieved when I told her that would be a good approach, and I helped her finesse her statement. I told her not to memorize it, because she didn't want to sound too rehearsed, and I suggested it might help to have a few key points in mind. I also said she might want to type up four or five bullet points emphasizing those remarks and hand the document directly to the reporter.

She seemed to like that idea. Most people were worried about misspeaking with the press, but it wasn't like the *Trib* was some muckraking rag. Whatever statement she gave them would be fine.

After assuring her it was okay to call if she needed my help, I headed downstairs, out the door, and to my car, mentally compiling a list of all the jewelry I needed to make once I got home that evening. I still had jewelry orders to mail, and I was determined to drop them off at the post office before my arts council meeting.

So I dashed inside the post office and got to my meeting five minutes late. Trish, who had recently agreed to serve a third year as president, was going over a few changes to the minutes. Martha was eating a doughnut, Shareta was uncapping some bottled tea, and Savannah and Gus were sitting side by side, leaned in as they appeared to be reading a flyer.

All eyes turned my way when I lumbered in with my giant purse-slash-tote bag. "Sorry I'm late. Had to squeeze in a post office run." I tried to slip into a seat a few spots down from Gus without causing any further commotion.

Trish smiled at me. "No worries. We were just amending the minutes to note that the treasurer's report hadn't been finalized in last month's minutes, and now it has been. At that point, we had a balance of nineteen thousand dollars and some change."

"That's great. Isn't that much higher than where we were at the same time last year?"

Trish nodded. "We've had an outstanding year. The spring art show and sale was a hit, and the quarterly gallery strolls brought in a lot of new members, too, including some new folks eager to support everything we do."

"Oh?" I hadn't yet heard any preliminary figures for the year.

"With the new sponsorships and the ones we already had, that gives us an updated balance of twenty-two thousand dollars, and we've gained seventeen new members over the past year, which I think is great."

Martha wadded up the napkin with her doughnut crumbs. "So does this mean we can give more art scholarships?" Martha might have a reputation as the council's curmudgeon, but she was our most passionate member when it came to promoting the arts among Roseland's youth. She liked nothing better than to stand on the stage at Roseland High each May and hand out art scholarships worth a few thousand dollars.

"Now, Martha"—Trish raised a hand—"I can't speak to that. The full board will have to vote on any effort to increase the scholarship commitments, although I, for one, would be happy to consider it. We've also got to look at those new expenses we'll have in the first quarter of the new year."

"New expenses?" Shareta's brow furrowed.

"The new website, remember?"

"Ah yes. We've been talking about it for so long that I'd forgotten."

"I think we'd all just about given up on ever getting it." Trish glanced at Bob Mathis. "But thanks to Bob here, we're finally going to get that long-overdue redesign."

"Don't thank me. A lot of people made this happen." Bob looked around the table. "All it took was a little campaigning from the artists... and a reminder to my little brother that he might want my help next time he's up for reelection."

Everyone laughed. Bob was famously proud of his brother's role as Roseland's mayor, and the mayor was in no danger of losing Bob's support.

"So Jim Mathis somehow helped us get the money for this? Or what?" Shareta looked puzzled, and I had forgotten that she was still new to the board.

Trish spoke up. "The city got a grant that was earmarked for promoting technology in the community. We agreed to find some local high school students who could help us with our technology project, and that made it clear to the city that the arts council website update would be a perfect fit. Kids get real-world design experience with working artists. We get a basically free website redesign and the opportunity to mentor students. We'll have some new hosting fees next year, but I think they'll be well worth it."

Shareta nodded and looked impressed. "Sounds like a win-win situation, then."

"It is," Trish replied. "And with the new website, we'll have the ability to showcase our artwork, feature artist profiles of our members, accept new-member applications online, host on-demand video art courses, create surveys about the community's art needs"—she paused for a breath—"and a lot of other cool things we haven't even dreamed up yet."

Savannah added, "Some of the students were there and filmed the grand finale at the Christmas bazaar, but of course now, that footage is in evidence over at the police station. We definitely don't want to splash that tragedy all over the internet."

Martha, who had just polished off a can of Coca-Cola, groaned. "I thought I'd seen everything in this town, but even I had never seen a murder onstage at a public event."

For a few moments, no one said anything.

Gus broke the silence. "Have the police gotten any leads about who killed her?"

"I hear they don't have a clue." Bob looked annoyed. All eyes were on him, and he obviously felt the need to clarify his remarks. "My brother hasn't mentioned it to me or anything, but from all the local rumors, it sounds like the police know she wasn't exactly the most popular person in town. But then again, not liking somebody and wanting to kill them are two entirely different things."

Before I could muse further on that, Trish asked who had something to share for show-and-tell.

"I do." Martha wiggled her head, and her tight gray curls bounced. "Let me just get it out of my bag over there."

An art quilter, Martha had started experimenting with collage-style pictorial quilts. I loved that our eighty-something member had such a loose, nontraditional style of quilting. She walked over to a large black tote bag, pulled out a quilt backed with red fabric, and shook it open to its full width.

"Martha!" Savannah's eyes widened.

"Is that who I think it is?" I couldn't believe what I was seeing.

Somehow, Martha had managed to cut out tiny strips of fabric and appliqued them in a design that bore a remarkable resemblance to her beloved cocker spaniel.

"If you're thinking Bitsy, you're right." Martha looked as pleased as punch.

Trish rose from her seat and walked over to the quilt, and after studying it for a few moments, she turned to Martha. "May I?"

"Certainly. It's not fragile."

Trish fingered one of the folds of fabric and appeared to examine the detail of the stitching. "You did this on your machine?"

"I sure did. You'd be surprised what all these new machines can do these days. And listen, feel free to touch it. It's sturdier than it looks. Kind of like me."

Gus laughed. "You know, I've seen a lot of art quilts in the galleries I've visited over the years, but this one is just the bomb."

"I'm glad you think so"—Martha pointed at Gus—"because your group is going to get it as a Christmas gift."

"Huh?"

"The Humane Society. To get him off my back, I promised Gerald that I would make a quilt for the society to use as a fundraiser. He hasn't even seen it yet, so I hope he likes it."

"If he doesn't love it as much as the rest of us do, he's off his rocker." Gus was never one to mince words.

"Maybe it'll put him in a better mood too," Martha said.

Bob looked confused. "Why is he in a bad mood?"

"Oh, that dustup with Miranda at the bazaar. Now he blames Happy Hometown for the fact that they didn't have as many pet adoptions there as he'd hoped this year. He's really got it in for her."

Savannah spoke up. "But the poor woman's gone now, Martha. Don't you think it's time he lets that go?"

"Sure I do, but I can't make him get over it. Before the bazaar, he seemed determined to prove that he was promised much more than the society got that day. He said he had some kind of contract from Miranda. A few of the members got angry about the situation, and I heard they were threatening to show up at a city council meeting to try to get her fired. Of course, there's no need now."

Apparently sensing that the conversation was going off the rails, Trish released the quilt to Martha's waiting hands. "This really is magnificent. I'm sure it'll be a hit for the raffle, and please let us know as soon as tickets go on sale."

"Yes!" Gus grinned. "I want the first ten."

Trish and Martha returned to their seats at the table, and Trish opened a folder. "Listen, everyone, I don't want to waste time, so here." She handed a sheaf of papers to Shareta. "This is a list of all the events we're planning next year. Everybody, take one and look it over. We've got lots of exhibits, some lectures, and scholarship night at the high school, and I'd like for us to take a Saturday for a council retreat sometime in March or April if we can find a date that works for everyone."

The room grew silent as we scanned the list. Within minutes, everyone was offering their thoughts on which activities were worth pursuing as a group and which ones probably weren't worth our time. I saw a couple of new events where I hoped to have a booth. The one in May would be a great place to sell jewelry before Mother's Day. I drew a star by that listing to remind myself to check into the festival registration ASAP. There'd been so much competition just to get into the Roseland Christmas bazaar that I wasn't going to sit around and let the slots fill up before I got my application in.

The rest of the meeting focused on board business and policy matters, like forming a committee to update the bylaws. Since I still enjoyed writing and found it less painful than the others did, I volunteered to serve on that committee. And at seven o'clock on the dot, Trish closed her notebook and asked if there was any other business.

As if on cue, someone knocked on the doorframe—that tall artist guy in the paint-splattered vest.

"Tyler, you came!" Gus sprang out of her chair, went to the door, and ushered him in. "Trish said I could introduce you to everyone at the close of the meeting, and this is perfect timing. Tyler, please meet my fellow members of the arts council."

"Have a seat." I pointed at the chair between Gus and me, and Tyler thanked me and sat down.

Tyler explained that he was back in town after having moved away for a few years. "Gus tells me this is *the* place for artists to be. I stay busy with my acrylics, just like all of you with your art, I'm sure, but I also want to get involved here in Roseland."

Bob was beaming. "I've been dying to get another male on this board, so if I can help make that happen, you just let me know what you need, brother."

Everyone laughed. As Tyler talked about his art education and training, I studied his vest. My mind wandered as I thought about how many paintings were represented on it. That dab of green could be a tree or a flower. The grays and blacks might be stormy skies. Not surprisingly, some stray threads and bits of white fuzz were sticking to a few blobs of paint. I could only hope he had some way of keeping the thing halfway hygienic.

"So that's my story, and I sure appreciate you folks letting me stop by tonight."

Trish adjourned the meeting, and while Bob was first to slip out, I noted that Savannah and Gus—especially Gus—seemed to have a lot of questions for Tyler. Soon, the three of them left together. Shareta and Martha spent a few minutes discussing what sounded like some sewing technique, then Shareta helped Martha refold her quilt and wriggle it back into her tote bag.

While they talked fabric, I sidled up to Trish and lowered my voice. "I'm assuming Erin told you that I'm the one who got her to forward those photos to the police department Saturday night. I hope you don't mind me asking her to send those on."

"Not at all." Trish smiled warmly. "But when I asked Erin how you happened to see those photos, she wouldn't look at me and was a little vague about it. What were the girls doing when you saw the photos?"

I sighed. "Just being teenagers. You know, passing around the photos like we'd have done at their age, right?"

Trish humphed. "Yeah, you're probably right. But anytime you see my kid doing something questionable, feel free to jump in. Or let me know. Or both. Okay?"

I helped her tidy up the remaining papers on the table and, since it was already dark outside, asked Shareta if we could walk out together. She agreed.

When we got outside the library, Shareta cleared her throat. "I didn't want to ask this in front of everyone else, especially considering what's still being said about Miranda, but I actually had terrific sales at the bazaar. If you don't mind my asking, it looked like you had pretty good sales as well. Yeah?"

I nodded. "It was my best event of the whole year, and I have zero complaints about my booth setup. Everything went off like clockwork."

Shareta wore a sheepish grin. "I hear you. It may have ended badly, but just between us, I couldn't have been happier with the crowd. Miranda might not have had very good people skills, but according to almost everyone I've talked to, it was a banner year for the bazaar. And more important, for the exhibitors and charities who benefited."

We said good night, and on the drive home, I thought about all I'd learned that day, from Gerald's still-simmering rage to the never-ending list of Miranda's enemies to Jen's news about possibly looking for a new job. The bazaar itself seemed so long ago, yet only two days had passed.

As soon as I walked into the house, Miriam Haskell rounded a corner from the living room and purred loudly.

"Miss me?" After cuddling with my kitty for a few minutes, I microwaved a cup of soup from the pantry and scarfed it down, hungrier than I'd realized. Miriam planted herself by the kitchen table while I ate, emitting enough accusing meows to remind me that I had been AWOL for too long to suit her.

Once I finished eating, I pulled out my jewelry supplies and got to work. Michele wanted more of my beaded bracelets and earrings for the Feathered Nest, and the faster I got them to her, the faster customers could scoop them up. I glanced at the clock. *Yikes.* I was way behind on work for the evening. Being my own boss was fine until I realized the boss had been a slacker, saying yes to everyone else and procrastinating with my own work.

As I worked at the kitchen table, my mind drifted back to Saturday's tragedy. *How could a person be so brazen and kill someone near such a well-attended Christmas bazaar? Who would plan to commit a murder in public like that?*

But perhaps the killer hadn't *planned* to kill Miranda at all. *What if someone got into a fight with her and it was a crime of passion?*

Once I finished threading beads onto a new bracelet and was pleased with the look, I tied off the elastic thread and secured the piece on an Emma Madison Designs card so that it was ready to go to Michele's shop the next morning.

Even though she hadn't done her shopping there until late Saturday, Michele had served on the organizing committee for the bazaar. I would ask about her experiences with Miranda in the weeks and months leading up to the bazaar.

Before I knew it, a dozen pieces of jewelry were finished and ready for customers. I gathered the designs, put them in a tote, and made a list of questions to ask Michele. A few simple inquiries wouldn't hurt anything.

And the sooner I got Miranda off my mind, the sooner I could focus on my jewelry business.

Chapter Nine

When I arrived downtown Tuesday morning, the electric company's bucket trucks filled the streets, and workers were busy hanging giant silver tinsel Christmas ornaments around the square. With the holiday season fast approaching, Roseland was teeming with shoppers. And no wonder, because during the holidays, Roseland outdid herself. Trees surrounding the old courthouse were dripping with garlands of twinkling white lights, and the trunks were wrapped in a spiral of illumination as well.

That fall, the Happy Hometown program had encouraged shops and offices to paint a wooden Christmas tree using one of the bases made from cutout pallets donated by a local lumber company. The trees were being used to encourage competition between the merchants and raise more funds that would benefit the area's foster children. Customers got to vote on their favorites by placing coins in a jar near the counter—with each cent equaling one vote—and after the coins were counted, winners would be named, and the proceeds would be used to provide a merry Christmas for local children. All the businesses wanted to win, and from what I'd seen on social media, the competition was getting fierce.

To absolutely no one's surprise, Michele Fairchild's Christmas tree entry outside the Feathered Nest was a stunner. She had spruced up the simple plywood tree with frosty paints in gumdrop shades of pink, turquoise, and lavender. Colorful miniature birds danced among the branches, and up top, in a nod to her store's name, baby birds sat in a nest, with fluffy white feathers blowing in the breeze. If she didn't take first place, that contest was clearly rigged.

Michele was proud of her shop's history, and her newly decorated Christmas window paid homage to its past as a millinery shop. She'd created a mini version of the old shop and had some darling miniature hats on display. Behind the storekeeper's wooden counter were beautifully dressed doll clerks, including one with a Gibson Girl upswept do, her leg o' mutton sleeves billowing over her full-length gown as she presented a miniature hat and hatbox to her customer. I wondered, and not for the first time, where Michele got all of her fabulous ideas.

Satisfied that I'd soaked up every last detail of her latest window display, I entered the store.

"Emma, I'm so glad to see you." Michele sidled up to me and handed over a small paper napkin with a cookie on it. "Have a pumpkin spice sugar cookie before I eat some more of them myself."

As I chomped a bite of cookie, I glanced at the napkin, a retro-looking design featuring what appeared to be a 1950s Santa Claus graphic. I swallowed the rest of the cookie and pointed at the crumbs. "Never had a pumpkin-flavored sugar cookie before, and I like it!" I was impressed. "And I adore these napkins. Please tell me they're for sale."

Michele pointed at a table stacked high with plates and platters, dip bowls and spreaders, and napkins in all shapes and sizes. "It's a new line I found at the mart earlier this year. Aren't they sweet?"

They were, so I snatched two packages of the Santa napkins in case the other shoppers heard us talking and got any wild ideas.

A gray-haired woman and a little girl stood near the register. Michele handed them each a cheese straw. "And these are made by a local woman using her great-aunt Josephine's secret family recipe. See what you think."

The woman and the girl accepted the samples, and Michele looked up in time to give me a smile and wave me over. "Come here. You have to try one of these too. They're getting rave reviews."

I accepted a cheese straw and took a bite. She was right—it was delicious, with just the lightest touch of cayenne pepper. "What's the cheese in these?"

Michele had popped one into her mouth as well. "Pimiento," she mumbled between bites.

The gray-haired woman spoke up. "My granddaughter and I are having a Thanksgiving tea party for her dolls this afternoon, so I'll take a package of these, too, please."

A few quick taps of the register and Michele had the woman on her way with a huge shopping bag that I assumed was packed with either Thanksgiving treats or Christmas gifts—possibly both.

"I hope you've brought me some more of those vintage-looking bracelets." Michele pointed toward the door. "That woman who just left? She has four daughters and bought one for each of them." Michele glanced over at the table where she displayed jewelry and accessories, and the rack that usually displayed my bangles had one lone bracelet left.

I held up my newly filled hamper.

"Your timing's perfect." Michele nodded at my red tote and bustled around the table as I hung bracelets on the display rack. "Let me put one of my holiday candles right here. When someone asks what that yummy scent is, and they will, I can tell them it's the same candle that's on the table with the locally designed jewelry."

"Clever." I loved all the creative ways that local shopkeepers enticed customers to make a purchase, especially when the purchase was my jewelry.

Michele spaced out the six new bracelets I'd hung and adjusted the beaded necklace-and-earring sets so that they filled the table. "There. Much better." No other customers had entered the shop, and Michele glanced toward the front door. "So, have you heard anything new on the Miranda Hargrove front?"

"Afraid not. What about you?"

"Zilch."

"Weren't you on the organizing committee for the bazaar this year?"

"Yes, but I didn't work closely with Miranda. And to be honest with you, that was probably best after the way she treated my child."

"What did Miranda do to Austin?" Miranda's precocious three-year-old was a mischievous little boy, but he wasn't a bad child.

Michele rolled her eyes. "I was biting my lip not to mention this at the luncheon on Sunday. Wells says I need to let this go, especially now that the woman's gone, but you know, when someone mistreats my son, the mama bear in me comes out. When she brought those plywood trees around for the decorating contest, Austin happened to be here, and he started dancing around with mine. You know how excited he gets over Christmas."

"Like about ninety-nine point nine percent of all kids?"

"Exactly. So when Miranda grabbed the tree from him, she snatched it away so quickly that he got a splinter in one of his fingers and started crying. I knew that wasn't going to kill him, but there's no excuse for a grown woman treating a little boy that way, and I told her so."

I grimaced. "Good for you. I'd probably have done the same thing if I had kids."

"And she didn't—how shall I put this?—respond well to the criticism. She said Happy Hometown had put a lot of effort into getting all those plywood pieces donated, and she didn't want to see one spoiled child damaging one and ruining the chance for all the less-fortunate children to have a happy Christmas."

"Whew." I let out a breath. "Let me guess that the conversation did not end well."

Michele crossed her arms. "It ended just fine for me. I told Miranda that if she was going to stand there and insult my child, especially here with the holiday season upon us, that she was welcome to hightail it back to Lake Wobegon, where the children are all above average."

I couldn't help snickering. "You didn't."

"Yes, ma'am, I most certainly did, and I'd do it again." Michele looked pensive. "But of course, I had no idea back then that she was going to an early grave."

I shuddered. I'd thought only my grandparents used that phrase. "So that was the extent of the exchange?"

She nodded. "Pretty much. I did mention to the mayor the next time I saw him that I didn't care for Miss Happy Hometown."

Our poor mayor. I wouldn't have his job for all the rhinestones in Austria.

"How did he react to that?"

Michele shrugged. "He got defensive and started telling me what a great job she'd been doing. I know for a fact that he'd already had a lot of complaints about her, though, so my beef was probably just one more added to a long, long list of them."

She reached across the counter and appeared to swipe something away.

"What're you chasing there?"

Michele shook her head. "Another stray feather. I bought a package of those white ones at the craft store to decorate our tree for the contest, and now I keep finding the little rascals all over the place. Only thing worse is glitter. See?" She turned up a palm and revealed a glittery pink spot. "I spilled some behind the counter when I was working on the tree, and I have never seen glitter spread through a place so fast. It keeps turning up everywhere. If you ever need any for your jewelry..."

I laughed. "Not sure I'll be using glitter anytime soon, but thanks. I'll keep that in mind."

The store's twittering chime signaled that more birds were entering the nest. Michele excused herself to go greet the new customers, so I looked around the store and gathered a few ornaments and tea towels to get a start on my Christmas list. The Feathered Nest was a treat to visit at any time of year, but it was a treasure trove during the holidays. Michele had a knack for knowing just what her shoppers wanted, often before they knew it themselves. I was grateful for her steady stream of customers, especially since one of the earlier ones had already bought some of my jewelry.

A forty-something woman with spiky blond hair picked up one of my jewelry sets, and Michele asked her if she would like to meet the designer.

"Sure. Does she live nearby?" the blonde asked.

"She definitely does, and she's standing right there." Michele laughed and pointed my way.

"I absolutely love the look of your jewelry." The woman held up a Ruby & Doris bracelet and sighed. Something about her looked vaguely familiar, but then I saw a lot of women, since they made up most of my customer base.

I thanked her for the praise, then she posed a question I hadn't seen coming.

"You were in that Christmas show this weekend, weren't you? And that lady in charge of it got in a fight with someone and ended up dead?" She looked so genuinely curious that I overlooked the crassness of her question.

I gulped. "Um, I was at the Christmas bazaar on Saturday. And yes, I'm afraid many of us were there when everyone learned about the death of the Happy Hometown program's executive director. I'm not sure I can speak to her getting into a fight with someone, though."

"One of my friends heard her get into a yelling match with the head of the Humane Society right before the show started. He told her that if she kept the pets out of this year's show, that would be the last show she ever directed." She tsked. "Everybody's talking about it."

The woman was a busybody, clearly, not that I held that against her. Then I paused to consider whether I wanted to hear one more thing about the murder. *Who am I kidding? Of course I do.*

"Would your friend be willing to tell the police what she heard?"

"I don't see why she wouldn't."

"Great." I pulled out a notepad and pen from my purse and handed them over. "I know one of the officers investigating the case, so if you don't mind giving me your friend's number, I'll have him get in touch with her."

Once I had the information in hand, I headed to the checkout counter and Michele. "I'm assuming you heard all that?"

"Oh yes." She grimaced. "And everyone knows how uptight Gerald Adams can be. He's always been an odd bird. Any grown man who still lives in his mother's basement, well, you've got to wonder. Loves his animals, but when he comes before the downtown merchants about anything, he usually rubs people the wrong way."

"How do you mean?" I placed my Christmas ornaments and tea towels on the counter.

"Let's see what we've got here." Michele tapped a few prices into her cash register. "Okay, so over the summer, the merchants were getting ready for our Back-to-School Bash, and Gerald wanted to have a pet adoption on the square at the same time. We were fine with that, but then, when we voted to set out collection cans to raise funds for school supplies for needy children, he thought we should have donations for pets too."

"But the pets weren't going back to school, so...?"

Michele frowned. "I know, right? So we told Gerald he could have his adoptions, and he did, but he'd branded us all as animal haters because we didn't focus our back-to-school event on pets too."

I shook my head. "That's crazy."

She nodded.

After Michele packaged my purchases, I said my goodbyes and headed to the police station. First thing, I stopped by Evelyn's desk and asked whether Detective Shelton was in.

"I think he is, hon. Let me ring his office and check." She punched a number into her desk phone. "Hey, Alan. Emma Madison is here and would like to speak with you. Do you have time? Okay, I'll tell her."

Evelyn hung up and said he was almost finished meeting with another detective and would come to the reception desk shortly. I had time to wait.

While we waited for the detective to arrive, Evelyn caught me up on her family. Soon, I heard footsteps coming down the hall. Detective Shelton said hello and asked how he could help me.

"Actually, I'm hoping I have something to help you." I held out the piece of paper with the phone number provided by the customer at the Feathered Nest. "Now, I don't want you to think I'm out there nosing around in your investigation, but—"

Evelyn's snicker caused us both to look her way. She feigned innocence and dove for a stack of files in her desk drawer.

"Let's step into my office," the detective said, and I followed him down the hall, walking at a clip to keep up. He ushered me in and motioned to a seat. "So, what's this about?"

"This may or may not be anything, but I overheard something this morning that I wanted to make sure you're aware of. You probably know this already, so forgive me if this is a repeat, but a woman at the Feathered Nest said her friend overheard Gerald Adams threatening Miranda at the bazaar on Saturday."

"Go on."

"So did you know about that already?"

"Now, Emma, you know this is an active investigation and—"

"Oh, good grief. If you've heard it already, I'll just throw away this woman's name and number. If you haven't, I'll give it to you. What do you want me to do, Detective?"

He bit his lip. If he said no, he hadn't known, he would be admitting he wanted my help. If he said yes, he did know, he would be disclosing information about his investigation.

Not surprisingly, he hedged his bets. "Whether it's something we already know or not, it's always smart to follow up with anyone who may have direct knowledge pertaining to an investigation." He sighed and held out his hand. "So yes, I would appreciate your giving me the information."

I met his eyes. "No problem." I reached into my purse for the piece of paper, suddenly grateful that I always kept a couple of notepads handy. I never knew when I might need to jot down a few notes about jewelry inspiration. *Or murder suspects, apparently.*

"Thank you. And..."

"Yes?" *Is he finally going to show a little gratitude for my help?*

"While I appreciate you bringing this to our attention, I'd just like to remind you that this investigation is being handled by the police department. We'd appreciate it if you kept in mind that a murder investigation is by definition a dangerous undertaking, so we strongly encourage civilians not to get involved."

I blinked. I'd just given him information for his case, yet he still couldn't resist giving me a lecture. And I couldn't resist letting him know precisely what I thought of that.

"Certainly, Detective. But just for the record, even as a 'civilian,' I'm more than aware that an investigation of murder might be 'a dangerous undertaking,' as you put it. But hey, I'll make sure I don't bother you again."

Humph. I turned and walked out of the detective's office. If that was his idea of gratitude, he wouldn't be getting any further help out of me.

AS I WALKED INTO MY house around noon, the heady aromas of curry and garam masala wafted through the air. Indian butter chicken was in the slow cooker, since Jen and Todd were coming over for dinner. I hadn't seen Todd in a while and thought it would be nice to dine with him, too, for a change.

While the spicy ingredients filled my house with the exotic scents of India, I wired a few more necklaces and earrings to make sure I had plenty of stock for the Foothills Gallery. After I completed five necklace-and-earring sets and packaged them all, I had time to catch up on the mail that was overflowing in the large basket near the front door. That day's batch alone was a four-inch-thick stack held together with a big rubber band.

I hefted the basket onto the kitchen table and quickly separated the week's mail into piles to save and to recycle. *Jewelry magazines, keep. Utility bills, pay and recycle. Junky coupon packs, recycle.* Then my heart skipped a beat when I saw the return address for the Jewelry Artisans of the Southeast.

Last month, I'd applied online to be in their spring show and snail mailed the required prints of my work. The photos were supposed to be returned by mail if I wasn't selected for the show, but the business-size envelope before me was thin, as if it held just a single sheet of paper.

Here it is. They're telling me whether I got into the show next May. With my sterling-silver antique letter opener, a gift from Carleen, I sliced into the envelope and took a deep breath. I promised myself not to be too disappointed if I didn't make it. It was a prestigious show. Not everyone could get in, especially not every newcomer to the jewelry design world.

"Dear Miss Madison, We are pleased to inform you that—"

"Yes!" Those were the words I'd been longing to read. Getting selected for the JAS show was a great honor for any jewelry designer, but I probably appreciated it more than most. Since I'd never gone to art school, I was still rather insecure around other jewelry artists with professional training. But then, not one customer had ever asked to see my credentials. They judged my work on its own merits, which was how I liked it.

The good news called for a celebration, and I knew just who I wanted to join me. I grabbed my cell phone and tapped a number from my contacts, and Carleen picked up on the second ring.

"Hi there. If you're not super busy at the Silver Squirrel this afternoon, any chance you could meet me for a coffee at Mavis's?"

Carleen said she was having a slow day and agreed to meet me there in fifteen minutes. I went to the bathroom to touch up my makeup, and since my hair looked a little unkempt, I ran a brush through it. Using a fabric-covered band that was the same honey-golden shade as my hair, I pulled it back into a sleek ponytail before heading to Mavis's.

When I got to the café—which still had a few whimsical ghost and goblin decals affixed to the windows—Carleen was waiting. I walked in and joined her at a two-seater. She'd already gotten her order of tea and a chocolate chip cookie, so I said hi to Mavis and ordered a salted caramel and pumpkin spice latte.

"What's up?" Carleen leaned in and raised an eyebrow. "You sounded excited about something."

"I am." I reached into my purse, pulled out an envelope, and handed her my acceptance letter from the Jewelry Artisans of the Southeast. "Check this out."

She slipped on her readers and pored over the letter. "Emma, this is wonderful!" She reached across the table and grabbed my hand. "What fantastic news."

Carleen and I enjoyed our treats as I babbled about my plans for the jewelry show. I explained that in addition to the pieces shown in the prints I'd sent—the jewelry I would be required to display at the show—I was also encouraged to take more of my work to sell.

"At a show like this, the quality of the work has to be exceptional, right?"

"Mm-hmm." I finished a sip of my latte. "They're definitely expecting some one-of-a-kind pieces. In my everyday work, I try to keep things unique but affordable. For this show, though, they say that high-end pieces sell best. You can bet I'll be using up my secret stash of the finest beads and stones I've had tucked away. I've never been able to work on pieces where price was no object before."

Carleen grinned. "This is really a dream come true for you, isn't it?"

"It is." I leaned back. "I don't want to get ahead of myself, but if I get the publicity and commissions I hear are typical at this show, I might have to consider scheduling shows at more high-end jewelry shops and art galleries."

Carleen's eyes lit up. "We'll do a trunk show!"

"What?"

"After your JAS show. We'll do a trunk show at the Silver Squirrel to celebrate your success!"

"Oh, I can't ask you to—"

"You're not asking me. I'm asking you. We don't have to nail down details right now, but after your big show next year, I'd love to feature you at my shop. Besides, I always have to work on getting word out that the Silver Squirrel sells more than just heirloom silver. I can work on adding to my fine jewelry and high-end costume jewelry between now and then. It'll be fun!"

Before my mind could venture too far in that direction, Carleen filled me in on her holiday schedule for the Silver Squirrel. She planned to close the week of Thanksgiving—a buying trip to Charleston was on her agenda—then she would come back and decorate the shop for Christmas.

Eyeing my empty cup, Carleen wanted to know why I hadn't ordered one of Mavis's treats to celebrate my good news.

"I'm saving my appetite for a nice dinner with Jen and Todd. They're coming over in a few hours."

"Just those two?" She had a twinkle in her eye.

"Yes, why?"

"I thought your new gentleman caller, Justin, might be there. Everything okay on that front?"

Then I realized why she was asking. She probably wondered why my "gentleman caller" hadn't been invited too. "Justin's at an art show in Colorado this week." I sighed. "I miss him, but his paintings have been a real hit at a couple of the finer galleries in Denver, so when he got invited to participate in several shows there, he didn't feel he could pass up the opportunity."

Carleen brightened immediately. "Good for him. Sounds like you're both on the path to becoming famous artists."

"I'm sure doing my part."

"And if you don't mind one more question..." Carleen stared intently at me.

"What is it?" I wiped the corner of my mouth with my napkin. "Am I wearing my latte?"

She chuckled and shook her head, her striking feathery gray hair swaying. "No, but naturally, the whole town's still abuzz about the murder at the Christmas bazaar. I just wondered whether you've cracked the case yet."

I humphed. "Hardly. I'm trying to learn something that might nudge the police along, but believe me, that last murder case was a one-shot wonder." Earlier in the year, Carleen's sole employee, who was also a dear friend, had been killed in what we thought was a botched robbery attempt. The killer had turned out to be the woman's sister, and while I'd helped solve the case, I didn't plan to make a habit of it.

Carleen narrowed her eyes as if she didn't quite believe me.

"When Harriet stopped by the store yesterday afternoon—"

"Wait a minute. Harriet stopped by *your* store yesterday? I remember you running into her at Mavis's, but she actually went inside the Silver Squirrel?"

Since Harriet operated the Making Memories Antique Mall, even if she admired the high-quality silver and other pieces Carleen sold, she rarely spent money with Carleen—or any other local business owners.

"Don't worry. She wasn't trying to score a deal or anything. She was still mad about Holly being excluded from the show and asked me if I knew anyone who might carry Holly's jewelry on consignment."

I wrinkled my nose. "Why would she think you could help her with consignments?" What an odd thing to ask Carleen. Everyone knew that she sold only quality antiques.

Carleen looked around the café and lowered her voice. "Those were my thoughts exactly." She folded her hands on the table. "I told her that since the jewelry wasn't antique, I didn't know of anyone appropriate for them to contact. I tried to be pleasant about it, although to be honest with you, Holly's jewelry isn't really my cup of tea. You know, lots of plastic beads and thick tassels made from what looked like ordinary yarn."

I frowned. "The mainstream craft magazines do seem to have gone overboard with tassel jewelry."

Carleen continued, "Harriet told me she gave an earful to the mayor when she saw him at the bazaar on her way out Saturday. She was all but demanding Miranda's head on a silver platter. You know, the mayor's family and Harriet's are related, although I forget exactly how, and I'll bet she bends his ear every chance she gets. Poor man."

Carleen glanced at her vintage gold Cartier watch and said she needed to get back to her shop for an appointment with a customer, so I waved her off. I got a glass of ice water from Mavis then sat back down to jot a few ideas in my design notebook. While Carleen and I were talking, a woman in a gorgeous bright-orange coat had sashayed into the café. Orange had never been one of my favorite colors, but it was popular in the design world, and I wanted to order some orange beads from one of my suppliers. Orange jewelry sets might sell well for Christmas.

I looked at my watch—unlike Carleen's elegant vintage model, mine was another whimsical rhinestone bracelet watch—and I still had a while before I needed to head home and get dinner on the table for Jen and Todd. That left plenty of time for a quick bead run.

Besides, I hadn't popped into Making Memories Antique Mall in a couple of weeks and wanted to be sure I wasn't missing out on some good junk. I was going there to shop, not to snoop. Harriet would likely know if there were any new bags of vintage jewelry I needed to check out. I'd let her know up front that I was in a hurry so that she wouldn't bring up the Christmas bazaar and the murder. It always helped to have a plan.

Chapter Ten

Some plan. Things went off script almost the moment I walked into the antique mall, and Harriet was as riled up as I'd ever seen her.

"Miranda really told you that Holly's jewelry was unfit to be in 'her' show?" I couldn't believe my ears.

"She most certainly did. A grown woman parading around in a silly Mrs. Santa Claus outfit like that. Channeling her inner Rockette, if you ask me. I'm sorry she was killed, but I did not care for the woman. Not one bit."

Harriet was cleaning the reading glasses she wore on a cord around her neck, and I was afraid she was rubbing so hard that she would pop the lenses out.

I would have felt guilty for the turn of conversation, but I hadn't been the one to bring up the Christmas bazaar. Once I'd told Harriet that I was in a hurry for more junk jewelry, she followed me to the aisle where a new dealer had just set out some bags that Harriet said looked promising. The seller wanted only eight dollars each for them, so I bought all five bags. That was a bargain for so many vintage pieces, and while the bags appeared to have lots of unstrung beads and broken brooches, I spotted some high-quality tidbits that I could either repair or repurpose.

While I examined the junk jewelry, Harriet chattered away about the bazaar, Miranda's insult to Holly, and the town hubbub over Miranda's death.

"I hope whoever they get to replace her has a much better attitude than she did. We need a friendly person in that job, not some cranky Yankee who's going to turn people off."

I stifled a laugh, because Harriet wasn't exactly the poster girl for Southern hospitality.

While she rang me up, Harriet was clearly not ready to leave the topic of the bazaar. She waved her hands as she spoke. "And to top it off, poor old Gerald Adams says he left his lanyard in the kitchen. It got wet while he was getting water for the pets, but he forgot it, and now the police want to know how that lanyard ended up around Miranda's neck."

So that's where the lanyard was.

"How do you think it got there?"

Harriet looked up from tearing my receipt off the register's printer. "No idea. But when you make a hobby out of offending half the town..." She shrugged. "And the killer wasn't necessarily someone here in Roseland, you know. A woman like that? She probably made enemies everywhere she went."

Harriet went off on a tangent about how she'd given the mayor a piece of her mind about Miranda, and if he'd fired her on the spot, maybe she wouldn't have been killed.

I bit my lip to keep from commenting on how ridiculous that was. Instead, I stole a look at my watch. "Oh, goodness, I didn't realize how late it's gotten. Listen, Harriet, I've got friends coming over for supper, so I'd better scoot."

As I dashed to the front door, I held up my newly purchased bag of jewelry supplies. "Thank that new seller for the great junk. Tell her I'll be back!"

ONCE HOME, I WALKED in and inhaled the decadent aroma of Indian spices. I was able to assemble the dish so quickly that I made it often. And while I knew my way around a kitchen, with all of my Christmas jewelry orders—not to mention my volunteer commitments—I didn't have a lot of time for hovering over the stove. A good slow cooker recipe was a lifesaver.

I peeked under the pot's lid, inhaled, and sighed. My stomach growled.

With thirty minutes until Jen and Todd arrived, I set out my vintage red Pyrex plates in the Autumn Bands pattern and added flatware, linen napkins, and retro water glasses. They were perfect at the Formica-topped table in my red-and-aqua kitchen with its fifties vibe.

I had just slid a pan of naan into the oven and lit the caramel-apple-scented candle in the foyer when the doorbell rang. "Come on in! Door's unlocked."

Jen popped into the kitchen and lifted her nose in the air as if following some magical scented trail. "What *is* that glorious smell?" She made a beeline for the slow cooker and lifted the lid.

"Indian butter chicken." I finished washing my hands and dried them on a dish towel. "Got the recipe from one of my online jewelry customers, Ginger in North Carolina."

"Tell Ginger I said thank you." Jen closed her eyes and smacked her lips.

I laughed. "But you haven't eaten any of it yet."

"I know, but I can already tell it's going to be great." She inhaled again.

Todd came over and gave me a hug. I'd known Todd even longer than I'd known Jen, and he was like the brother I'd never had.

"How's the real estate business going these days?"

He and Jen exchanged glances.

"What?" I looked between them.

"Todd is thinking of making a career change."

"You're kidding. You've worked there what? Eight years now? You're practically an institution in this town. I thought you loved selling houses. Why would you stop?"

He shrugged. "Same reason you left your old job."

I grinned. "Why, Todd, I had no idea you've always wanted to design jewelry."

He waved away the comment. "You know better. I've been beefing up my web skills, and I want to create a new real estate website that covers not just Roseland but also the entire North Georgia Mountains region. Something very modern, very interactive. With its own mobile app and everything."

"Sounds like you've given this some serious thought. And I know you majored in business, but didn't you minor in PR and marketing?"

"Sure did."

Jen chimed in, "We've been talking about this idea for months. Todd likes the real estate business, but he really loves crunching numbers and running analytics and using data to sell houses. That's Todd's passion." She reached over and squeezed his hand.

I loved seeing the two of them so happy together and hoped for a marriage like theirs someday.

"You guys go ahead and sit down." I gestured toward the table. "I'll put the crock from the slow cooker on the table, and you can scoop up the chicken yourselves. I think the bread's ready too."

Jen and Todd took their seats while I grabbed a pot holder and removed the pan of flatbread from the oven. "Mm, perfect. I love naan almost as much as I love this chicken." I slid the wedges of bread onto a waiting platter on the table.

Soon, we were digging into plates of chicken and basmati rice, and I was pleased the meal was a hit.

"So, about this career move"—I looked at Todd—"are you planning to have advertisers or sponsors on your new website?" In the

South, it was considered impolite to come right out and ask about money, but approaching the topic sideways was permissible.

Todd finished chewing a bite of naan. "I've already got the first three advertisers lined up. The Ross County Association of Realtors, a local decorator I went to school with, and the guy who last owned our home, a fellow Realtor." He paused and scooped up another bite of sauce. "Man, this stuff is great, Emma."

"Thanks." I loved it when guests enjoyed my cooking.

Jen turned to Todd. "Tell her about that other big project you've got lined up."

"With Gerald?"

"Yeah." Jen nodded.

Todd turned to me. "How well do you know Gerald Adams?"

"Not well, but I bump into him around town every now and then."

"Turns out he has an interesting past, and he comes from a family that's been in the real estate business for a century. Started one of the most popular real estate companies in Atlanta, in fact, back in the eighties—the 1880s."

"Okay." I wasn't sure what Gerald's family history could possibly have to do with Todd and real estate.

Jen turned to Todd. "Emma doesn't care about real estate history, so fast-forward to the good part."

"So, here's the deal." Todd steepled his fingers. "Gerald and I go to the same gym, right? Well, the other day, he told me he's always wanted to write something about his family's business history but didn't know where to start. So I told him about my PR background. Basically, I'm going to help him compile a history of his family's real estate business and develop a new website. The one they're using now was designed by his late father back in the nineties. I mean, it's still got a hit counter and everything."

"A what?"

He shook his head. "Never mind."

Jen chimed in. "Anyway, Gerald's going to pay him big bucks to do all that."

I was impressed. "So when do you start?"

Todd furrowed his brow. "I'm not sure yet. He said my first job is to help him get the history written, then we'll make a plan for the website launch. He wants to start next Monday because he said he had something to finish up this week."

Like hiding his tracks after murdering someone with a lanyard? No. That's ridiculous.

As I cleared our plates and set out dessert, my first pumpkin pie of the season, I wondered whether to tell Todd that Gerald had gotten into it with Miranda on Saturday.

Todd rubbed his hands together. "Excellent choice."

"And there's whipped cream in the fridge. You guys want some?"

Todd's eyes grew wide, and he and Jen both nodded, so I fetched the container and a spoon and set them on the table.

"So, Jen"—I made eye contact—"I'm assuming Todd knows the rumors about Gerald?"

"Oh, get real," Todd scoffed. "Yeah, she's already told me the gossip about him that came into the newspaper office, but be serious. Gerald may be socially awkward, but he's no killer. I'm not worried about that." Todd leaned in and speared a bite of pumpkin pie.

"If he turns out to be a serial killer, you can't say you weren't warned." I grinned.

We talked about our holiday plans as we lingered over dessert and coffee until Jen commented that she had a meeting with the boss early the next morning and needed to get to bed. She didn't seem to want to talk about it, and I hoped the news operation wasn't facing more budget cuts.

After Jen and Todd went home, I hand-washed my Pyrex plates and thought about Todd's new gig. If Gerald had done anything nefarious, surely he wouldn't be focused on writing his family's business history and updating a website. So he'd been a successful businessman before he became president of the Humane Society. Depending on how successful he'd been, his time in the business world could have left him comfortable.

I shook my head. Todd was right—it was crazy to imagine Gerald as Miranda's killer. But someone had killed her, and so far, I hadn't heard of any arrest. Detective Shelton wasn't my favorite person, but I hoped he'd made some progress on the case.

After washing the last of the evening's utensils, I stored the leftover chicken in the refrigerator. Before hitting the hay, I checked my phone and found a text from Trish asking me to call her. It was only ten o'clock, but I wondered whether that was too late to call.

I texted her instead. *Just seeing your message. Give me a ring if you like.*

Within a minute, the phone rang. "Emma, I'm so glad you're still up. Got a huge favor to ask you."

"Sure. What's up?"

"I've been asked to fill in for someone at a pottery show in the mountains, and I know this is terribly last-minute, but it opens at eight o'clock tomorrow night. I can leave after my all-day shift at the gallery tomorrow and still make it in time, but I'd love to head up in the morning if I could get someone to fill in for me and—"

"Consider it done," I said. "I don't have anything scheduled tomorrow that can't be moved to later in the day." *Like, well, my jewelry designs. But I'll make it work somehow.*

"You're a lifesaver." Trish listed a few tasks I would need to tend to once at the shop, and I wrote them down so that I wouldn't forget. I chose the blouse and slacks I would wear the following day, laid out the matching jewelry, and settled in bed next to Miriam, who'd already claimed her spot for the night.

I turned off the bedside lamp, scrolled through some jewelry posts in my Instagram feed, and tried to force images of Gerald's lanyard—and Miranda's lifeless body—from my mind.

Chapter Eleven

D espite the late night spent lingering over dinner with friends then talking with Trish, I woke early the next morning. I showered, dressed, and made sure Miriam had plenty of food and water for the day. Then I headed to Mavis's to grab a hot beverage and something sweet before going to the gallery for my second volunteer shift of the week. The morning was unexpectedly and blessedly chilly, so the café's business was even more brisk than usual, with everyone picking up hot coffee to go.

In a nod to the season, I opted for a pumpkin spice scone with sea salt caramel glaze. I forked over my debit card so that Mavis could ring me up—for that and a pumpkin spice latte. After all, peppermint season was fast approaching, and I wanted to enjoy the fall flavors while I could.

"Emma, I need to see you for a minute before you dash out of here." Mavis swiped my card then handed it back. She lowered her voice. "I've got something important to ask you."

Mavis had been saying for months that she wanted to place a few special orders for Christmas, and I feared she had finally made up her mind, but I might not be able to help her. Half my Christmas inventory was already gone, and I made a point of not taking new orders after the first of November. I could probably make an exception for Mavis, but I hoped she didn't want anything elaborate.

"Now then," she called once she'd packaged my treats. "Come over here a minute, will ya?"

Curious, I did. Mavis handed me a business card for a Shane McLoughlin, vice president of the Greater Atlanta Happy Hometown Program.

I looked up. "Why are you giving me this?"

"Because Caitlyn Hill dropped it when she left here late yesterday." Mavis narrowed her eyes.

"Caitlyn came by again?"

"That girl's here most every day." Mavis pursed her lips. "And yesterday, she seemed awful friendly with this man nearly old enough to be her father. He had on a wedding ring too. But he bought her lunch, kissed her cheek when he left—"

"Now, Mavis." While I didn't mind the occasional business gossip, I tried not to know too much about the personal lives of people in town. As nosy as I already was, I didn't need one more secret to keep.

"Like I said, they were pretty tight, but that's not why I saved the card for you. It's what I heard her tell him."

I sighed. "Go ahead. What did you hear?"

"She told him, 'Now that Miranda's gone, there's no reason you can't come by the office as often as you like.' Emma, she must be having an affair with that man!"

The oh-so-public meeting didn't sound prudent, but I wasn't sure the comment necessarily indicated anything malicious on Caitlyn's part. Skeptical, I frowned at Mavis and tried not to blurt what I was thinking—that she was making a mountain out of a molehill.

She plopped a large take-out box onto the counter. "Listen, I've been watching the movers and shakers in this town for longer than you've been alive, and I know an affair when I see one. Those two were sitting a little too close, if you ask me, and he was patting her hand. Something's not right. I'm telling you. You're good at this investigatin' stuff. Take this card and go check the man out."

I glanced at my watch—I had ten minutes to open the Foothills Gallery. "Even if they are having an affair, that's not illegal, you know."

Mavis slapped the flaps on the take-out box. "Well, it's certainly immoral."

Personally, I agreed with her. Professionally, I had no reason to go around sticking my nose into people's affairs, literal or figurative. I barely had time to tend to my own business, much less anyone else's. But the best way to get Mavis off my back was to take the card, conduct a little research, then assure her that nothing devious was going on with Caitlyn and the Happy Hometown office.

I tucked the card into my purse. "I'll let you know what I find out. I'm sure it's nothing, but if it'll put your mind at ease, I'm happy to help."

Mavis's bear hug nearly choked the life out of me, and I promised to get in touch if I learned anything.

With my hard-earned scone and latte in hand, I headed a few doors down and opened the shop for the day. New gold lettering on the glass door proudly proclaimed Foothills Gallery. Smaller black letters read Home of the Award-Winning Ross County Arts Council.

As I stepped inside, I took a deep breath. Crisp fall mornings at the gallery smelled different, as if the hundred years of history embedded in those old wooden floors were rising to celebrate the season with us. Our window displays were filled with rich jewel-toned arts and crafts, from Trish's pumpkin-colored pottery to Shareta's regal yellow-and-orange handwoven baskets to Martha's latest quilt, its golden batik fabrics featuring elaborate freeform stitching in variegated earth tones. Some topaz-colored paper-bead necklaces I'd gotten obsessed with making last summer spilled over a section of the quilt, the colors blending beautifully.

Soon the doorbell announced the first visitor of the day, and it was a fellow artist, Gus. She wedged the door open with her body since her arms grasped an enormous frame. I dashed to the door to help her in.

"Whoa, Trish told me a few of you might be bringing in new pieces this morning. What've you got here?" I held the door open wide to allow her to pass through. "Your latest masterpiece?"

After carefully setting the piece on the floor, Gus paused to catch her breath. "I hope so." She adjusted the ruffled scarf she was wearing with a lace-trimmed blouse and fall-toned patchwork skirt. "I just finished it last week, and it's taking up too much space in my studio."

Gus pulled a ponytail holder off her right wrist and used it to corral the mass of auburn curls framing her face. "Weird, isn't it? As soon as I put the final touches on a piece, I'm over it and start getting excited about the next one."

The doorbell chimed again, causing us both to turn. That time, Bob Mathis was struggling through the door with a huge cardboard box.

"Here, let me help you." I again sped for the door.

Bob dipped his chin as he entered the shop. "Appreciate that." He headed to a display table near the front window and shoved the box against the wall. "Had so many pieces left over from the bazaar this year that I've got to get them out of the shop so I'll have more room to work." He shrugged out of his Georgia Bulldogs windbreaker, pulled a bottled water out of his box, and guzzled the drink.

Gus left her artwork propped against a wall and walked over to Bob. "I almost hate to ask"—she tucked a wayward strand of hair behind one ear—"but how did you end up doing at the show?"

Bob snorted. "Losing my old spot put a huge dent in sales. I got home and had one man call and ask why I wasn't there. Said after he walked past the spot where I usually was and didn't see my bowls and lamps, he went home."

I fingered one of the smaller bowls Bob had placed on a display shelf. "But he does know they're available here now, right?"

"Yeah, he knows." Bob jerked a thumb toward the box he'd just brought in. "That's one reason I wanted these bowls up here before the weekend. That man has always been one of my best customers. An Atlanta mortgage banker. Likes to buy something handmade for all those city slickers who come to Roseland looking to buy a weekend home."

I grinned. "City slicker" was a term I didn't hear much anymore, but I knew what he meant. Each year, more and more Atlantans discovered our area as the perfect spot to get away from the busy metro area south of us.

"And I might as well say it." Bob held up a hand. "I know a lot of folks are upset that Miranda got killed at the show, but no one in this town is going to miss that woman."

He looked from me to Gus, and I didn't know what to say. It wasn't like Bob to be so harsh and cold, especially when a woman had just lost her life.

Gus cleared her throat. "Well, now that that's out of the way—" She went over and plopped a hand on the large canvas she'd brought in. "It's time for me to get this artwork up."

I looked at Bob, and he lowered his eyes as if he knew he'd crossed a line. I followed Gus to the only open expanse along one of the exposed-brick walls and helped her remove bubble wrap from her latest piece.

"Whoa," I said as my friend finished uncovering her new work. "This is fantastic."

Plenty of modern art assemblages incorporated old magazines and newsprint, but Gus had used the narrow lines of type to create the branches in a forest of trees.

"I've titled it *Reforestation*." She grinned. "Call me crazy—and yeah, I know that some do—but I hope someone will look at it and think about all the trees that are dying just so we can have more magazines and newspapers and junk mail show up in our mailboxes each day."

I had mixed emotions about her reasoning. I still looked forward to getting the newspaper on my porch each morning, and when Roseland's *Thrifty Shopper* landed in my mailbox, I read it from cover to cover for the events and local columns and business openings. And of course I subscribed to a few jewelry design magazines to stay abreast of industry trends, but I understood Gus's point. Whatever her impetus for creating the piece, the result was stunning.

We both looked at the artwork and appeared to come to the same conclusion: it would require a large stretch of wall space.

I glanced around. A little farther along the wall was an old, chipped white shutter serving as a display rack for some of my jewelry.

I pointed at the shutter. "Why don't you take that spot? I've gotten bored with that display anyway."

"You don't mind?" Gus seemed appreciative.

My display was seriously overdue for a revamp, and giving her that wall space was the push I needed to get going on it.

"Not a problem." I tapped her on the shoulder. "Here, help me get that shutter down, and it'll be the perfect spot for your piece."

Jewelry jingled and jangled as we slowly slid the shutter off the nails drilled into the wall.

"Where should we put it?" Gus looked around the shop. "Do you know which table you'll be using?"

I nodded at the one nearest the counter. That had long been one of my sweet spots for jewelry sales. Gus helped me transfer the shutter, and because we moved it so carefully, not one bracelet or necklace had gotten tangled.

"There. That wasn't so hard, now, was it?"

The front door opened again, and that time, it was the unmistakable figure of a new artist in town—one whose denim vest had colorful splotches of dried paint all over it.

"Welcome to the Foothills Gallery." I gave him a smile. "I hope you don't mind, but a couple of us are switching out some work this morning."

He crossed his arms and looked between Gus and Bob.

Bob's face broke into a huge smile. "Tyler, good to see you again, son."

Gus looked radiant, and unless I was imagining things, she was starstruck by Tyler. "If you decide to hook up with one of the local galleries, it had better be this one," she told him.

I couldn't help noticing the easy rapport between the two of them, and I smiled at the romantic notion of two talented artists falling in love.

Gus must have noted me watching them. "Emma, help me convince Tyler he needs his work in here." She slipped her arm into his. "Tyler has been painting since he was old enough to hold a paintbrush, and his acrylics are highly prized by collectors. He'd be a great addition to the gallery here, wouldn't he?"

"Sounds like we definitely need to talk about—"

My cell phone rang, so I stepped behind the counter to answer it and saw that Caitlyn was on the line.

"Hi, Caitlyn. What can I do for you?"

"The Roseland PD seems to think I killed Miranda. You've got to help me!"

"Oh no. What are you going to do?" I barely knew Caitlyn and wasn't sure why she was calling me.

"Go talk to them, I guess." She sighed. "What else can I do? But listen, I heard how you helped solve that other murder case in town a while back, and I was wondering—"

I cleared my throat and tried to put a stop to that line of thinking. "Look, I'm sorry you're having to deal with the murder, but that other case I helped solve was just a fluke. I am not an investigator, and the police need to solve this case, not me."

"But you used to be a reporter," she said.

"A lot of people used to be reporters." *What does she expect me to do?*

Silence. I feared I'd prompted her to end the call. "Caitlyn? Are you still there?"

I heard a sniff. "Are you sure you won't help me? I'll never be able to do my new job if I'm seen as a murder suspect, and I just know that with your help, we could figure out who killed Miranda."

Oh great. Nothing like a little guilt to get me to volunteer for one more thing.

I sighed. "Call me when you get through talking to the police, and if I can, I'll stop by for a few minutes." I jotted a note on a scrap piece of paper. *Go see Caitlyn after her interview.* "I can't imagine I'll be much help, but I'll be glad to listen."

After thanking me profusely, Caitlyn hung up.

As soon as I stepped out from behind the counter, Bob held out his hands. "Well? Do we have to beg, or do you want to save us the trouble and tell us what that was all about?"

Clearly, I'd said enough during the call for them to know something was going on. I briefly recapped Caitlyn's side of the conversation.

Gus shook her head. "Even in death, Miranda Hargrove is causing trouble. How fitting."

"The woman has died, Gus." I bit my lip for a moment and tried to rein in my comments. "I mean, I know she rubbed people the wrong way, but don't you think she's paid enough of a price for whatever trouble she caused?"

Gus shrugged. "I'm just saying she made a lot of enemies, and I don't see all that many tears being shed over her death. Tyler just told me she kept him from being in the show this year too. He heard the same thing Savannah did, that his application wasn't in on time, and she wouldn't budge on his."

"And apparently, my artwork was a little too 'moody' for Miss Hargrove." Tyler chuckled. "But you know"—he turned a smile on Gus—"I didn't really have the time to be in that show, anyway, so it wasn't a huge deal. She might have done me a favor, because I got more work done when I would have been turning out small pieces for the bazaar."

Bob cleared his throat and fussed over his display of wood-turned bowls. He probably shared Gus's sentiment. Tyler walked over and examined Gus's new artwork, so I assumed he didn't have anything to add to the conversation.

After she straightened her piece on the wall, Gus and Tyler continued to talk quietly while I greeted new customers. Soon, she gathered the few supplies she'd brought with her and told Bob and me goodbye. "Tyler's treating me to lunch so that we can catch up, so wish me luck in getting him on the arts council and in the gallery."

"You don't stand a chance, son." Bob smiled. "I'll save you a seat at our next meeting."

Tyler shook Bob's hand then mine. "It was nice seeing you again, Emma."

"You too. Good luck surviving lunch with Gus, and I look forward to seeing you at your first arts council meeting." Unless my radar was off, though, Gus was interested in more than just getting Tyler to join the group.

As soon as Gus and Tyler left, two women came in to browse. Soon, Bob left too. He waved at me as he headed out. I still didn't know Bob that well. I'd served on the arts council with him for more than a year, but outside of his work there, I didn't know his character.

With the gallery momentarily quiet, I started working on my jewelry display. It always helped to freshen the presentation. Sometimes, just moving an item to a different spot in the shop made customers think they were seeing something new.

Around lunchtime, the gallery's traffic picked up, with a nearly constant flow of shoppers entering and exiting, most of them leaving with stuffed gift bags. The gallery offered free gift wrapping all year round, and at Christmastime, we used distinctive kraft paper bags with rustic-looking red and green stars on them.

During the only brief lull of the afternoon, I got one of the small gift bags from behind the counter, tucked in a few sheets of red tissue, and let a few bracelets and necklaces spill out of the top. I finished fluffing it just in time. Four women entered the shop together. I welcomed them and thought I heard the *ding* that indicated I had a cell phone message. After tucking the stack of tissue paper beneath the front counter, I reached into my purse and grabbed the phone. I had a text from Jen.

Dinner? Todd and I are having homemade pizza. Join us?

I quickly tapped my reply. *Sure! Time?*

The answer came quickly: *6ish.*

I sent back a thumbs-up and tucked the phone away. Then the front door creaked open again, and Mavis came bearing one of her signature yellow boxes and held it out to me.

Eagerly, I accepted it. "For me?"

She looked around and grinned at the busy store. "Yes, ma'am. Figured you might enjoy one of my bananas Foster cupcakes as an afternoon snack. You know, to help you keep your strength up."

I gave Mavis a hug. "No wonder you're this town's favorite baker."

She brushed away my comment. "I'm also this town's only baker, so don't you go trying to flatter me, young lady."

I lowered my voice and indicated for Mavis to follow me to a spot near the counter. "Okay, I've got a quick question for you."

Mavis's eyebrows shot up.

"Bob Mathis. How long have you known him?"

"Oh, forever. He was one of my first customers when I opened the bakery, and he's been eating there ever since. Always been partial to my raspberry-jelly-filled powdered doughnuts." A note of pride crept into her voice.

I shrugged. "Just wondering if you've ever seen him lose his temper or hold a grudge against someone."

Mavis paused and stroked her chin. "Can't say I have. Bob's always been easy to get along with and a big supporter of the town. Of course, some of that's probably because he's the mayor's brother." She narrowed her eyes at me. "Why are you asking?"

"No particular reason." I tried to blow it off. "I saw him get kind of mouthy about Miranda this morning, and I just wondered if that was typical of him."

Mavis patted her ever-present gray bun. "I wouldn't make too much of that, hon." She tapped my arm. "Now, with this many women in here already, I'd better start shopping."

Mavis scurried to the table with hand-knitted scarves, which I could have predicted. She was passionate about color, so with one glance at those brilliant reds, blues, and golds, she was clearly hooked.

"My sister up in Kentucky will love this." She fingered a lacy scarf in a soft lavender mohair and draped it over an arm. "And her teenage girls will love these black ones." She grabbed two more and added them to her collection.

"Take this"—I handed Mavis one of the store's canvas shopping totes—"and feel free to fill it up. We'll make a dent in that list of yours."

Mavis's eyes were gleaming. She spent so many hours baking cupcakes and sweets that whenever she got a chance to go shopping, she sometimes went overboard.

A group of teachers came in. One of them mentioned that they were meeting for dinner that evening and had decided to head over as soon as school was out and attack their Christmas shopping lists.

"Do you happen to know what china pattern this charm is?" one woman asked.

"I sure do." I walked over to her and pointed at the back of the card displaying a broken china charm. "Spode's Christmas Rose. A friend of my mom broke a plate and asked if I wanted it to make charms out of."

The woman held it up in the warm afternoon sunlight streaming through the windows. "You made this? It's charming."

A colleague punched her playfully. "No pun intended, right?"

Another of the women approached me and smiled shyly. "I was at the Christmas bazaar on Saturday and thought you had one of the best booths in the whole show. I bought some earrings from you and—"

"I was just asking myself where I knew you from." I held out a hand. "I'm Emma Madison with the Ross County Arts Council. Thanks for coming to the bazaar."

The woman shook my hand. "I'm Cindy Mathis Green, and I think you probably know my dad, Bob Mathis."

I gulped. Thank goodness I hadn't been talking too loudly about him to Mavis.

"Cindy?" Mavis's strong voice rang out. "Do you mean to tell me you're that little girl I used to bake the Strawberry Shortcake doll birthday cakes for all those years ago?" She stepped past a few tables and gave Cindy the once-over.

"Hi there, Miss Mavis, and yes, I'm the one. I moved away after college and haven't lived in Roseland in ten years. My husband and I moved back over the summer so that I could take a job with the Ross County School System. We wanted our two girls to grow up closer to my dad now that my mom's passed away."

Mavis hooked an arm through Cindy's. "You've obviously turned into a fine young woman, and I'm sure Bob is thrilled to have you home. What did you end up teaching? Art?"

Cindy smiled and shook her head. "Dad got all the artistic talent in our family. Like my mother, I'm all about the cooking. I'm a school nutritionist now."

"It's sure great to see you again. Stop by the bakery sometime. Come in, and I'll give your girls a free cupcake to welcome them to Roseland."

"We will. Thanks."

Mavis returned to her shopping, and she and the teachers continued to browse the jewelry, scarves, and artwork.

Cindy looked over at Mavis and smiled fondly. "I'm so glad to be back home, and I have to admit that Miss Mavis's treats are one of the many reasons I'm glad we've moved to Roseland. I'd hoped to stop by the bakery Monday morning, but I got summoned to a meeting in the kitchen at Ellis Middle School since..." She lowered her voice. "Not to be morbid, but we had to do a deep cleaning there after what happened over the weekend. The lunchroom manager wanted me there for moral support, I guess."

I was glad Cindy was so forthcoming. "Speaking of that, I hope I'm not out of line for asking, but has anyone figured out how the murderer managed to get Miranda's body onto the stage without being discovered?"

Cindy looked surprised. "Then you haven't heard?"

"Heard what?"

She looked around then whispered, "The police said Miranda probably died right there in our kitchen. Some pots and pans had been knocked to the floor, and a corner on one of the stainless steel tables had blood all over it along with a few long auburn hairs, presumably Miranda's, since the lunchroom ladies all wear hair nets. I had to go over there to make sure a new table got installed properly and to replace some of the other equipment that got carted off as evidence."

I kept my voice low but couldn't hide my astonishment. "The police actually told you all this?"

Cindy nodded. "They had the crime scene tape removed by late Sunday afternoon, and once they cleaned up the kitchen, the lunchroom supervisor and I had to go in and see what was what."

Cindy's eyes darted left and right. "Please don't mention this to anyone. The scene was pretty grisly, and the last thing we want is those gory details getting out to the kids or their parents."

I pantomimed zipping my lips. "Mum's the word."

Mavis headed our way with her gift-laden basket and smiled at Cindy.

"So, if you're the nutritionist now, you work with what we used to call the lunchroom ladies, right?"

"Yes, ma'am."

"A couple of 'em were in the café this morning and told me what a mess y'all had to clean up. I'd have had a fit if someone had messed up my kitchen like that!"

Thanks a lot, Mavis!

Cindy's shoulders slumped. "I'm not really supposed to be talking about that, and..."

"It's okay. I've probably heard most of the story, anyway, darlin'." With a final pat on Cindy's arm, Mavis headed to the counter with her purchases.

Before I stepped away to ring her up, I whispered to Cindy, "What can I say? Word gets around in a small town."

Cindy sighed. "That's what I was afraid of."

Chapter Twelve

Right before closing time at five o'clock, I got a call from Caitlyn that made my day. She'd finished meeting with the police, and apparently, she'd jumped to conclusions and wasn't on their suspect list after all. They'd quizzed her on some details about Miranda's background, which she found odd, but she told them what she knew. As a result, she didn't need me to stop by her office.

Hallelujah! I needed to run by the house and check on Miriam, anyway, since I'd accepted the dinner invite from Jen. When I got there, Miriam stood in the kitchen and meowed loudly next to her water bowl, which I'd forgotten to check before I left that morning. Like most Siamese cats, Miriam could be quite vocal about her needs.

"I guess you're glad to see me." I stroked her fur then refilled her bowl. After quenching her thirst, Miriam curled up at my feet while I thumbed through a new jewelry-supply catalog that had arrived in the day's mail. For once, I focused on the more expensive beads, charms, and findings. With the Jewelry Artisans of the Southeast show on my horizon, I needed to think about more upscale designs.

I also needed to figure out how to catch up on my current jewelry orders for the week when I kept saying yes to everyone around me—and to dinner with friends.

But that bananas Foster cupcake I'd eaten around four o'clock was long gone, so after I changed into jeans and a comfy top, I drove to Jen's house and was more than ready for dinner. As I stepped through the front door of their fixer-upper, the aroma of garlic and onions made my stomach growl. I'd been so busy at the shop all day that by suppertime, I was famished. I entered Jen's farmhouse-style kitchen, closed my eyes, and inhaled deeply. "Mm. The pizza smells divine."

When I opened my eyes, Jen had an arm extended and touched one of my beaded oval earrings. "Cute! A new design?"

"Yep. Sold six sets just like these at the gallery today."

Todd nodded. "Very nice. I know your gallery sells arts and crafts, so are you considered an artist or a craftsman?"

I humphed. "That's a great question. The difference between a crafter and an artist is often in the eyes of the beholder, but I like to think I'm a jewelry artist. And"—I waited till both Jen and Todd were looking at me—"I want you two to be among the first to know that I've been accepted to the Jewelry Artisans of the Southeast's spring show."

Jen squealed. "What? Why haven't you told me about this already?"

"Yeah, that's awesome," Todd said.

Jen and I looked at him.

"I mean, I guess it's awesome. Right? What's the Jewelry Artisans of the Southeast?"

I laughed. "You have to send them images of your work and fill out this detailed application online, and you're competing with some of the best amateur jewelry designers in the whole Southeast. It doesn't matter how much money you've earned or how many thousands of followers you have on Facebook or Instagram. It's a really big deal, and I'm still stunned that I got in."

Todd interrupted his pizza making long enough to slap a dish-cloth across his shoulder and give me his full attention. "Sounds like those folks aren't easily impressed. You're entering the big leagues now, aren't you?"

"I don't know about the big leagues, but I mean it when I say it's an honor to be chosen."

"You won't forget us little people after you're rich and famous, will you?" Todd grinned.

"We'll help keep her humble." Jen handed me a knife. "Here, Jewelry Queen. How about chopping the lettuce and tomatoes for our salads?"

While I attacked a head of lettuce, Todd whipped up a quick herb-and-vinegar dressing. I loved to watch him work. With a flourish, he poured his oil into a wooden bowl before adding freshly chopped herbs. He had just plucked a stainless steel whisk from the utensil crock when Jen stopped him.

"Nope." She handed him a plastic-coated whisk. "Use this one instead."

Todd looked puzzled. "Okay. But why?"

"I don't want to scratch the interior. Bob Mathis put a lot of heart into that bowl, you know." Jen peered inside, then I did too.

Sure enough, the inlaid interior told me it was my friend's work. I usually thought of Bob's bowls strictly as art pieces, so I was surprised to see one functioning in its utilitarian purpose. "It's safe to actually use these?" I fingered the smooth-as-silk rim of the wide bowl.

"Oh yeah. And Bob encourages it."

"I didn't know that. Yet he's *my* friend."

"He's not just *your* friend." Jen laughed. "Bob's friends with half the town. He likes everyone."

I raised an eyebrow.

"What does that mean?" Jen looked curious.

I shrugged. "Bob doesn't like everyone. Miranda, for instance. He and 'Miss Rochester,' as he called her, didn't exactly hit it off."

Todd piped up, "She *was* quite a looker, though, wasn't she?"

Jen and I gave him the stink eye.

"Sorry." He draped the dishcloth over his face, and we laughed.

I drummed my fingers on the counter. "I still can't understand why someone with her experience would have taken a relatively rinky-dink job like Happy Hometown director in Roseland."

Jen frowned. "You're not dissing Roseland, are you?"

"You know better. I adore this town, just like you guys, but I'm well aware some folks move here with the goal of turning us into something we're not. Didn't it strike you as odd that a New Yorker would arrive in town and constantly talk about how great Rochester was, showing up to meetings in her tailored suits and designer pumps?"

"Hey." Todd clapped. "Enough about the late Ms. Hargrove. Pizza's ready."

I joined Jen on one side of their bench-style seating at a distressed wooden table that they'd had forever, and I leaned in so all three of us could hold hands while Todd said grace.

At the conclusion of the prayer, I squeezed both hands I'd been holding. "With all due respect, I'm starving, so amen and dig in."

Todd and Jen must have been as hungry as I was, because we polished off that first pizza in record time. Todd's pizza crust used an old family recipe he protected like the formula for Coca-Cola. Jen and I were only too happy for him to keep it a secret, though, because that meant he had to make the pizzas himself. Our job was simply to eat them.

The first pie had sausage, mushrooms, extra cheese, and a rich marinara sauce. The second one was a pizza margherita with the classic thin crust and loads of gooey mozzarella. I gave Todd my compliments for the millionth time.

After my third slice of pizza, I leaned back in my chair and groaned. "Wow, that sure hit the spot."

"Sure you don't want some more?" Todd asked.

"Or more salad?" Jen tipped the bowl in my direction.

I declined both offers, but I traced a finger along the top of the pretty bowl, which reminded me of my earlier conversation with Bob Mathis. I faced Jen. "I didn't know you were friends with Bob. How did that happen?"

She swallowed a last bite of pizza crust. "He comes by the office to bring us press releases and photos about the arts council. He's always stayed on top of the group's PR, which is great for helping us fill up holes in the paper." She frowned. "And did I tell you that the company has cut back on our budget for stringers? I guess that's one reason I appreciate folks like Bob so much."

That didn't surprise me. Bob was a loyal member of the arts council and never missed a meeting. He was always first to sign up for assignments, and if he said he would do something, he did it. I supposed that being on the arts council had given him something to do after his wife died a few years ago. And that reminded me that I'd just met another member of his family.

"Did you know Bob's daughter recently moved to Roseland? She stopped by the gallery this afternoon with a group from the school system."

"Can't say I've ever heard him talk about her, but then he never stays long when he drops by the office." Jen stacked our plates in the dishwasher while Todd stood at the sink and hand-washed his huge pizza stone.

I set the salad bowl on the counter next to him. "Do you know Bob too?"

"Nope." He looked up from the suds. "Never met him. But I do like his stuff."

Jen reclaimed her seat at the table. "He's always been nice to me when he comes by the paper, but you know how that is. Everybody's nice when they want something out of you."

"And nice is good." Todd cocked his head. "Something our friend Gerald needs to learn."

That got my attention. "Wait a minute. Last night, you said what a great guy he was. What's changed?"

Todd rolled his eyes. "I spent an hour on the phone with Gerald this morning. Turns out that one reason he wants to do this family history is to embarrass some Adams cousins he doesn't think are pulling their weight in the family business. I tried to discourage that, naturally. The dude has some anger issues, and I'm starting to wonder whether I should have agreed to help him."

"Are you seriously rethinking the new project?" I asked.

Todd shrugged. "I hope his attitude doesn't end up being a problem. I was at his house one day when we first talked about the website, and the mailman dropped off a package and didn't ring the doorbell. The minute Gerald got an alert on his phone saying a package had been delivered, he ran to the door, threw it open, and yelled at the guy, saying he should have notified Gerald that he'd delivered something."

I humphed. "Seems a little overbearing."

Todd's eyes widened. "A little? He definitely has a short fuse."

And all Miranda had done to light it at the bazaar was simply request that the nicest animals be the ones brought indoors. I wondered why Gerald had come unglued over that. *And whether he was angry enough to commit murder.*

Shaking off the thoughts as the result of an overactive imagination and a long day, I thanked Todd and Jen for dinner and headed home. Once I got there, I changed into pajamas then went into the kitchen to make my nightly cup of chamomile tea. Miriam Haskell looked up at me with her beautiful deep-blue eyes. No wonder Siamese cats had once been the favorite felines of royalty. I reached down to give her a rub, and she rewarded me with a satisfied purr.

"Miriam, I wish I could talk to you about all the murder suspects in town."

She replied with a spirited meow.

"Oh yeah? You think I'm a little nuts for suspecting half the town of murder?"

Miriam rubbed against my leg and swished her tail.

"You may be right, but..."

Miriam's head jerked up at me as if she were truly considering my words.

"But somebody killed Miranda on Saturday, right? And I haven't heard about an arrest being made, so clearly the murderer is still out there."

Miriam apparently preferred a more upbeat bedtime story, because she wandered off to the living room, leaving me alone with my questions.

I was tired of thinking about the case. When I finally climbed into bed, all I knew was that if I didn't fulfill the jewelry orders I had promised to make, the holidays weren't going to be very happy ones at all.

Chapter Thirteen

I opened my eyes, reached for my cell phone, and peeked at the screen—7:23. Sheesh, I was going to have to start setting an alarm. I would have to hop to it in order to make and deliver all the jewelry I needed to that day.

Bleary-eyed, I slogged to the kitchen. With a punch of a button, I got the coffee brewing, then I quickly scrolled through the morning's emails and my Facebook feed. After the brew was ready, I spooned some Greek yogurt into a vintage Pyrex berry bowl, sprinkled strawberry-and-dark-chocolate granola on top, and scarfed it down.

By eight o'clock, I was dressed in jeans and a cozy blue sweater and seated at the kitchen table, coffee and supplies at hand, ready to create another dozen Ruby & Doris bracelets. After the vintage designs had been such a big hit at the bazaar, I wanted plenty of stock for the Foothills Gallery and Michele's shop.

A plastic bag of my latest junk jewelry from Making Memories sat before me, and I reached into it to fish out the best vintage clip-on earrings to embellish the bracelets. I heard a crunch of gravel at the kitchen door, then I stood up and peeked out the window—Michele was hurrying up the driveway.

I opened the door. "This is a surprise. Who's running the store?"

"The Christmas helpers are full-time these days, so I can take some time off when I need to." She looked troubled. "Have you got a few minutes? I really need to talk this out with someone."

"Have a seat." I gestured to the table, where we both sat down.

Michele took a deep breath. "It's about Miranda Hargrove. You know I didn't care for her."

I nodded.

"But you also know I didn't kill her, right?"

I held a spool of elastic beading cord in midair. "Have you been accused of something?"

She frowned. "Not directly. But you remember the other morning when that customer told you what her friend overheard Gerald say at the bazaar?"

"Mm-hmm."

"After you took that info to the police department, Alan Shelton stopped by. Silly me, I thought he was there to Christmas shop."

"He wasn't?"

She shook her head. "Somebody, and I can't figure out who, told him about my run-in with Miranda over the way she treated Austin."

I rolled my eyes. "Oh, good grief. Nobody in their right mind would accuse you of murder because of that."

"Somehow the police got wind of it. Alan wanted to know what time I got to the bazaar, where I went while I was there, the time I left, and if anyone could vouch for where I was after the show."

"Surely Wells can tell him when you got home and—"

"But I didn't go straight home."

I raised an eyebrow. "Because?"

"Because I drove to Atlanta to pick up a Christmas gift for Wells. He and Austin were visiting the railway museum in Duluth all afternoon, so I knew I wouldn't be missed. There's a shop in Acworth that sells all of Wells's favorite imported English goods—like the socks and handkerchiefs he's so fond of—and I'd arranged to meet the shop owner at closing time to pick up my order."

"Then can't the shop owner vouch for your whereabouts?"

"She's gone back to London until after Christmas, and I don't know the people who run the place in her absence."

I sighed.

Michele's eyes widened. "And the more I think about the murder, the more I think Gerald could've done it."

I rolled my eyes. "You can't be serious."

"I'm dead serious. In fact, if you can take a short break..."

"What?"

"I was thinking of driving over to Gerald's house to see if he's still living in his mom's basement."

Michele was going a little cray-cray. "Do you have some reason to doubt him?"

"Have you ever seen her?"

"No, but I'm not exactly part of Gerald's inner circle."

"Hear me out. I'm just saying he strikes me as the kind of guy who could be all lovey-dovey with pets then have his mama's body locked in the basement freezer."

"Oh, for heaven's sake, that's—"

"Five minutes. That's all it'll take."

"How do you propose we check this out, Miss Marple? What'll we say if Gerald shows up and sees us snooping around his house?"

She threw up her hands. "Won't be a problem. I saw him at the post office this morning, and he said he was headed to Atlanta for the day on business, so it's the perfect time to nose around. It's just a few streets away, so run over there with me."

If it'll get her off my back, why not? "Your car or mine?"

Michele smiled for the first time that morning. "Mine. I backed it into your driveway, hoping you'd say that."

As we buckled up in her SUV, she told me she'd already looked up Gerald's address in her store records. True to her word, we were at his house in five minutes. No vehicles were in the driveway. Michele parked on the street and jerked her head at me. "Follow my lead."

We walked to the front door, and she pressed the doorbell button. I hoped she had planned what to say, because I had no idea how to ask some nice old lady whether her son was a murderer.

No one answered. Michele rang the doorbell again, and a female voice called out, "Hold your horses, people!"

Click. The door opened but only wide enough for us to see a length of chain and an attractive gray-haired woman peering out from behind it.

"Can I help you?"

"Are you Mrs. Adams?"

"I am. Why? Nothing's happened to Gerald, has it?"

"Oh no, ma'am." Michele shook her head. "I'm Michele Fairchild from the Feathered Nest downtown"—she handed over her business card—"and this is Emma Madison, another local business owner."

I dipped my head in acknowledgment.

"She designs jewelry that's in all the best shops in the area."

I appreciated the plug, even if the circumstances were less than ideal.

Michele continued, "We're friends with Gerald, and as big-time pet lovers, we were thinking of making a gift to the Humane Society in his honor this Christmas. We wondered whether that would be a good idea or if he would prefer something more personal."

The chain came down, and the door whipped open. "How thoughtful! My Gerald would love for you to donate to the society in his honor. Listen, would you ladies like to come in and have a cup of coffee? I've got a pot brewing in my apartment down in the basement."

"You live in the basement?" Michele asked.

The woman chuckled. "Ironic, isn't it? But yes, Gerald renovated it last year and set me up in my own apartment. Hired an interior decorator and everything. Not many sons are thoughtful enough to do that for their mother, are they? Now won't you come in for a cup of coffee?"

I gave Michele the side-eye. I hadn't signed up for a coffee klatch with Gerald's mama.

"Maybe some other time, Mrs. Adams. We've both got businesses to run, but you've been a huge help. And please, we want to keep this a surprise for Gerald."

Her eyes widened. "Oh, I won't say a word."

Michele and I said our goodbyes, and I held my tongue until we got in the car. "Happy now? Mrs. Adams looks pretty good for a woman who's been living in the basement freezer, don't you think?"

Michele glared at me then drove down the street. "Don't be so crabby. At least now we know. And since—" We were almost to my house when she looked over my shoulder at something, hit the brakes, and pulled to the curb.

I followed her gaze, and Shareta Gibson was jogging by in hunter-green sweats as she tried to keep up with her chocolate Labrador retriever. I caught her eye and waved as Michele rolled down the window.

"Morning, Shareta!" She leaned over me. "Who've you got with you here?"

Shareta halted with her dog, and once again, I was envious that Miriam wasn't the kind of pet that could join me in the great outdoors.

"This is Indiana Jones—Indy, for short. He loves to go on adventures."

He was certainly a handsome boy.

"So what are you two up to?" Shareta leaned in and cocked her head at me.

"Just running a few errands." Michele looked at the cloudy sky. "Think you'll get your run in before the rain comes?"

Shareta smiled. "We're gonna try."

"They say it's bringing cooler weather with it, and I'm glad. Guess we'd better let you get back to your run, then. Have a good one."

As we pulled away, Michele rolled up the window. "I still can't believe Miranda told her to change the colors of her baskets. Good grief. Didn't the woman know how offensive that would be to an artist?"

"You heard about that too?"

"Oh yeah. Shareta was hot about it. She was in the shop yesterday and mentioned it. And Miranda hadn't been very nice to her when she first applied for the bazaar either."

"Yeah?"

"Mm-hmm." Michele made the turn into my driveway, so I was only minutes away from getting back to work. "Something about how miniature African baskets might not do so well at a Christmas bazaar."

"Why on earth not?"

Michele shrugged. "Who knows why Miranda saw anything the way she did?"

She turned off the engine. "Thanks for going with me, but I'd better get back to the shop. I guess I was wrong, and Gerald didn't make up a story about his mother living with him, but oh well. I'm just ready to find out who killed Miranda so that we can all move on."

"And we can get that donation on its way to the foster kids."

"Is that in question?"

I nodded. "Latest I'm hearing is that the city is asking for an audit before any money from the bazaar goes out."

After promising to see her the next evening at her open house, I sped inside to get out of the mist and spotted a familiar-looking blue-and-white bubble mailer propped against the kitchen door. Amazon must have dropped off that spool of copper jewelry wire I'd ordered the other day. How odd that they would leave it by the kitchen door, though.

As the floodgates unleashed, I scooped up the package, unlocked the door to dash inside, and set the package on the kitchen table. I shrugged out of my jacket and shuddered from the sudden chill.

When I turned on the electric teakettle to heat some water, Miriam sauntered into the kitchen. "Hi there, beautiful." I reached down and petted the silky-soft fur on my feline friend. "Did you miss me?"

She meowed.

Once I'd prepared a cup of Japanese sencha, my favorite green tea, I reached for some scissors and sliced open the package, but oddly, the end was taped over as if the mailer had been used before. The only thing inside was a piece of paper. *Did they bungle my order and forget to place the wire inside?* Then I noticed that the mailer had no address label on it, only the sticky remnants where a label had once been attached.

I unfolded the paper, and it was a résumé for the late Miranda Hargrove—except it listed her last name as Horgrave. The name of her last employer was circled in red marker, and the job wasn't the one I'd expected—assistant manager of a discount clothing store at a mall in Pittsford, New York.

Perplexed, I read the rest of the résumé, and a picture began to emerge. Miranda *Horgrave* hadn't been a successful downtown development staffer after all. She wasn't even from New York. According to the sheet of paper, she'd graduated from high school in Virginia, taken classes at a community college for two months, and gone straight to work at the mall in Pittsford, which a quick online search revealed was a suburb of Rochester. She'd apparently volunteered once for a fundraiser with the Happy Hometown program in Rochester, but that was it. And there was nothing wrong with any of that experience—except that she'd apparently lied about it.

After shoving a few jewelry supplies out of the way, I retrieved my laptop from the living room and made room for it on the kitchen table. I searched for Miranda Horgrave in Pittsford, New York, and after clicking through a few press releases in which she was listed as the contact for various store promotions, there it was—a photo of Miranda with a Jennifer Aniston "Rachel" haircut in a photo that looked at least ten years old. And she was indeed Horgrave.

I clicked through another page of links and found one that led to an article in a Pittsford community newspaper. "Pittsford Woman Arrested for DUI," it read. According to the police report, Miranda Horgrave had been spotted weaving between lanes around eleven thirty on a February evening several years before. Her blood alcohol level was .08.

I did another search for Miranda Horgrave, adding the words *Pittsford* and *DUI*, and I learned she'd been sentenced to community service. No further charges came up in my search, so perhaps that arrest was a one-time deal.

As fascinating as it was to discover that Miranda Hargrove-slash-Horgrave hadn't been who she'd claimed to be, I found some disturbing questions bobbing around in my head: *Why did I get a copy of her résumé? Who delivered it? And more important, what am I supposed to do with it?*

Actually, I knew full well what I was going to do with it. I would swallow my pride and pay Detective Alan Shelton another visit to turn over the mailer and the sheet of paper. But first, I scanned the résumé with the Notes app on my cell phone and saved a copy of it. Just because I wasn't officially investigating didn't mean I wasn't curious.

Chapter Fourteen

Once I set the résumé aside, it was crunch time on getting my jewelry photographed to send to the Jewelry Artisans of the Southeast. After two hours of photographing necklaces, bracelets, and earrings from every angle imaginable, I had no time to prepare a meal, even though I'd invited Justin over for dinner to celebrate him getting back into town. Instead, I ordered Chinese takeout.

When I got home from picking up the food, I curled up on the living room sofa with Miriam and thumbed through a new bead catalog while I waited for Justin. Still thinking about the Miranda *Horgrave* résumé, I tossed the catalog aside and retrieved the envelope with the mysterious piece of paper in it.

Someone wanted me to see this. If it was the killer, how does he or she even know that I'm interested in this case?

Before I could muse any further, a rap on the front door signaled Justin's arrival.

As soon as I opened the door, he gave me a kiss on the cheek and stepped inside. Then he sniffed. "Whatever you cooked smells delicious."

"Actually, I ran out of time and didn't cook at all, but our friends at Little China did, so you're in luck."

Like me, Justin was a fan of the Chinese restaurant's moo goo gai pan. I motioned for him to follow me to the kitchen, where I prepared a small pot of green tea before we filled our plates and sat at my retro dinette set. I preferred to use chopsticks when eating Chinese, but Justin opted for a fork.

"So I want to hear all about Denver." I popped a water chestnut into my mouth.

Justin eagerly gave me the scoop on his recent show. He said he'd made some great contacts, and after talking with them, he wanted to get more involved with the local arts council, which was music to my ears.

Justin poured himself a refill of tea. "And at this one gallery I liked, they have five artists who travel around doing shows together. I'd love to hook up with some of the other artists in the area and do something like that."

I considered the idea. "Savannah would probably be up for it, and she'll know which other painters in town might be interested."

Justin swallowed a bite of chicken and continued, "So she's the only fine artist on the board?"

I pretended to be offended. "I must point out that we all like to think we're *fine* artists, but yeah, she's the only painter on the board right now. Although hopefully, that may be changing soon. I guess we skew heavily to the crafts side of things, now that you mention it."

"Nothing wrong with that." Justin grinned. "And by the way, I think you're pretty fine too."

I hadn't been fishing for a compliment, but I could feel my cheeks flushing. I turned my attention to my chicken and rice. "You might be interested in knowing that there's another painter who's thinking of joining. It's Tyler Montgomery, and he's an old friend of Savannah and Gus. Ever heard of him?"

Justin shook his head. "Nope. What's his art like?"

I perked up. "I haven't seen it myself, but I'm told it's these wonderful moody acrylics. I hear he's got a big following, so that sounds like just the kind of person who might fit in with your group of exhibiting artists."

"Have you met him?"

I swallowed a sip of tea. "Briefly. He was at the last arts council meeting, and he dropped by the gallery the other day. I think he and Gus may have something serious going on."

"Really?" Justin raised an eyebrow. "I don't guess I've ever seen Gus with anyone, now that you mention it."

"I've only ever seen her with the guys she volunteers with or serves on boards with. Nothing romantic at all. I hadn't even heard of Tyler until he showed up at the bazaar on Saturday. Savannah was excited about him being there and gave me the scoop on him and Gus. She said his appearance was definitely one of the best things that happened on Saturday."

"Speaking of, have the police made any progress on figuring out who killed Miranda?" he asked between bites. "I saw a lot of references to it on social media once I got back in town."

I shrugged. "I haven't heard anything new, except..." I'd debated whether to tell him about the résumé. I bit my lip.

"What's wrong?" Justin furrowed his brow.

I got up from the table. "I want to show you something." I stepped to the entryway, retrieved the padded mailer, then returned to the kitchen and handed it over. "Take a look."

He fished out the paper, unfolded it, and began to read. After a few minutes, he looked up. "I thought Miranda was some Happy Hometown legend who came from New York. I was under the impression that Roseland was lucky she'd decided to grace us with her presence."

"That's what I thought too." I told Justin what else I had learned about Miranda from my internet search.

Justin refolded the paper, tucked it back into the mailer, and set the package on the table. "How did you get this?"

I explained that I'd found the mailer at my back door earlier in the day. "And no, I have no idea why it was dropped off here."

"I don't like this, Emma." The set of his jaw told me he meant business.

I grimaced. "You don't like what?"

"I don't like that someone overly interested in Miranda's murder, maybe even her killer, dropped off her résumé here at your house. It's like someone knows you're going to do his dirty work for him."

"Or her."

"Huh?"

I shrugged. "We have no idea whether the killer is male or female. It could be a he or a she."

Justin sighed. "I suppose you're right. But please tell me you're taking this to the police."

I nodded. "That's exactly what I'm planning to do. First thing tomorrow morning."

"Promise?"

"I promise. As a matter of fact, I feel kind of creepy having this, now that you've mentioned some of the same thoughts I was already having."

As we polished off a second pot of tea, we left that unpleasant topic and brainstormed about the group of fine artists he hoped to assemble. Then we moved to the living room to check out a new series on Netflix, and by the time the first two episodes ended, I was stifling a yawn.

"I saw that." Justin grinned. "You've had a busy day being a businesswoman, jewelry marketer, and amateur sleuth. I think it's time we called it a night."

I couldn't argue with that.

"We're still on for The Loft tomorrow night, I hope," Justin said as he headed to the front door.

"Wouldn't miss it." The Loft was our favorite restaurant in Roseland, and I always looked forward to going there, especially with him.

He fingered my chin and stared into my eyes. "You know I love my work, but I've missed you this week, Emma. Thanks for dinner tonight." Then he tucked a wisp of my hair behind my ear and gave me a kiss that made my stomach do backflips. I was still determined to take my time on our new relationship, but it was nice to be missed—and even nicer to be kissed. He stepped away and headed down the steps. I savored the kiss for a moment then waved him off as he pulled away from the street, but as soon as I closed the door, my thoughts drifted back to the résumé.

Something had been rattling around in my head ever since I'd read it, and I finally realized what it was. City leaders had supposedly chosen Miranda from a host of other applicants for the new job, and surely they'd seen a copy of her résumé before they hired her. But they couldn't possibly have viewed the same one I'd received. Somehow, I needed to find out what they'd seen, so I put that on my list of things to check out.

After Justin left, I tidied the kitchen before settling in the living room, where Miriam curled up next to me on the sofa, both of us quite content. Pets really did give back so much more than they asked for.

I flipped through a few channels and tried to decide between some HGTV and a new episode of the *Great British Bake Off*, then my cell phone rang. The display said it was the Happy Hometown office, so it had to be Caitlyn. How odd that she was calling at almost ten o'clock in the evening.

"Hey, Caitlyn. What's up?" No answer came.

"Caitlyn? Are you there?"

I barely managed to hear her frightened whisper. "I-I'm here at the office and..."

My senses tingled. "What's wrong? Are you okay?"

"Y-Yes. But something terrible has happened. It's Gerald. He's—"

The call abruptly ended, and I called her back. One ring. Two. Three. Four. Five. I was already fishing the car keys out of my purse.

Gerald! So Michele was right about him after all. If he's there with Caitlyn, what's he doing to her? He's got to be stopped!

I called 911, and with my phone pressed to my ear, I locked the kitchen door and got in my car as I reported an emergency at the Happy Hometown office. I told the dispatcher I suspected a woman was in danger, and she said someone was already headed there.

Why? Did Caitlyn call 911 before she called me? I sure hope so.

After clicking off the call, I cranked my car and backed out of the driveway. I was too worried to be scared about what I would find at the Happy Hometown office.

Gerald. I should never have given him the benefit of the doubt. He'd pretended to care about all the pets in Roseland, but obviously, he had little regard for human life. As I squealed away from a stop sign, I prayed that police would get there before something happened to Caitlyn.

The street in front of the building was completely deserted except for a black Malibu, maybe Caitlyn's, two Roseland PD cars with lights flashing, and an ambulance. No lights were on in the street-level offices, but the second floor was lit up like a Christmas tree.

What's going on?

The building's front door was open, so I cautiously walked inside. "Hello?" I called. I felt safer knowing the police were there, but I still didn't know what I was walking into. The crackle of a police radio came from nearby, and I spotted a uniformed officer.

"Ma'am, this building is closed right now and—"

"I'm a friend of Caitlyn Hill from the Happy Hometown office, and she just called me a few minutes ago and sounded scared. Is she okay? Have you found Gerald Adams?"

"Found him?" The officer looked confused. "What's your name, ma'am?"

"Emma Madison."

"Come with me, please."

We walked upstairs, and Caitlyn cried out the second she saw me, "Emma! I'm so sorry I hung up in the middle of our call, but I thought Gerald was dead!"

Gerald Adams lay on his back on the floor, clutching his chest and squinting as if in pain. A paramedic wiped blood from a gash on Gerald's forehead and said they needed to get him to the hospital.

Caitlyn looked dazed. "He'd been knocked out, so I was calling you when I heard him groan out in the hallway. I rushed over to see if he was going to make it."

"Why is he here? And what happened?"

She shook her head. "I don't know what happened. I was up here working late, and I guess Gerald must have seen my car outside, because he called and asked if he could come up and make a copy of the minutes from our last board meeting. Since it was after hours, I went downstairs to let him in, and while he was working in the office, I asked if he would mind me running to a drive-through for some supper. When I got back just thirty minutes later, the office had been ransacked, and he was out cold on the floor out here." She lowered her voice. "I was honestly afraid he was dead, so I'm glad he's going to be okay." She chewed her lip and appeared to be on the verge of a crying jag. "Just take a look in the office."

I stuck my head in the door, and the place was utterly trashed. Chairs had been overturned, and a sea of papers and file folders littered the floor. Plaques and certificates on the wall had been smashed, and even the coffee counter had taken a hit, its mugs slung to the floor. I walked over to a framed diploma that dangled precariously on the wall, its glass cracked. It was Miranda's diploma from Reederton Community College.

"Who would do this?" Caitlyn surveyed the destruction, clearly dismayed.

I shook my head. "I have no idea, but I'm sure the police will—"

"Caitlyn Hill?"

The familiar voice made me cringe.

Emma turned and looked at Detective Alan Shelton. "Yes, sir?"

"I'm going to need to get a statement from you." He looked at me. "And is there any particular reason you're here, Emma?"

I met his gaze. "I came because Caitlyn called me, and I thought she was in danger."

He humphed. "I see. Then I guess I'll need a statement from you too. Please have a seat in the lobby while I talk to Caitlyn."

While I waited downstairs, I pulled out my cell phone, which I'd tucked into my coat pocket. I had a text from Jen. *What's going on at the HH office?*

I wrote back, *Vandalism and an attack on Gerald.*

She sent back a wide-eyed emoji followed by a thumbs-up.

The paramedics came downstairs with Gerald on a stretcher, and I stayed out of their way while they carried him out the door and into the ambulance. A female paramedic told one of her colleagues that she suspected Gerald had suffered some broken ribs.

Soon, the detective sent an officer downstairs for me. When I got to the office, Caitlyn was gathering papers and file folders and plopping them onto her desk. Detective Shelton pointed at Caitlyn's now-upright guest chair and asked me to have a seat.

"So tell me how you got involved in the evening's events," the detective said.

I gave him the rundown, and he wrote some notes in his pocket-sized spiral notebook. "And what was the situation when you arrived?"

"An officer asked what I was doing here, and I explained that Caitlyn had just called me, so he let me come upstairs."

He nodded. "Anything else? Did you see anyone leaving as you were coming in?"

I shook my head. "I'm afraid not."

"Any idea who had it in for Gerald Adams or the Happy Hometown program?"

"No, but Gerald's on the board, you know. And so am I."

He wrote that down.

"After Saturday, it sure looks like someone has a grudge against the Happy Hometown program. Don't you think?"

The detective didn't even look up from his notebook. When he did, he flipped it closed and smiled.

"Thanks for your comments, Emma." He whispered, "Now can you help me convince Caitlyn to go home for the night?"

I nodded. When I walked over to her overflowing desk, Caitlyn looked weary.

I tapped her on the back. "Let's call it a day, okay?"

She spread her hands over the disarray. "Look at this mess. There's no way I can face all this in the morning and—"

"Then don't. I'll meet you here, and we'll clean it up together. That'll be safer, and we'll both feel better after a good night's rest."

Reluctantly, she agreed to leave. The detective said he wanted to follow her home, which I thought was a wise move, considering. I told Caitlyn I'd meet her at the office at eight o'clock, and I couldn't wait to get home myself. I had a lot of thinking to do.

Gerald wasn't our killer after all, and it was time to strike him from my suspect list.

Chapter Fifteen

It seemed I had barely closed my eyes when my phone rang at 6:02 a.m. *Who on earth?* I answered the call and croaked out a sleepy hello.

"Hey, is Mike there?"

"No, there's no Mike here."

"Sorry. Must have the wrong number." Then dead air.

Thanks a lot.

My mind started racing with all I wanted to get done that day, so I was unable to go back to sleep and catch the thirty minutes I had just been cheated out of. Since I was already up, I would try to get a little work done before meeting Caitlyn at her office.

My mind replayed the events of the previous evening, and I wondered how Gerald was doing. I felt guilty for ever considering him a suspect in Miranda's murder.

After a quick shower, I downed a cup of coffee and some scrambled eggs for breakfast then wired a few pairs of earrings. I loved making those, and they came together so fast.

Since I was meeting Savannah for lunch, I slipped on gray slacks, a hot-pink sweater, pearl stud earrings, and a simple pearl charm necklace before I headed to meet Caitlyn.

When I arrived downtown, the wire frame of the Roseland Christmas tree was under construction, and thanks to a few lookie-loos showing up, only one parking spot remained near the Happy Hometown office. Fortunately, I got it and was soon on my way up to see Caitlyn and help restore order to the plundered office.

When I got to the door, a clipboard with a visitor sign-in sheet was mounted to the wall outside, so I paused to write my name. *A response to last night's rampage, maybe?*

I knocked on the door, and before it even opened, "I'm glad you're here, Emma" came from the other side.

I was sure I had a puzzled look on my face when Caitlyn opened the door. "How'd you know it was me?"

She pointed at a far corner of the upstairs waiting area. "One of those doorbell cameras. The city had it installed early this morning. Mayor's orders."

"They don't waste time, do they? When did he hear about what happened last night?"

She smirked. "Seriously?"

I had to laugh. "What is it they say about small towns? You don't have to mind your own business, because everyone's always doing it for you? But I guess it's nice that the mayor cares what happens to you."

Caitlyn brushed a strand of hair out of her eyes. "Frankly, I think it's more that he's concerned about a liability issue. He said that for the time being, I'm not to work up here without having another board member in the office. I got permission to come in early only because the workers were installing the camera, and I promised them you'd be here at eight." She glanced at her watch. "And of course you are. Listen, thanks again for coming up here last night. I'm so sorry about everything that happened."

"Don't give it another thought. Have you heard an update on Gerald this morning?"

"Mm-hmm. I just got a call from that detective, and he said Gerald got stitches for the gash on his head. He has some broken ribs, too, and he's going to be in the hospital a few days, but he's expected to make a full recovery."

"That's great news." I smiled. "Now..." I looked around and sighed.

"Yeah, that was my reaction when I walked in and saw everything." Caitlyn waved her hand over the files as well as numerous stacks of paper on her desk. "We've had quite a few cards and memorial gifts come into the office since Miranda's death, and I've tried to stay on top of the thank-you notes and acknowledgments, but now I can't tell what's what."

"I guess not." I considered the scene again. "Let's get everything off the floor first, then I'll help you figure out how to get it organized and put away."

"Sounds like a plan." Caitlyn bobbed her head. "Then I can get back to settling up with everyone from the bazaar." She blew out a breath. "Keeping up with all the accounting is definitely beyond my skill set, and the mayor's office is sending someone from the finance department to do an audit before we see about the donation that goes to the foster parent association, paying our vendors, getting the refund for the rental deposit... I never realized how many things Miranda took care of behind the scenes."

That was just the opening I'd been hoping for.

"I imagine she did a lot of stuff that many of us weren't aware of." I scooped up a pile of papers that had landed on a windowsill. "If I recall, she came highly recommended from some downtown development program up in New York, right?"

Caitlyn chewed her lip. "Um, it turned out that she was familiar with the program but was actually hired because of her... event-planning and... networking skills."

What a crock. Caitlyn was trying really hard *not* to say something. I just couldn't figure out what.

"Really? How interesting." I looked off to the side, hoping Caitlyn would take the bait.

She did. "Why do you ask? Is her background important?"

"Maybe. Maybe not." I shrugged. "On one hand, she was a highly acclaimed downtown development staffer, or so I'd heard. But on the other hand, if things were so wonderful up there, why did she move to a small town like Roseland?"

Caitlyn picked up some pieces of a broken coffee mug and dropped them into a big black plastic bag. "I wouldn't know about that."

"So you don't remember where Miranda last worked?"

She shook her head. "But I imagine her file's somewhere in this office." She gave me a wry grin. "And right now, your guess is as good as mine about where that file is."

"Why don't you take that side of the office"—I pointed her way—"and I'll gather the papers and files over here. I've always liked to divide and conquer."

"Sounds good."

Caitlyn started on the side of the office nearest the hallway, and I worked on the opposite side, where the windows faced the street.

I didn't pay close attention to the papers and files I picked up, but many of them seemed to pertain to businesses submitting bids for catering, office supplies, consulting, and other expenses the program had on a regular basis. I recognized a few of the papers as applications for exhibitor spots at the Christmas bazaar, including mine. Out of curiosity, I scanned my application, and someone—Miranda, I imagined—had written the day and time it came in on the upper right corner of the page.

After two tedious hours of cleanup then sorting the folders, we had made excellent progress and were nearly done. One of the last folders I came across was marked Personnel, and it appeared to have most of its contents intact. I held it up and got Caitlyn's attention. "Is it okay if I look at this?"

She shrugged. "Suit yourself."

I peeked inside, and there was Miranda's résumé, which was formatted just like the copy I had received the previous day. This résumé, however, said that Miranda *Hargrove's* last job was with Happy Hometown in Rochester, which was apparently untrue. Prior to that, the résumé claimed, she'd worked as an events planner for five years. She had included a lot of details about her high school and college achievements as well.

I wondered whether anyone had ever bothered to contact the references she'd listed on the next page or if they were legitimate. I thought of asking Caitlyn to call them but didn't see the point. Miranda had obviously been afraid she wouldn't get the job in Roseland if they knew she didn't have experience in downtown development, and she might have been concerned about her DUI showing up as well.

When I looked up, Caitlyn was studying my face. "Anything of interest?"

"Not really." But on a hunch, I added, "And I'm assuming you already knew about that DUI in Miranda's past, didn't you?"

Caitlyn looked down. "Yes."

That was as good a time as any to surprise her with the questions I'd wanted to ask all morning. "Let me just be up front with you, Caitlyn. I understand you and Miranda argued quite a bit. Is that true?"

I'd expected Caitlyn to squirm. Instead, she looked me straight in the eyes. "Yes, we did. In fact, we had quite a few arguments before she—" She pursed her lips. "Before the bazaar."

"What did you argue about?"

Caitlyn teared up, and I wondered whether I had crossed a line. *Sheesh.* Our conversation wasn't going anywhere if I upset her. *Maybe Detective Shelton's right that I really ought to leave the investigating to the professionals.*

"If that's too emotional to talk about..." I wanted to give her the opportunity to clam up if she wasn't prepared to go on.

"No, it's okay." Caitlyn reached across her desk and pulled a tissue from a box. She blew her nose then cleared her throat. "Miranda and I had quite a few run-ins in the weeks before she died. I thought she offended way too many people with her efforts to turn this year's bazaar into some regional spectacular."

I raised an eyebrow. "It wasn't wrong to want to raise the profile of the show, was it?"

She shook her head and fiddled with the collar on her blouse. "But it *was* wrong to tick off half the town, people who've worked so hard over the years to make the show the success it's always been."

I leaned forward. "What about the registration for Harriet Harris's daughter? How'd that get so bungled?"

"Truthfully, I expected some trouble with Mrs. Harris after Miranda tossed Holly's application into the trash and told me not to even call to say we didn't receive it in time."

"Whew. Bad move on her part," I agreed.

Caitlyn nodded. "Mrs. Harris was one of the teachers when I was in elementary school, and I know she can be an old battle-ax, but she still has a lot of influence in Roseland. It's not smart to get on her bad side. Then came the controversy with the Humane Society where—"

"The day of the show, you mean?"

She shook her head. "No, during the registration period. Gerald got his application in early, just like always. For some reason, Miranda decided we shouldn't have pets at an arts-and-crafts bazaar. She said pets were neither arts nor crafts and that it was ridiculous that they'd ever been included in the first place."

I rolled my eyes. "Let me guess. She wasn't a pet lover, was she?"

"How'd you know?" Caitlyn smiled tentatively. "The one time I came into the office to pick up my check before vacation and had Mitzi, my Yorkie, in my arms, Miranda nearly hurt herself getting to the threshold, telling me I couldn't bring 'a wild animal' into the office."

I laughed. "A Yorkie? A wild animal?"

My regard for Miranda, God rest her soul, was not improving with the new information.

Caitlyn shrugged. "Some people are like that. Their loss, right?"

I nodded. *Maybe Miranda would have been a nicer person if she'd had a pet.* "So did she ever actually tell the Humane Society they couldn't participate?"

"She tried. After Gerald and the Humane Society got word that they couldn't be in the bazaar, he went straight to their board and instigated an email-writing campaign demanding that Miranda reconsider."

"And she did, obviously."

"Oh yeah." Caitlyn's expression turned serious. "Some of the society's most influential board members were so upset that they threatened to boycott the show and run newspaper ads claiming that the Happy Hometown program was hostile to the entire Roseland pet population."

I frowned. "Oh no." One thing I remembered from my newspaper days was that ticking off pet owners was never, ever a good idea.

"So"—Caitlyn held up her hands—"that was probably the biggest blowup the two of us had, the time we argued the most, and she said to let the Humane Society run their ads if they wanted to. I finally convinced her that Happy Hometown would be ridiculed if things turned nasty. In fact, when I mentioned that the Atlanta TV stations might pick up on it and come up here to investigate, she changed her tune pretty quickly."

How intriguing. "Why do you think that was?"

"She told me she was uncomfortable with the idea of some reporter in a TV news van showing up and sticking a microphone in her face."

I'll just bet she was.

"I thought it was odd, too, because Miranda always seemed to like being the center of attention," Caitlyn said. "But then I learned about that DUI, and I decided that was what she didn't want people to find out."

"Who told you about that?"

Caitlyn clammed up. "I'm... I'm really not supposed to say."

Okay, then. But no wonder Miranda had felt threatened by the idea of Atlanta media attention. If she became the subject of a local controversy, some hard-nosed reporter might be tempted to look into her background and spot a few troubling items on her résumé.

I had another question for Caitlyn. "I know what you thought of Miranda professionally, but personally, what did you think of her? Did you ever like her?"

Caitlyn was quiet for a moment. "Honestly? I felt sorry for her. She seemed to be trying so hard to prove something, and I knew that wasn't going to turn out well. I mean, I certainly never dreamed she'd get killed. But I also knew that she had already rubbed a lot of people the wrong way. A *lot* of people."

It was time to go big or go home. "So you didn't kill her, then?"

Caitlyn's mouth flew open. "No, of course not!"

"I didn't think so, but I had to ask."

The desk phone rang, startling me.

Caitlyn pointed at the phone. "Mind if I get this? It seems people are expecting work to go on as usual, and—"

"I've got to run anyway, so please, take your call."

While Caitlyn looked hurt about what I'd just asked her, she was still professional enough to motion to the stack of folders. "And thanks for that. I appreciate the help."

I opened the door of the Happy Hometown office and headed down before passing the library director on the stairs. *Guess she gets to babysit for a while.* When I got downstairs and exited to the street, a chill in the air made me wrap my trench coat tighter around myself.

With a sigh of resignation, I fished the mysterious résumé from my purse and headed to the Roseland Police Department. Considering I'd seen him only twelve hours ago, I hoped the person I was going to see wouldn't lock me up when he saw me again.

Chapter Sixteen

When I walked into the police station, Evelyn tapped away at her computer as a girl who appeared to be in her late teens complained about the cost of a speeding ticket. By the set of Evelyn's mouth, I could see she wasn't in the mood to hear the complaint.

While I waited, I listened to the scanner on Evelyn's desk. The only breaking news was that a traffic signal near the hospital wasn't working, and officers were on the way to direct traffic.

Finally, stone-faced, the girl paid the fine and pranced out.

As soon as she'd left, Evelyn met my eyes and lowered her voice. "Guess we'll never get to stop explaining to eighteen-year-olds that going sixty-five in a thirty-five zone is indeed speeding." She shook her head. "So, what brings you here today?"

"Nothing I was out looking for. I promise you that. For some reason, I received anonymous information about the late Miranda Hor—*Har*grove, and I thought the police department might want to see it, since it could be relevant to the case." I explained about finding the copy of Miranda's résumé at my back door the previous day.

"Oh yeah, they'll want to talk to you for sure." Evelyn used the eraser of her yellow pencil to tap three numbers on the phone. "Hey, Alan, it's Evelyn, and I've got someone up here you're going to want to talk to. It's Emma Madison, and... Yes, actually, it is about the murder investigation. Anyway, I'm going to send her down to your office, okay? Thanks."

She looked up at me. "He's expecting you, so go on back."

I thanked her and headed down the hall, biting my lip like a naughty child headed to the principal's office. I hadn't done anything

166

wrong. In fact, I was there to do something right. I had no reason to feel nervous.

When I got to the detective's office, he stood in the doorway with his arms crossed. "Funny, I could have sworn I just saw you last night."

I rolled my eyes. "And last night, we were both busy with another matter entirely, as I recall."

He humphed. "Evelyn tells me you have some information related to the Miranda Hargrove case?"

I shoved the blue-and-white mailer in front of him and pulled out the piece of paper. "This. It came to my house. I don't know why. I don't know who sent it. I thought you ought to have it."

Why am I speaking like a robot?

He scanned the paper then looked up at me. "A résumé?"

"Mm-hmm. And from what I know about Miranda Hargrove, or Horgrave, apparently, this isn't the background she claimed to have."

"How do you know that?" He raised an eyebrow.

"Detective, you live in Roseland. Everybody knows everybody else's business here. Miranda evidently got under a few people's skin with her 'New York' ways, only it turns out she wasn't from New York at all."

The detective stuck a hand into his pocket and rattled some coins while his gaze scrolled over the résumé again. "Says she worked in retail previously. Interesting. Did you know that?"

I shook my head. "Like everyone else, I had no reason to question her background. We've certainly had pushy newcomers move here before, so that was nothing new."

He peered back down at the paper. "You said you received this anonymously?"

"Mm-hmm. It was propped against my back door when I got back from running an errand yesterday."

"And you didn't see fit to mention this last night?"

I frowned. "I was rather preoccupied there at the Happy Hometown office, if you'll recall."

He humphed. "I'd like to keep the paper and the mailer, just in case whoever sent this has some connection to the case."

"Be my guest." I waved a hand as if dismissing both pieces of evidence—or possible evidence.

"So you have no idea why these were sent to you?" He squinted as if he thought I was holding back on him.

"Well, I..."

"Yes?"

"Look, I was a newspaper reporter for a few years, and everybody knows that all small-town reporters are basically cheap, low-rent celebrities. A lot of people know me. Maybe somebody remembered that and knew I would do something with this. Like share it with the newspaper, maybe."

He nodded. "But you didn't, right?"

"No, I came right here."

"You didn't mention it to anyone else?"

I took a deep breath. "I showed it to my boyfriend, but he suggested I get it to you as soon as possible. Which, by the way, I was already planning to do."

"Okay, then."

Having done what I'd gone there for, I was ready to leave. "So, is that it? That all you need from me?"

Detective Shelton stood from his desk. "I do have one more thing."

"Yes?"

He cleared his throat. "I don't know how I can make this any plainer, Emma, but you need to stop your amateur sleuthing—before someone gets hurt."

"But I haven't been—"

Detective Shelton's baby-blue eyes turned dark and bored a hole through me. "I'm not sure what you're doing and saying all over town, but once again, you've somehow ended up right in the middle of our investigation. I don't know why others think you need to be the point person on this case, but need I remind you that there's a penalty for interfering with a police investigation? And if I have to assign an officer to watch you twenty-four, seven to get you to back off, I'll do it."

Seething, I counted to five, because I didn't have the patience to count to ten.

"If you're suggesting I *asked* for this information to be delivered to me, Detective Shelton, you're completely out of line, and I resent being blamed for something that literally showed up at my back door. If I happen to come across any other evidence, I'll certainly keep it to myself to avoid inconveniencing you."

I whirled around and heard, "Emma, wait..."

Halfway down the hall by then, I couldn't get out of that building fast enough. Evelyn had stepped away from her desk when I marched past, and I was glad she was gone. Too bad she had to work with such an arrogant, incompetent detective.

How dare he accuse me of involving myself in his precious case.

Outside the building, I was so rattled that I looked around and tried to remember where I was headed next. Since I'd silenced my cell phone while I was at the police department, I checked for messages and had one from Savannah, confirming that we were still on for lunch and asking whether I'd heard about some vandalism at the Happy Hometown office.

I wondered what had taken her so long to ask. It had already been more than twelve hours since Gerald was assaulted and the office was trashed.

I tapped a quick reply. *Will fill you in at lunch. Mama's Place at noon still okay?*

Savannah replied with a thumbs-up.

With only ten minutes before time to meet her, I window-shopped the downtown stores and tried to clear my head.

What was I supposed to do with that information, Detective Shelton? Sit on it? Throw it away? That wouldn't have been very bright.

Speaking of bright, the sparkle of gemstones distracted me from my replay of the morning's events. Lamberson Jewelry had a sign up announcing a special Thanksgiving promotion. For each in-store purchase of two hundred dollars or more, they would donate a turkey to Roseland's famous Turkey Toss campaign to feed the hungry, which was coming up that weekend. What a great idea, and it reminded me that I'd been meaning to stop by to make a few fine jewelry purchases for those on my Christmas list, and—

"Boo!" A poke at my back nearly sent me sailing through the plate glass window.

"Savannah!" I clutched my chest. "You're going to give me a heart attack. And right now, that wouldn't take much."

Her mischievous grin vanished. "Why? What's wrong?"

I looked around. "I just came from the police station, where I once again got a lecture from Detective Alan Shelton."

"What on earth about?"

I scowled. "I'm not supposed to talk about it."

She eyed me up and down. "And it doesn't look like you *want* to talk about it."

"Nope."

She studied me for a moment then nodded. "Okay, then. Want to head to Mama's?"

"Sure do." At some point, I would tell her about my kerfuffle with the detective, but right then, I was ready to move on. The local meat-and-three diner, one of Roseland's hidden gems, was located in an alley a few doors away. All the tables were taken when we got there, so while we waited in line, I told Savannah what I knew about the incident at the Happy Hometown office.

"Good grief. Is Gerald going to be okay?"

I sighed. "I hope so. Caitlyn said she heard he would be in the hospital for a few days."

"I wonder if he saw whoever attacked him."

"He was completely out of it when they carried him out on a stretcher last night, so I doubt he was able to tell them if he did."

Surveying the packed dining room, I said, "Business is sure booming today. I'm glad we didn't wait any longer to show up."

No matter what had happened earlier that morning, I fully intended to make the most of lunch at Mama's Place. The lunchtime patrons were already chowing down on the day's special, meatloaf, and nursing tall tumblers of the best sweet tea in North Georgia.

After we'd waited for five minutes, a middle-aged man I recognized as a local judge got up and left a table where he'd been sitting with another man, who appeared to be in his twenties. He was probably some aspiring legal eagle.

Savannah and I grabbed the newly vacated table and looked over the diner's photocopied menus, which always had a Bible verse printed at the bottom. The verse for the day read "This is the day which the Lord hath made; we will rejoice and be glad in it. Psalm 118:24." I grinned. My sour attitude sure wasn't doing me any good, and Mama and God—not necessarily in that order—had obviously known that I would need an attitude adjustment.

Savannah set her menu on the table. "I know I shouldn't, but I'm having the fried chicken. What about you?"

I sighed. "Still can't decide." *How long has it been since I've had the meatloaf here? Oh, and there's baked fish today too. That would be a healthy choice. With a side salad and some green beans.*

Mama herself, LaNelle Jenkins, came to our table, her mint-green order pad in hand. "Welcome, ladies. What can I get for y'all today?"

I nodded at Savannah. "You go ahead. I'll make up my mind by the time you're through."

"I'll have the meatloaf, squash casserole, and fried okra. And sweet tea to drink."

"You got it, babe. And you, Emma?"

I stared at Savannah. "You said you were getting the fried chicken, so *I* was going to get the meatloaf."

"So get the meatloaf, sugar." Mama's pen was poised over her order pad. "I've got enough for both of y'all, you know." She grinned.

"I know. I just always like to order something different from the people I eat with. But you know what? I wanted the meatloaf, so I'm sticking with that, and—"

"And you'll have macaroni and cheese and fried green tomatoes for the sides. And sweet tea. Right?"

I smiled as LaNelle hurried off with our orders, then I looked around and spotted some familiar faces, including Savannah's sister, who appeared to be enjoying another lunch date with Tyler Montgomery. Despite the bad things going on in Roseland, I was heartened that both my and Gus's love lives seemed to be moving in the right direction.

I leaned over and looked past Savannah until I caught Gus's eye and nodded at her nearly empty plate. "I'm a fan of the meatloaf too. Up to the usual standards, I trust?"

"As always. I used it to nudge Tyler along about joining the arts council."

"Oh?" I nodded at Tyler and raised an eyebrow. "And has she been successful?"

Tyler grinned. "Gus is the kind of woman who doesn't take no for an answer."

Savannah joked, "You're not telling me anything I didn't already know."

Gus rolled her eyes, but she was smiling. She closed the pastel floral notebook she'd had open on their table, and she and Tyler stood and headed to the door.

When they were out of earshot, I turned to Savannah. "Looks like those two are getting on well, huh?"

"Shh, don't jinx it. I can't remember the last time a guy worked out for Gus. She's had some of the worst luck." Savannah shook her head. "But I've sure got my fingers crossed this time."

One of Mama's daughters arrived at our table with two plates of meatloaf and vegetables. Mama's meatloaf was so good that I almost forgot about the unpleasant encounter at the police station that morning.

Savannah was halfway through her meatloaf and making headway on her squash and okra. As she speared a bite of meatloaf, she laughed. "It just hit me that Gus has been thinking of going vegetarian. If she's bribing Tyler with Mama's country cooking, I guess that means she's ditching that plan, at least long enough to get Tyler on the arts council."

That reminded me of Justin's idea about assembling a group of fine artists. "Speaking of artists and the arts, I was supposed to ask you something. What would you think about joining forces with some other fine artists in the area and staging your own shows? Does that appeal to you?"

"Sure. What've you got in mind?"

I cocked my head. "It's only an idea at the moment, but Justin wants to gather a group of local artists who exhibit together and support each other's work. I told him I'd ask you about it, and of course he's hoping Gus will participate too."

Savannah was all smiles. "I love Justin's work, and yeah, I'd be extremely interested in that. When do we start?"

I pulled a notepad out of my purse and scribbled down his number. "Here's his contact info. Text him or give him a call, and maybe the two of you can brainstorm how this might work."

Savannah eagerly accepted it. "Will do."

"And one more thing. When Justin and I talked about this last night, I also told him about Tyler. Would he be interested in joining? Would he be a good fit?"

"Hmm, good question. Tyler's unbelievably talented, but he's always done his own thing. I'll run it by Gus first and get her to see if he's interested. The worst he can do is say no."

"Exactly."

LaNelle made the rounds again and walked by our table while holding up two slices of pie. "We've got both apple and pumpkin today, ladies. Can I interest you in a slice?"

Already stuffed, I declined. Savannah said she would like some later then asked whether she could purchase a whole pumpkin pie to take home with her. LaNelle said she'd get it ready for her.

"You must like that pumpkin pie a lot."

"I do, but enough about pie. Are you going to tell me what had you so rattled earlier? Something to do with Alan Shelton?"

I waved it off. "No big deal, really. I had a lead on something that might be related to the murder, and when I stopped by his office to share it, I got a lecture about keeping my nose clean and staying out of his investigation."

Savannah pursed her lips.

"What is it? You're not on his side, are you?"

She clasped her hands on the table. "Look, I'm not on anybody's 'side.' But if you're investigating again when he's asked you not to..."

I huffed. "I promise I am not intentionally investigating anything. But when information literally lands at my back door, what am I supposed to do with it? Ignore it?"

"Here you go, lady." LaNelle plopped a paper grocery bag in front of Savannah and said she'd wrapped the pie in double layers of foil to keep it fresh.

We headed to the cashier, and after we paid for our food, Savannah tapped my arm.

"I believe you when you say you're not trying to investigate the murder, but even if something 'lands at your back door,' as you put it, be careful, okay?"

I assured her that I would watch my back, and as I left the restaurant, I took that promise to heart. The morning's weather report had said more rain was coming, and the dark-gray skies made me believe it. A chill crept up my neck—along with the strange sensation that I was being watched. But that was ridiculous. I looked around and saw only the usual hustle and bustle of holiday shoppers going in and out of the downtown shops.

A chill in the air. That's all it was.

I hoped.

Chapter Seventeen

What a day! Vandalism cleanup, a dustup with a detective, then a nice lunch with a friend. I entered the house through the back door, put my purse on the counter, and was welcomed by a sea of red fuzz sprawled across my kitchen floor. *What on earth?*

"Hey, you!"

Miriam's head jerked up from the kitchen doorway.

"What have you gotten into now?" The roll of red raffia I'd been using to make bows for my Christmas jewelry packages was shredded to pieces—no doubt by little kitty claws—and half the contents of the spool were curled around a chair and past a table leg then, helpfully, right up to the kitchen garbage can.

"Miriam Haskell!"

She looked at me as if to say, "Huh? What'd I do, Mom?"

So much for knocking out more jewelry. Cleanup would have to come first.

After I searched in vain for the ribbon's end, hoping to salvage some of it, I reached into the junk drawer for my all-purpose scissors and sliced the nearest spot of raffia. I had just started winding a length of it around my fingers when the doorbell rang. As I headed to the door, I wound faster, and the knocking grew louder.

"I'm coming!" *Jen, maybe?* But Jen rarely had time for a visit on Fridays, since she was busy editing stories for the weekend newspapers.

When I peered through the window, Detective Alan Shelton was standing there.

I opened the door and glared. "Yes?"

His eyes followed the streamers of shredded raffia in my hands, and he must have wondered what I was doing. "Oh, this." I nodded at the ribbon. "My cat got into some of my craft supplies while I was away."

"I just need to ask you a few quick questions."

"About?"

"Can I come in for a few minutes?"

I huffed and motioned to the living room. "Wait in there. I need to throw this ribbon away."

In the kitchen, I untwirled enough ribbon to easily shake it off, then I washed my hands and scooted to the living room.

"Now, what is this about?"

"It's about the Christmas bazaar photos you had the teenage girl send to our office the other night following Miranda's murder."

"Do forgive me if I'm misremembering something, but I believe that this very morning, I was asked—no, make that *ordered*—not to have anything further to do with this investigation. Did I dream that conversation?"

The detective frowned. "No, but this time, I'm coming to you, so it's different."

"Is that so?" But curiosity got the better of me. "Anyway, what was your question about the photos?"

"How well did you look at those before she sent them our way?"

"I barely glanced at them. Once I saw Miranda's arm dangling out of Santa's bag, I knew you'd want to see them yourself and not have... *the public* trying to solve the case themselves."

"So you didn't make or keep copies?"

I felt my face heating. "What do you mean, 'make copies'?"

"Did you have her forward them to you then have her send them to Evelyn? Did you get prints made or keep the copies on your phone?"

Barely concealing my aggravation, I replied, "No, Detective, I didn't make copies. No print copies, no cell phone copies. No copies period."

I could've sworn I heard a forlorn sigh, then he said, "Good. That's what I was hoping to hear."

"Is there some reason you're asking me this here, at my house, on a Friday afternoon when I've got a million things to do?" I had a hand on my hip.

"A person of interest was in one of the photos and—"

"Oh yeah?" *Now, that's news!* "Who was it?" He was implying that somebody who'd been at the bazaar was on the police department's radar.

"You know I can't disclose details of an active investigation."

I tried another tactic. "So, exactly what difference would it have made if I had kept copies of those cell phone photos? You thought that if I knew who was in those photos, I might be in danger, didn't you?"

He ignored my question. "The girl's mother, I believe, serves on the arts council with you. Do you happen to know whether Mrs. Delgado looked at those photos?"

I had to think about that. "I honestly couldn't say. She knows about my getting her daughter to send them to you, and we talked about the photos at our meeting the other night, but I don't think she specifically mentioned seeing them herself."

"Who all was at that meeting?"

"Besides Trish and me? Savannah Rogers, Gus Townsend, Bob Mathis, Martha Barnes, and Shareta Davis."

"No one else?"

"Nope. Oh, wait. A potential new board member, Tyler Montgomery, came by at the end. But he was really there just because he's seeing Gus. So do you think the killer's after us?"

"Fortunately for you and everyone else, the killer can't possibly know who all snapped cell phone photos that night. I'm hoping the person has no reason to suspect you of having an interest in the case. At least, no more so than any other curious person here in Roseland."

"Curious." I smiled. "Sounds slightly better than nosy."

The detective gestured to a renegade raffia streamer that Miriam had just trailed into the living room. "I guess that's my signal to go and let you finish cleaning up your craft supplies."

"So that's all you had to ask?"

He nodded. "That was it. Enjoy your afternoon."

The detective was gone in an instant, and I found it odd that he'd come to my house to question me. If I didn't know better, I would have sworn he was genuinely interested in my safety.

JUSTIN HAYES AND I had been seeing each other for months. While we'd gotten past the butterflies-in-the-stomach stage of dating, my heart still flip-flopped whenever he looked my way. That night, he had picked me up in the pouring-down rain for dinner at The Loft. He had arrived promptly and escorted me to his car as he held a huge golf umbrella over our heads.

Within minutes, we were out of the car, out of the rain, and soaking in the cozy atmosphere of The Loft.

As our server seated us, I glanced around.

"Hey," I whispered, causing Justin to look up from studying his menu. "Have you noticed how sparse the crowd is tonight? I wonder if the rain is keeping everyone away."

Justin grinned. "I know you're a fan of The Loft, but you do know it's not a crime if they have a slow night, right?"

I smiled back. "I suppose you're right."

He continued to study his menu, and I gave full attention to mine. Then I sensed a presence near our table.

"You guys having an early dinner too?" A female voice caught my attention.

Savannah and her husband, Paul, had a black to-go bag from The Loft, presumably transporting leftovers of whatever delicious meal they'd just consumed.

"I shouldn't have eaten such a big meal at lunchtime then come here for dinner." Savannah patted her stomach. "You probably feel the same way."

"Speak for yourself." I laughed. "Nah, I'll probably end up with a to-go bag, too, but I can never resist an invitation to dine here."

"We were just checking out the menus." Justin gave a nod to his. "Got a recommendation?"

Paul tapped the bag. "I highly recommend the New York strip, if you're thinking of having the special."

"Good to know. And thanks for the advice."

Savannah and Paul said their goodbyes, and before they reached the front door, our server returned, and both Justin and I had decided to have the steak special.

"So." Justin handed the server our menus then turned to me. "If I know you, you've been thinking about the Miranda Hargrove investigation some more. Correct?"

"Who, me?" I feigned my most innocent look, and he chuckled.

"Just as I thought. What does Roseland's Nancy Drew think is going on? Who killed Miranda, how did they do it, and how did they get away with it?"

"It was Colonel Mustard, in the conservatory, with a..." I slumped in my seat and confessed, "I have no idea. And it's been further complicated since you and I spoke last night."

"Oh?"

I filled him in on what had happened since I last saw him, including the attack on Gerald at the Happy Hometown office then my unappreciated visit with the detective, including his follow-up visit in the afternoon.

Our server brought our bread and salads and slipped away.

Justin tore off a piece of bread. "Okay, so let's hear who your suspects are now."

"I'm thinking we need to look closely at the list of people who didn't get their usual spot at this year's show, like Bob Mathis—not that I actually believe Bob's a murderer. But if the artist was someone who relied on this show for a chunk of their annual income and they didn't do as well as usual, that would certainly give that person a motive for wanting to get back at Miranda. Plus, they might have found it embarrassing to get knocked out of their old spot."

"Someone like Savannah?"

"Yes. Well, no. I mean someone *like* Savannah but not Savannah, obviously. She wouldn't hurt a flea. So someone who was chosen for the show but who didn't get the booth that they did in years past."

Justin stared into space as if pondering that idea. "How would you find out who was in the show in the past but didn't get their previous spot? That would be hard to figure out, wouldn't it?"

He'd just given me an idea. "Caitlyn would definitely know, or she'd at least have access to the records of who set up where last year. On Saturday, Miranda had Caitlyn go around to all the booths to make sure everyone was in the location Happy Hometown had assigned them. So she would have had a list of who had what spot last year and what they were assigned this year."

"Then I sincerely hope someone talks to Caitlyn soon. If she has that information, and if the killer knows she does, then that could be what made her a target last night."

I wondered if Caitlyn had considered that. She was only a year or two out of college, and since she was fairly new to the job, she might not be aware that she had anything to worry about. I didn't want to frighten her, but Justin's comment was sobering, and I planned to call her as soon as I got home.

Soon, our server arrived with our steaming steaks. Mine was medium rare, just like I liked it, and Justin said his—ordered well-done—was cooked perfectly as well. We ate in silence for a while, and I was pleased to see the restaurant traffic had increased significantly.

"Now that our appetites have been satisfied"—Justin had a mischievous look in his eyes—"tell me how the jewelry biz is going. The last time I mentioned your work, you promised to fill me in on some design news."

I held out my arm. "It was this." I had on a new leather cuff bracelet that had a large center oval of hand-forged silver. "I made it in a workshop last month. What do you think?"

Justin reached out and gently touched the bracelet, brushing my skin. Inwardly, I sighed, though on the outside, I aimed for calm, cool, and collected. He gave a low whistle. "Stunning."

He wiggled his eyebrows, and I could feel myself blushing. *Is he talking about the bracelet or me?*

"Thanks. I'm pretty pleased with how it turned out."

Justin dipped his head. "You should be. That definitely looks like a high-quality piece. So are you going to make more?"

I shook my head. "Right now, I can't. I'm up to my elbows in Christmas designs. But taking a new course fills the well, if you know what I mean, and any technique I learn seems to inspire some future project, so it's a good career investment. Does that happen when you take classes?"

"Absolutely, and when—"

"Well, hi, you two." Gus Townsend had stopped at our table. I always loved to see what outfit Gus dreamed up next, and she was wearing a denim jacket with a crazy-quilt-style bodice, a slim-fitting denim skirt, and granny boots with velvet-trimmed socks.

"You here with someone?" I glanced around but didn't see her new companion.

"No, alas." She grimaced. "Tyler said he had to work on a commission tonight. But Savannah and I are planning a big fiftieth-anniversary party for our parents next year, and I came by to drop off some menu ideas so that I can get a catering quote."

"This would be a great place for that." Justin nodded. "Have you heard about that new rooftop patio they're working on? I hear the plans for it are spectacular."

Gus bounced on her feet. "That's where we're hoping to have it. We'd like something more upscale than chicken dinners for seventy-five at the country club, if you know what I mean. We're hoping for something more intimate here, and Savannah put me in charge of the food."

"Fun job." I had known her parents for years, so I hoped to be invited when the big event rolled around.

"It'll be fun when the sampling time arrives." Gus chuckled then stole a glance at her watch. "Speaking of the parents, I'm headed there for dinner, so I'd better run." She looked at Justin then me. "Enjoy the rest of your dinner, you two."

Justin's eyes followed her out of the room, then he lowered his voice. "Have you heard that some of her pieces are going to Washington for a congressional art exhibit?"

"Seriously? No. How did you hear about it?"

"One of the regional art magazines had an article on her. I was impressed with how far she's come with her art. And it mentioned she's become quite active in the local Humane Society, even donating some of her pieces to help them raise money for the no-kill shelter."

"Gus never mentions any of this at our arts council meetings." Nearly stuffed, I folded my napkin and set it to the side of my plate. "I can't believe I'm in an arts group with someone who hasn't been shouting this news from the rooftop. And I'm wondering why on earth not."

"It's the same dilemma we all have." Justin's baby blues were aimed right at me. "How do we acknowledge our success without sounding like we're bragging?"

I understood his concern. I'd already gotten several awards for my work, but I didn't want to contact Jen and the newspaper every time I was honored. She was already stressed out since subscriptions continued to decline. If she felt compelled to use the precious space in the newspaper to promote her best friend's achievements... well, I didn't want to be the source of more stress.

Then a thought came to me, and I narrowed my eyes at Justin. "You're not holding back on me, are you? Have you won some big award that I'm going to read about in the newspaper or a magazine?"

His eyes sparkled. "I wish, but no, no big awards lately."

The server delivered our check, and Justin accepted the black leather folder and took care of our bill.

"Nothing major"—he slid the receipt into his wallet—"but I have been chosen for another juried show, one down in Seaside the week before Christmas. And this one has some of the best artists in the whole South lined up, so I'm really psyched about it."

I would be visiting my parents in Pensacola that week, and Seaside wasn't that far away. I wondered whether it was too soon to suggest that Justin meet us all for dinner one night and—

"Emma?"

"Sorry. My mind wandered there for a minute. What?"

He smiled but had a puzzled look on his face. "I was just saying how I think we ought to have a juried show in Roseland sometime. Would the arts council go for it?"

"Hmm." I would have to think about that. "The topic's come up several times before. We used to have a juried show years ago, but interest petered out, and people moved on to the next big thing.

The same three or four volunteers kept it going, and you know how well that works out. But I'm still thinking this artists-society thing of yours may be the way to go."

The waitress asked if we needed refills, and Justin assured her that we were about to leave. He had treated me to lunch and dinner so many times lately that I was probably overdue for having him over for another home-cooked meal rather than just takeout. The last meal I'd cooked for him had been weeks ago. And I would definitely cook for him again. Just as soon as I got caught up on making Christmas jewelry—and figured out who had committed a murder and some vandalism.

Before we walked out into the rain, Justin reached for the umbrella, which he'd tucked into a stand inside the restaurant's front door. "You still want to run by your friend's open house for a few minutes?"

I nodded. "If you're sure you don't mind."

He smiled. "Your chariot awaits, m'lady."

Under the protective cover of Justin's umbrella, we made it to his car, drenching the interior as we clambered into our seats. We'd been circling the square while looking for a space near Michele's shop and were stopped at a red light when a tall man at the front of Sombrero caught my eye.

"Justin, that's Tyler!" I pointed at the covered awning where the dark-haired man dressed in a paint-splattered vest was standing.

"Didn't Gus just say he was working tonight?"

"Yeah, so he must be picking up some takeout." We continued to watch Tyler, who appeared to be looking for someone. A few seconds later, Caitlyn walked up, and he gave her a peck on the lips.

Justin looked at me. "Uh-oh."

My heart sank.

Gus might have thought Tyler was serious about dating her, but it sure didn't look that way.

Chapter Eighteen

Normally, I would have taken time to admire the window displays at the Feathered Nest before going into the holiday open house, but I was still bummed about what I'd just seen outside Sombrero. And at the moment, I was more concerned with escaping the monsoon roaring around us. Justin let me out in front of the shop's door and promised to join me shortly.

I stepped into the store, and it was a different scene entirely. *Ah.* The scents of peppermint candles and simmering hot chocolate mingled pleasantly in the air.

"Have a sip of this and get warm." Michele rushed up and stuck a paper cup of cocoa into my hand.

"It's not that cold outside, just messy and wet." I wiped away a few raindrops snaking down my neck.

"Here." Michele used a golden paper napkin with a cornucopia on it to wipe the last of the rain off my arms. I'd worn a ruby-red blouse with three-quarter-length sleeves because it allowed me to show off one of my red Christmas necklaces, but I hadn't planned on getting drenched on the way in.

"Thanks." I smiled as she tossed the wet napkin into a wastebasket behind the counter. "I know we've needed the rain, but sheesh, it could have held off until your open house was over."

"Definitely agree with you there, and—Austin! Don't touch that cheese ball!"

Michele dashed behind the counter, where her three-year-old had his fingers poised above a pumpkin-shaped mound of cream cheese with a bell-pepper stem. "No, son." She took his hand, walked out from behind the counter, and headed over to Wells, who'd been engrossed in a conversation with a couple near a display of Christmas candles. She tapped his shoulder. "Honey, would you mind keeping an eye on him?"

Wells scooped up the little boy.

"I told you if you don't watch him like a hawk, he'll get into everything."

"Sorry, dear." Wells cradled their son. "We'll head to your office and look for a lollipop. How about that, son?"

Austin nodded.

Michele grinned and shook her head. "I knew he was going to be a handful, but Wells was bored and didn't want to stay home with him tonight when our sitter canceled on us at the last minute." She paused to admire my necklace and glanced at the table where my jewelry was displayed. "This reminds me—I've sold several of your sets already today, so keep an eye on your inventory. I predict we'll need to restock again soon."

"Will do. But please don't mind me. Don't you need to get back to your guests?" A sweep of the room revealed that Michele already had a few dozen people packed inside.

"You're my guest, too, you know. And I thought you said Justin was coming."

"He's parking the car and should be here any minute."

She grinned then lowered her voice. "You won't believe who's just past the alcove and in the next room. It's Harriet and Hubert." Her eyes traced their path through the shop. "They never spend any money downtown. Just here to scope out the competition, no doubt."

I felt someone bump against my back and turned around. "Oh, hey, Martha."

"Good to see you, Emma." She held up a tiny paper cup. "Have you tried some of these salted-caramel pecans? Mighty tasty."

I shook my head. "I just got here, but Michele told me about the recipe. Pretty good, huh?"

"Yes, and I may have to grab another sample or two before I go."

Martha walked on to get her refill. Michele winked at me as, obviously determined to spread the holiday cheer, she headed over to the Harrises with a tray of cookies. I had taken a peppermint macaron myself before Martha made another run on the platter.

The teenage girl serving refreshments smiled shyly. "Can I get you anything else?"

"No, this is plenty, but thanks." After that hearty lunch at Mama's and dinner at The Loft, I wouldn't need to eat again for a week, but no one could resist a sweet treat during the holidays.

I glanced around the store, and quite a few friends had stopped by to join in the fun. Trish and Shareta were there.

Evelyn from the Roseland PD carried an armload of soaps and candles to the checkout counter. "You'll hold these till I finish shopping, won't you?"

Michele nodded eagerly. "Absolutely. And don't forget to draw a coupon out of the basket here." She gestured toward a large red wicker basket shaped like a sleigh. "Everybody gets a discount tonight. At least ten percent off, and two of the coupons are for fifty percent off."

Evelyn beamed. "If I've already saved ten percent, I'm getting another candle for myself. As much as I'm spending on everyone else tonight, I deserve something too."

Michele always hosted the first holiday open house in Roseland, and she knew how to get a head start with holiday shoppers. She had as much decor for fall as she did for Christmas. Thanksgiving was still a few weeks away, and the Feathered Nest offered velvet pumpkins, gorgeous golden ceramic pie plates, wooden cutting boards in the shape of Georgia—which were disappearing fast, thanks to the popularity of charcuterie boards—and of course, candles.

"What? You're not checking out the jewelry bling?"

Inwardly, I sighed, but I turned around with a smile plastered on my face. "Hi there, Harriet."

Her husband, Hubert, stuck out a hand. "Always good to see you, Emma."

"I wouldn't miss one of Michele's open houses. Last year, she had some gift wrap that was perfect for my jewelry customers, and if I hadn't been here that night, I would have missed out. Look at how many folks have their shopping baskets full already."

Harriet peered around the room and nodded. "'Tis the season. We've already seen an uptick at the antique mall too. Everybody's buying new furniture in time for Thanksgiving, for some reason. Which reminds me." She turned to Hubert. "What was that woman telling you when she left today? The one who picked up the Hepple-white chairs?"

Hubert, whom I'd gotten to know during another recent murder investigation, caught my eye. "Oh yeah." He lowered his voice. "You know how the people at the antique mall tell us everything. So"—he looked between Harriet and me—"this gal who was in today tells me the Miranda Hargrove killer is still on the warpath and even broke in on Caitlyn at the Happy Hometown office last night."

I bit my lip. "Is that right?"

Hubert nodded. "That's what she said. The police were called, so that's how the word got out."

"Hmm" was my noncommittal reply.

Harriet peered at me as if I puzzled her. "For a gal who used to be a newspaper reporter, you sure don't seem to know much about what's going on these days."

I stifled a laugh and changed the subject. "The jewelry business keeps me plenty busy, and I'm up to my ears in Christmas orders. You guys are probably busy selling more holiday items, too, aren't you?"

Hubert jumped in. "Boy, are we. If I had a hundred vintage aluminum Christmas trees, I'd still have a waiting list of people who want them."

I had to smile. "Some people like those vintage decorations. I may obsess over vintage jewelry, but when Christmas rolls around, I want to smell the needles on a live tree. Besides, I don't like getting shocked by static electricity from a fake tree that looks like aluminum foil."

Eyes twinkling, Harriet said, "Christmas is my favorite time of year, and I'm with you on the trees. We sell a bunch of fake ones every year, and the bigger, the better, but I think they're hideous."

Hubert patted her arm. "Now, don't say that too loudly, sweetheart. If any of these fine shoppers want a fake tree, I want to sell them one."

She rolled her eyes. "And considering what happened in Roseland last week, I want people to start thinking about a *merry* Christmas, not a *Murder, She Wrote* Christmas, like some nasty people were talking about on Facebook."

I grimaced. "They were? That's tacky."

Harriet appeared to agree with me. "At any rate, we've got plenty of events coming up between now and Thanksgiving to help get everyone in the right frame of mind. Of course, it'd sure be nice to have the crime solved by then."

"I'm with you."

Out of the corner of my eye, I saw Justin enter the store and pause to accept a complimentary cup of cocoa. Meanwhile, Michele made a beeline for me, and I was grateful for the rescue I hoped was underway.

Michele stopped beside the Harrises and me and sounded breathless. "Forgive me, folks"—she gave Hubert and Harriet an apologetic smile—"but I need to have a quick word with Emma about some more jewelry I need before Christmas. Do you mind?"

They bowed off, and as Michele and I headed to the jewelry display area, I whispered, "Do you really need me to make some more jewelry, or was that an excuse to get me away from the Harrises?"

"Both." Michele's eyes twinkled, and she subtly nudged me to the front of the store, where Justin awaited. "They seemed to be monopolizing you, and I thought you might need a break. But"—she waved at a jewelry rack—"I also noticed that we've already sold half a dozen of your new bracelets here tonight."

I scanned the rack, and she was right. All the Ruby & Doris bracelets had vanished. She was also nearly wiped out of simple silver charm bracelets with soldered hearts made of old Christmas china. Only three were left, so they were going fast too. "That's terrific. I'll get going on some more and have them to you by the first of the week."

Michele smiled. "Perfect. That's just what I was hoping you would say."

Peering over my shoulder, she said, "You did come! Great to see you, Justin."

She gave him a hug, then she turned to me and lowered her voice. "So, I hear that someone tried to attack Caitlyn last night, and somehow Gerald was there and got hurt. Do you know anything about it?"

"Yeah, and I was there afterward, actually. Caitlyn called me, and when I heard her say the name Gerald and end the call, I thought..."

Michele looked sheepish. "Mama in the freezer?"

"Or Caitlyn in the freezer. At least, that's what I was worried was about to happen. By the time I got there, police were already on the scene, and Gerald was still knocked out cold."

"What was he doing there, then?"

"Caitlyn said he came by to copy the minutes from the last board meeting, so unless another tenant in that building was working late, she doesn't know how someone got into the building to attack him."

Michele shook her head. "That's scary. You have to wonder if they intended to kill Gerald. And maybe Caitlyn too."

Yet another reason to call Caitlyn as soon as I get home.

"And if I know Gerald, what's going to bother him the most is that someone else will have to look after his pets while he's gone." She snapped her fingers. "Speaking of pets, come over to the counter for a sec."

I did, and Michele reached beneath the counter and handed me a small bag.

"For me?"

She seemed pleased with herself. "Open it now."

I pulled out a beautiful glass ornament of a gray Siamese kitty, which bore an incredible resemblance to Miriam Haskell. "She's perfect! I can't wait to put her on my tree."

Michele looked alarmed. "Please tell me you don't have your tree up yet. Even I don't put up a tree at home until Thanksgiving night."

"Nope, no tree yet. And if I don't get cracking on some jewelry tonight"—I glanced at my watch—"I won't have time to put up a tree or any other decorations next month."

I shooed Michele away to mingle with the other customers, and I purchased a few jars of pear-pecan preserves to have on hand for hostess gifts over Thanksgiving and Christmas. I'd told Justin that I couldn't afford to stay at the open house for longer than thirty minutes, max, because I needed to finish some jewelry designs. He offered to pull the car around for me, but the rain was barely a trickle by the time we walked out.

When we got to my house, the rain had completely stopped, and since I'd confessed I was way behind on jewelry making, Justin walked me to the door and made no move to come in.

"So, this volunteer thing we're doing tomorrow"—he scratched his cheek—"we're just going to meet there, and you'll fill me in on everything?"

"Yep." I smiled just thinking about it. "And trust me. You're going to love it."

We shared a good-night kiss, and I waved him off.

Before I started working on jewelry, I had planned to call Caitlyn to tell her my concerns about her possibly knowing who the killer was, but it sure looked like she'd had a dinner date with Tyler.

I grimaced. *Why is he leading Gus on if he isn't interested in her?* I didn't have an explanation for that.

Even though I didn't expect Caitlyn to answer, I called her cell phone and left a voicemail asking her to call me when she got in, and although I was up working on jewelry until almost midnight, she never called.

Hoping I would hear from her the next day, I finally climbed into bed and anticipated my favorite volunteer stint of the whole year.

Chapter Nineteen

The whole town must have been praying overnight, because Saturday dawned clear, sunny, and cool, ideal weather for the Turkey Toss. I smiled from ear to ear when I looked out the kitchen window and saw brilliant blue skies and not a single cloud. *Perfect!*

But before I'd even finished my first cup of coffee, a text from Jen arrived.

Can you meet me at the café this morning? It's important.

What on earth? Jen and Todd usually spent Saturdays together, and it wasn't like her to want to meet so early on a Saturday. But I had a fairly leisurely—for me—morning planned, and I could visit with Jen and still have plenty of time to get ready for the Turkey Toss at noon, so I texted back, *9:30 okay?*

She replied with a thumbs-up.

It was a jeans-and-sweatshirt kind of day, so I got dressed and headed downtown.

As soon as I walked into the café and glanced at Jen, I knew something was wrong. Her eyes were red and swollen, and she looked miserable.

"What happened? Are you and Todd okay?"

She nodded. "Yeah, we're fine. He's fine, but..."

I motioned for her to continue. "Well, what is it?"

"The company wants to promote me."

Of all the terrible things I had imagined, that possibility wasn't even in the running. "That's great news! So why've you been crying?"

She swiped at a few tears. "The job is in Mississippi. It's a larger paper, one that's still daily."

"Oh." I forced a smile. "What does Todd say about it?" That was a great opportunity for Jen and, in the current publishing climate, one she probably couldn't afford to pass up. But I didn't want to lose my best friend. One reason I was so happy in Roseland was that I loved hanging out with my BFF and her husband.

"That's the thing." Jen's tears cranked up. "He's been at some web design seminar in Atlanta for the past two days, and I got the offer late yesterday. I don't want to tell him and distract him while his classes are finishing this morning."

"Wise move." I stood and tapped her shoulder as I headed to the counter to place an order. "This calls for caffeine. I've gotten addicted to that new cinnamon-flavored coffee Mavis started offering last week. You want one?" I held up my wallet. "My treat."

"That would be great."

I returned with two to-go cups of cinnamon coffee. Jen sniffed and smiled. "Emma, I don't want to leave Roseland."

That made me hopeful but also feeling like a lousy best friend. A good friend would think about what was best for Jen and her career. "With all these budget cuts at the *Trib*, you've been stressed out for the last few months," I gently reminded her. "Don't you think you might enjoy a new challenge? A new city? And hey, Mississippi's not that far away. I mean, it's not like you're talking California or South Dakota or something."

"South Dakota?" Jen looked at me like I'd lost my mind. "Where'd that come from?"

I laughed. "I just got through reading a great romance novel about a wheat-farming family in South Dakota. Guess it's still on my brain. Now, back to this new job of yours..."

"I haven't accepted it yet, so don't say that."

"What do you think Todd's going to say?"

"I've been wondering about that. Since he was already urging me to find a new job, he'll most likely say I should consider it."

She was probably right. "But Todd was also talking about launching that new real estate website. Is that a concern?"

"Sure it is, and I know we'll have to talk about that."

I was quiet for a moment—clearly too quiet, because Jen looked at me over her coffee. "What are you thinking? I know something's up in that head of yours."

"Just wondering what it might be like to get a fresh start in a new town. That's all. It could be great, you know."

Jen shrugged. "Or it could be a colossal mistake. On the other hand, staying here could be the big mistake. And after the kind of morning I've had..."

"Other than the job offer, what's up?"

Jen brightened. "I can't believe I forgot to tell you. One of the reporters got a tip from someone who says Caitlyn Hill got into a huge fight with her boss just two days before Miranda was killed."

Oh. That wasn't news. "I heard about that, too, and it didn't sound like that big of a deal."

"Really?" Jen looked skeptical. "Because the source told our reporter than Caitlyn has some sort of skeleton in her own closet, and Miranda found out about that and threatened to expose her."

I'd stood to get refills on our coffee and looked over my shoulder. "Skeleton? Like what?"

"Like the fact that Caitlyn didn't get hired because of her qualifications but because of some family connection. When Miranda learned why Caitlyn was hired at the same time she was, she and Caitlyn nearly came to blows over it."

I set our mugs on the table. "What was Caitlyn's big 'family connection,' then?"

Jen's eyes widened, and she shook her head. "Shh."

"Huh?"

"Don't look now, but ..." Jen wrapped her hands around her coffee cup and slowly scanned the front of the café.

It took every ounce of self-restraint I had not to turn around.

"It's Caitlyn," Jen whispered. "And she's with some older man." She looked back at me but continued to glance toward the front of the shop. "Okay, they're looking at something, so you can turn around now."

When I did, the handsome gray-haired man was showing Caitlyn what appeared to be a magazine article.

"I know just how to handle this."

I went to the counter and ordered a cranberry-oatmeal cookie. Mavis stopped boxing doughnuts long enough to ring me up. As I headed back to my table, I looked in Caitlyn's direction, and when she glanced up, I pretended to have just seen her.

Then I handed my cookie over to Jen and swept past our table. "Be back in a jiff."

"Well, hi there," I said as I approached Caitlyn.

She looked happy and didn't seem at all concerned about being seen with the older gentleman. *But didn't I see you out with Tyler last night?*

"Hey, Emma. Shane, I'd like you to meet Emma Madison, one of our new Happy Hometown board members here in Roseland."

He held out a hand, and I shook it. "Nice to meet you, Shane."

"He's the head of the Greater Atlanta Happy Hometown Program... and I guess it's safe to tell you that he's also my stepdad. Miranda didn't want anyone to know that Shane helped me get the job, which I always thought was silly."

I looked at Shane and shrugged. "Miranda had some interesting ideas about things, didn't she?"

He replied with a wry grin.

Caitlyn added, "Shane and my mom got married last year. She's still shopping back at the Feathered Nest. And I know I owe you a phone call. I didn't return it last night because I was out with a new friend, and we got home late after seeing a movie. I didn't know whether it was too late to call. So, what can I help you with?"

I still wanted to warn Caitlyn that she might be on someone's radar because of her familiarity with the bazaar's exhibitor list, but I wasn't about to go into all that in front of her stepdad. I also wondered whether she considered Tyler serious boyfriend material. I certainly hadn't imagined that kiss between them outside Sombrero.

"It can wait until, um..."

Mavis provided the diversion I needed. She was carrying a small bud vase of fresh fall flowers and put them on a table next to Caitlyn's, but I knew exactly what she was up to—eavesdropping. I would save her the trouble.

"Mavis," I called.

"What? Oh, and hi there, Caitlyn. I didn't see you come in, hon."

Liar.

Caitlyn motioned Mavis over to her table. "I'd like you to meet my stepdad, Shane McLaughlin."

She shook his hand. "Pleased to meet you, and thanks for coming to the Cupcake Café."

"Shane works with the Greater Atlanta Happy Hometown office." I looked Mavis in the eye and made no effort to hide my smug grin. "Isn't it great to have him here in town for a visit?"

Unperturbed, Mavis smiled back. "So nice to have you here. And I thought you looked familiar. You've been in before, haven't you?"

Shane nodded. "I told Caitlyn that I wanted to come back for one of your bananas Foster cupcakes. I hope you've got some of those today."

"I sure do." Mavis beamed. "In fact, let me go get you one right now. On the house."

With her back to them, Mavis winked at me as she walked past.

"I'll let you two get back to your visit, then." I tipped my head at Caitlyn and her stepdad. "I'm catching up with a friend over there. And again, it was nice meeting you, Shane."

So much for Mavis's gossip about Caitlyn and the married man.

When I returned to our table, Jen swallowed a sip of coffee. "Want to tell me what that was all about?"

I smiled. "Funny you should ask, considering what you just told me. I was getting the scoop on Caitlyn and her stepdad over there. He works for the Atlanta office of Happy Hometown, and that's how she got the job. Her folks are here visiting for the weekend."

Jen grimaced. "Shoot. No scandal there, then." Jen's phone beeped, and she pulled it out of her pocket and glanced at the screen. "Oh no. It's one of the photogs saying there's some problem with his camera, and he's supposed to cover the Turkey Toss. I'd better get to the office and see what's going on."

"Go." I waved her off. "But call me later and let me know how you're doing. And I want to know what Todd says about the job offer."

"Will do!"

Since I still had almost two hours until time to volunteer, I headed home to squeeze in some more jewelry designs. Maybe it was the caffeine from all the coffee, but my mind was running a mile a minute. Learning about Caitlyn's stepdad made me less inclined to question her ambition. Like a lot of people, she had taken advantage of a family connection to get a job. Miranda might not have liked it, but it certainly didn't mean Caitlyn was incompetent and didn't deserve the job.

Once back in my kitchen, I pulled out a container of red beads and spilled them into an empty trench on my bead board. *Maybe the mayor's brother killed Miranda, and ooh, what if the mayor is helping with the cover-up?*

Clearly, I needed to stop reading *National Enquirer* headlines while I was in line at the grocery store.

Then my mind returned to the image of Tyler and Caitlyn outside Sombrero the previous night. How odd that he'd been upset about being excluded from the show but was seeing—or at least interested in—Caitlyn. And she was a good ten years younger than Gus. Maybe he was one of those guys who just liked women too much to settle down with one. Still, I hoped nobody would end up hurt, and if someone did, I suspected it would be Gus.

My worry list had grown to include more than just Miranda's murder, in which neither the police nor I seemed to have made a bit of progress. I clenched my jaw, aggravated that my list of serious suspects was dwindling.

Something kept bothering me, though. Miranda had disappeared from the floor of the cafeteria for several hours late Saturday afternoon, and no one had ever mentioned precisely where she was supposed to be during that time. That had to be crucial information. I wondered who might have seen her then.

I shook my head, trying to clear the cobwebs, and got to work. With a spool of elastic beading cord next to some beads lined up for a new bracelet, I was set to stab the first bead with my needle when the doorbell rang.

What now? This house has had more comings and goings than Hartsfield Airport this week.

I set the needle aside and headed for the front door, and when I looked through the glass windowpanes, Savannah stood there. She waved a white plastic bag.

I opened the door. "A gift?"

"Just found this at Second Chance for a dollar. I think it's some kind of vintage rhinestone chain." She handed over the bag. "After all the old sewing tools you've found for me over the years, I'm happy to find something for you for a change."

"Cool." I opened the bag and was rendered almost speechless. "Oh, wow! This is a steal. I don't even see this stuff on eBay or Etsy very often."

"Really?" Savannah shrugged. "Didn't know if it was something you could use, but if you like it, they've got spools of it in several other finishes. I told Marge to hold them behind the counter for you."

I was already reaching into my purse for my car keys.

"You're going there right now?" Savannah looked confused.

"You bet I am. Wanna come with me?"

"I'd better not." She looked at her watch. "I need to spend some time in the studio today."

"Me, too, but I'm going to get that chain before somebody else does."

MARGE, THE GRAY-HAIRED volunteer I'd gotten to know over the past few years of shopping at Second Chance Thrift Store, tucked a tissue into her denim shirt pocket. "Donations are flooding in this fall. People used to wait and clean out after Christmas or maybe in early spring, but thanks to that woman's book about 'tidying up,' we can barely process the donations fast enough."

I laughed. "One man's trash..."

"Hey, I'm not complaining." Marge put a hand on her ample hip. "With all these donations, we're able to keep our prices low and move stuff in and out pretty quickly."

Second Chance used its proceeds to benefit the women's shelter in a neighboring county, so that had to be good news.

"I know folks are getting some ridiculous deals. But to be honest with you, I don't have time to do more than guess about the value and slap a price sticker on things."

"And on behalf of your grateful customers, thank you." Then I pointed behind the counter. "Savannah says you've set aside some jewelry supplies for me."

"Oh yeah. Now, where did I put those things?" Marge's head bobbed from box to bin beneath the counter as she unearthed who knew what. Most thrift stores wouldn't hold items for customers, so I marveled at her ability to keep up with the inventory.

"Here." Marge whipped out a large plastic bag and handed it over. It was full of spools of skip chain—silver chain with rhinestones, gold chain with rhinestones, and gold chain with rubies. My heart sped up at finding the mother lode of vintage chain. In a flash of inspiration, I envisioned a necklace I would make for the Jewelry Artisans of the Southeast show next spring.

"I'll take it all." I set the bag on the counter. "How much?"

Marge tapped a finger to her chin. "Eight dollars for the whole kit and caboodle?"

"Sold. And I'll leave it here while I buzz through a few aisles. Since I'm here, I might as well see if you've got anything else I need."

I headed down the housewares aisle, my fingers crossed. *Is that a bit of turquoise I see peeking out?*

And there it was, another turquoise Pyrex Cinderella bowl. I slid it off the shelf and smiled. Another score. I'd found the same color bowl in a smaller size the previous month, so I'd wondered when the large bowl would show up. If I visited often enough, I could complete my set.

I didn't spot any other vintage Pyrex, but they sure had mountains of china. I picked up a teacup with pale-pink roses and mossy green leaves and turned it over—Haviland. I was about to text a photo to Carleen, who was passionate about old Haviland, when a similar piece of china caught my eye. That design also featured pale-pink roses. If I wasn't mistaken, it was Rosalinde, the same pattern Carleen had used when I was invited to tea at her house a while back.

What I'd first thought was a teacup was actually a cup with double handles—cream soup bowls—and all with matching saucers. Eight sets of them sat on the shelf, taped haphazardly together. Matching cream soups were often hard to find in any pattern. *Ten bucks for the lot? Yes, please.*

"Emmaaa, finding anything good over there?"

Inwardly, I rolled my eyes. *Not her again.* That woman had a sixth sense when it came to the bargains around town.

I turned slowly, balancing the cream soup bowls inside my vintage Pyrex. "Hi, Harriet. So, you're out thrifting today, too, huh?"

She nodded. "Decided to get out of the shop and see what's out here. Get a little fresh air, you know." She didn't even try to hide her curiosity about my purchases. "Pyrex and fine china both? You're covering all your bases today."

I tipped my head at the items. "It's always hit-or-miss at places like this, but today's definitely a hit."

It dawned on me that I didn't really know anything about Harriet's own collecting interests. "I'm after vintage Pyrex, the occasional china, and old jewelry. What do you look for?"

Harriet looked around as if making sure we weren't being overheard.

My eyes tracked her gaze. "What? Is it a secret or something?"

"No." Harriet paused. "It's just that if my regulars ever find out what I collect, I'm afraid they'll up the price when they try to sell these to me."

That was a valid concern, and I certainly wasn't going to beg her to spill. But then, as if I'd twisted her arm, she came out with it. "Okay, I'll tell you. Since I've always loved dogs, I collect dog figurines."

"Seriously?" Harriet had never struck me as a pet lover. "Do you have a dog now?"

Harriet whipped out her cell phone, and before I knew it, I was laughing over pictures of JoJo, her Pekingese. She definitely wasn't the sort of dog I would have expected to find at Harriet's house.

"So, china figurines? Ceramic? What?"

"As long as it's old and cute, I don't care." Harriet held out her hand. "Like this little guy."

The tiny bone china collie couldn't have been two inches high. "I have an antique display cabinet in my sunroom that's overflowing with the things, and I love looking at them."

While I'd never really understood people who preferred dogs over cats, Harriet's stock rose the minute I learned she was a pet lover. "What does JoJo think about them?"

Harriet grinned. "JoJo runs our house, so as long as Hubert and I jump when she tells us to, she doesn't care what I bring home. Well, except for that time I tried fostering a puppy for Gerald Adams. That didn't go over so well with JoJo."

"I didn't realize you fostered pets. Gerald signed you up?"

"Yep. Tugged at the old heartstrings till I couldn't say no. Gerald has done more for the Humane Society than any president they've had in years."

My dishes were getting heavy, so I asked Harriet to give me a minute to unload my stash at the front counter.

Harriet called, "And they're saying that adoptions are way over where they were this time last year."

"I heard that too," I said as I returned to the china aisle.

"We have Gerald to thank for that." Harriet fingered a pink milk glass candy dish that I wished I'd seen first. "I'm still concerned about his getting attacked at the Happy Hometown office."

"So am I."

"When Hubert and I left the movies last night, we ran into Caitlyn Hill and told her she'd better be careful, since someone seems to have it in for that program."

So Harriet had had the same thoughts Justin and I did. "What did she say when you told her that?"

Harriet scoffed. "Didn't take it too seriously, if you ask me. She had her parents and that new boyfriend, Tyler Montgomery, with her, so I think she was more concerned about—"

"Excuse me?"

Harriet's brow furrowed. "What? Did I say something wrong?"

"No, I just wondered if you're sure about Tyler Montgomery being her new boyfriend."

"The artist? Usually wears those tacky vests with paint all over them? That's who I'm talking about. Lived here most of his life, though I can't say I know him well. His mother has bought a few Early American pieces from me over the years."

My heart sank. From what I'd learned in the last twenty-four hours, Gus was going to be so disappointed. When I saw her at The Loft, she'd said Tyler wasn't with her because he was working that night. He didn't have to marry her, but he didn't have to lie to her either.

A commotion at the front door drew our attention. A pickup truck had backed up to offload some donations.

I turned to Harriet. "It's been fun talking to you, but I need to get going. Gotta head over to the Turkey Toss. Good luck finding your figurines."

I left Harriet to plunder for more canine china while I checked out with my housewares and the vintage skip chain.

On the drive across town, I found myself more concerned about Gus's love life than Miranda's murder, which was an odd turn of events. Before Justin had even assembled his group of artists, one of them was causing a disruption.

I tried to shake off my worries. Like Scarlett O'Hara, I would have to think about that another day.

After all, I had some turkeys to toss.

Chapter Twenty

Justin had never been a part of the Turkey Toss in Roseland, so as we waited for the event to kick off, I gave him a brief history of the annual turkey giveaway. As volunteers, we sat in metal chairs behind a folding table that had been set up in front of Hutchinson Law Offices.

"You ever had a reason to visit this building?" I asked.

He shook his head. "And I kind of hope I don't, if you get my drift."

I grinned. "Back in the thirties and forties, this was known as the Hutchinson Dry Goods building. In those days, farmers came to Roseland with their cotton money on Christmas Eve, if they got to do any Christmas shopping at all. One year, the merchants on this side of the street got together and decided they needed a way to lure folks downtown on Christmas Eve, so Mr. Hutchinson came up with the idea of tossing turkeys off the roof."

Justin cut his eyes at me. "You're pulling my leg."

"Would I do that?"

"Yeah, I think you would."

I snickered. "You're probably right, but I'm not pulling your leg right now. They really did have a turkey giveaway, and they really did toss live turkeys off the roof of this building." I shuddered. "Poor things. If you go by the *Daily Trib* sometime when Jen is there, she can show you an old photo of it."

"Wow." Justin seemed at a loss for words. "That's got to be the craziest turkey story I've ever heard."

I beamed. "Yeah, we're pretty proud of it. But I'm glad the turkeys aren't live anymore." Then I looked in the direction of the turkey van. "Listen, if you're ready to help"—I handed him a stack of plastic bags—"start separating these and get them ready for frozen-turkey bagging."

A van from the town's utility company rolled to a stop in front of the offices. Their team of volunteers followed, piled out of three SUVs, and unloaded the coolers. Within five minutes, they'd set up folding tables in front of the building and unloaded all the turkeys. Based on my past experience, it was a safe bet that within thirty minutes, the turkeys would be tossed in front of the old Hutchinson Dry Goods building once again—but from street level.

Shareta, who seemed to be showing up everywhere that fall, was head of the Turkey Toss committee. She wore a long-sleeved T-shirt depicting a cartoon turkey and had accessorized with cute dangling turkey earrings.

She walked over and gave me a hug. "I see you convinced your friend to help this year." She smiled at Justin.

I gave her the side-eye. "With you in charge, I was afraid not to."

"Smart girl." She surveyed the table in front of Justin and me. "If you guys are okay with bagging the turkeys for the first shift, I'll leave you to finish setting up."

"We're good." I clasped my leather-gloved hands. I'd told Justin to bring his gloves, too, so that his hands wouldn't freeze, which was the only job hazard when volunteering at the Turkey Toss. The weather was glorious, with sunshine and temps in the high sixties, but frozen turkeys were frozen turkeys, no matter what the weather was like.

Sooner than I'd expected, the starting whistle blew—a turkey call, in honor of the event—and we were off.

The first hour of the Turkey Toss each year was reserved for those referred by one of the local nonprofits. Like a golden ticket in a Wonka Bar, those orange slips of paper ensured that the recipient left with a turkey and extra treats provided by Roseland's civic clubs. That year's goodies were homemade pumpkin pies and jugs of apple cider.

"Have a happy Thanksgiving," I told the first smiling face in line. Justin joined in, too, with send-offs of "Have a Happy Turkey Day."

During a brief lull, he asked if I'd known we had so many needy families in Roseland.

"Oh, sure." I picked up a pile of plastic bags and prepared to send another few dozen turkeys on their way.

"I wouldn't have suspected it." Justin looked embarrassed. "I guess I've been so focused on my art and the galleries that I haven't thought about those who aren't as fortunate as I am."

He seemed so sincere, and I was touched. "Well, you're thinking of them now, so don't be too hard on yourself."

A weary-looking blond woman came up. She was holding a toddler's hand and had a baby wriggling in her other arm—along with the turkey she'd just gotten at a table near ours.

"Here, where are you parked?" I offered to take the bagged turkey from her. "Let me carry this to your car."

The woman lowered her eyes. "I don't have a car. I walked here from my apartment." She gestured toward a public housing unit located behind an old mill.

Justin piped up, "Emma, didn't you say we take a break for a shift change in about five minutes?"

"Yep."

He turned to the woman. "Ma'am, we'll be happy to give you a ride, if you don't mind waiting here for a bit. Would that work?"

The woman teared up. "I'd sure appreciate it. We can just wait on that bench right over there, if that's okay."

When she and the children walked away, the turkey in her protective custody, Justin was so earnest that he almost made me cry.

"Man," he said.

"It gets to you, doesn't it?"

"Yeah." He bit his lip. "That woman must have really wanted that turkey to walk all the way up here with her kids then be willing to carry all that back home."

"Kind of gives you a new perspective."

As the end of our shift neared, Martha Barnes came by and handed us cups of coffee and some banana-oatmeal muffins. They were Courtesy of the Cupcake Café, according to the labels on them.

Justin left to give the woman and her children a ride home. Since I needed to remain on duty at our table, Martha agreed to join him in case the woman was uncomfortable getting into a car with a man she'd just met, volunteer or no volunteer.

I wondered who would relieve us. No new volunteers appeared to be on deck, which was unusual. Volunteers usually competed for the best spots that day. A few minutes later, Caitlyn walked up, but no parents—and mercifully, no Tyler—had joined her.

"Hey. I wouldn't have expected to see you here with your folks in town. Are you volunteering?"

She frowned. "Yes, unfortunately. I didn't know I would be expected to come do this on my day off. The mayor called this morning to say I ought to make an appearance on behalf of the city."

Okey dokey, then.

I handed her a clipboard with a sign-in sheet for the day's volunteers. "At any rate, I'm glad to see you. And besides, it's really fun." I pointed at my colleague over at the volunteer sign-in table. "Shareta has this thing running like clockwork, and if she says you'll be done at five o'clock, you can take it to the bank that you'll be out of here by then."

"That's good"—Caitlyn looked around—"because I've got a ton of stuff to do at home between now and Thanksgiving."

"Having company over the holidays?"

"Um, no. Just... I just have a lot going on right now."

"Do you know who's working your shift with you?"

"Shareta said it's Trish somebody from the arts council. I was hoping she'd be here by now, since I have no idea what I'm doing."

I patted her on the arm. "Trish Delgado. And she'll be here. No worries."

Caitlyn sighed. Miss Happy Hometown didn't seem too happy—or too into her town, for that matter.

"Sorry I'm just getting here," Trish said as she walked up. She took a deep breath and slung her purse under the table. "Was waiting for my new kiln to be delivered, so I had to deal with that before I left." She turned to Caitlyn. "I hear you're my partner for the afternoon."

Caitlyn offered a weak smile. "Looks like it."

"Great. So here's what we need to start doing..."

Since Trish was off and running, I wandered over to Shareta's table and dropped into the empty folding chair beside her. Some clouds had rolled in, but the sun was still out. "Hiya."

Shareta looked up from the pages of a catalog. "How'd it go?"

"Great! As always, those who got the turkeys seemed very thankful for them, and I love knowing that we'll help some folks have a happy Thanksgiving."

"Me too." Shareta closed the catalog and plopped it on the table. "I'm just killing time now while I wait for the next volunteers to arrive. I need to order some more basket-making supplies, and this catalog has so much stuff I want. Just look at all the gorgeous baskets on that cover."

I picked up the catalog. "That's how I feel when I get a new bead catalog in the mail. If I had a million dollars, I still wouldn't be able to afford all the supplies I want."

A gust of wind rustled papers, blowing away some brochures and tipping over an empty paper cup. Shareta snatched them up, and I grabbed a blue-and-white Amazon mailer that had apparently been beneath the catalog and fluttered to the ground.

"This yours too?" I asked as I picked it up and noticed the mailing label was missing.

"Yeah. I save those things and recycle them after I peel the label off and—"

I was handing it to her when my hand froze in midair. Shareta stared at the mailer and bit her lip.

"You... you always peel the labels off?" I looked her straight in the eye.

She looked at her lap. "Yeah. I do."

I took a deep breath. "Why did you send me that résumé?"

To her credit, Shareta didn't attempt to deny that she had. "Because I knew you'd make sure it got to the right people. Emma, Miranda was a horrible leader. She was incredibly offensive when she talked to me about my baskets, and I've worked so hard to be good at my craft."

That, I understood.

"So after hearing from some past exhibitors who didn't get accepted in the bazaar, I called her the week before to confirm that I got the space I had last year. Not only did she rudely inform me that no, I didn't, she said I should be grateful I was exhibiting at all. When I got there and learned she'd put a hold on my registration—she wanted to see my baskets before I put them out, if you can believe that—I called her right there from the lobby and let her have it. But you know what she said? She told me not to 'go there' with her after we'd had words the week before."

So, that's who Savannah overheard Miranda talking to that day.

"By the time she was killed, I'd already looked into her background and knew something wasn't right. An old friend of mine worked for Happy Hometown's regional office in New York, and he did a little digging for me. I told Caitlyn about all of this, but she seemed unable to make a decision on it and didn't know what to do with the information. And after Miranda died, I didn't want to give the résumé to the police or anyone else in case they thought I was sticking my nose in where it didn't belong."

"Well, now the police think that about *me*!"

She placed a hand on my arm. "I know I should have been up-front with you. Can you forgive me?"

Before I could answer, Justin and Martha returned and asked if there was anything they could help us with.

"You were right." Justin grinned. "This was even more fun than you said it would be. And that woman Martha and I took home? She said her family was almost out of food for the month, so this turkey and pie were lifesavers for her. I'll run by the grocery store and get some things to drop off at her apartment later today."

Justin's heart was even bigger than I'd imagined. No wonder I liked him so much. "That's terrific."

"And Shareta"—Justin turned to her—"my hat's off to you for or-ganizing everything this year. Martha just told me you lobbied hard for more food to give away—and got it. So thanks for all your hard work."

"My pleasure."

Justin said he'd go get our gloves and my purse from our table.

Shareta's smile disappeared. "Are you still mad at me?"

I grimaced. "You could have told me sooner."

"I know." She twirled one of her turkey earrings. "Look, next time there's a murder and I learn something about it, I'll go directly to you first."

I huffed. "Next time? There'd better not *be* a next time."

Justin arrived with my bag in hand. "Are we good to leave?"

He looked at Shareta, and she nodded.

"And thanks, both of you, for everything."

I still wasn't thrilled Shareta had put me in the awkward position of taking that résumé to the police. On the other hand, it was a relief to know that a murderer hadn't made a delivery to my back door.

Justin and I walked to a nearby parking lot for our cars. He was headed to the grocery store, and I had agreed to meet Carleen for coffee before he and I had a cookout with Jen and Todd.

CARLEEN AND I WERE the only ones in the café at A Likely Story, where I'd promised to tell her about my newest jewelry line.

"Now, which one was Ruby, and which one was Doris?" Carleen peered at the two faded images of my great-grandmothers.

"Ruby was the great-grandmother on my dad's side, and Doris was the one on my mom's side."

She traced the worn edges of the photos. "I love old images like these. I don't even have photos of any of my great-grandmothers, so you're awfully lucky to have them."

"I know." I frowned. "I just wish I could have known them longer."

Carleen's brow furrowed. "Do you mean to tell me that you actually knew both of them?"

I swallowed a sip of pumpkin spice coffee. "I have photos of both of them holding me when I was just a baby, but of course I don't remember those times. Still, I'm glad to have the pictures as proof that we actually knew one another."

Carleen sighed. " I love their names. You don't see very many women with names like Ruby and Doris anymore, do you?"

I agreed. "That's one reason I decided to name this jewelry line after them." I held up a bracelet I'd made with vintage charms, buttons, and the jeweled fronts of old clip-on earrings, all in pearly pastel hues.

Carleen reached for the bracelet. "So this is a Doris and Ruby original?"

I shook my head. "Other way around."

"Ruby and Doris."

"Uh-huh. That gets them in chronological order, since Ruby was born before Doris."

"Too bad you didn't have a grandmother named Pearl." Carleen smiled, and I was about to ask for her thoughts on the bracelet—it was a little froufrou, even by my standards—when Nichole sidled up to our table.

"Here. And don't say no." She plopped a plate full of cookies before us. "I don't like to sell anything more than a day old at the bookstore, and we'll be closed tomorrow, so if y'all don't eat these, they're getting tossed."

I reached for one with great big chunks of chocolate. "Far be it from me to let your reputation get tarnished." I took a bite. "Mm-hmm. Delicious, as always."

Carleen was quick to reach for a cranberry-and-white-chocolate-chip cookie. "You had some of these left over?"

"Business is a little slow this afternoon. Maybe everybody's at the Turkey Toss." Nichole wrinkled her brow. "I sometimes wonder if I've lost my mind for opening an indie bookstore when everyone's become so used to buying books online and from big-box retailers."

Carleen reached for her hand. "I'm thrilled you've opened A Likely Story. I shop online just like everyone else, but I adore walking into a bookstore and seeing and touching the books. Not to mention"—she glanced past the café area and at the rest of the store—"you've got great gift items here too. Your journals and bookmarks are awesome, and I love that you have all those stuffed animals related to children's books."

"Thanks." Nichole looked pleased. "I'm trying to beef up the gift section, and speaking of bookmarks, Emma, I was hoping you might be able to make some for me."

I was always open to new business opportunities. "Jeweled ones? What do you have in mind?"

Nichole held up a finger. "I'll be right back. Just a sec." She headed to the store's checkout counter, rustled through some papers underneath, and came back with a printout. "Check out these lovelies."

I accepted the sheet of paper and whistled. "What great ribbon bookmarks. Look, Carleen."

I passed her the sheet, and she, too, looked impressed. Short lengths of thick, elegant velvet ribbon had metal clamps attached to the ends, and from the clamps hung charms, beads, and other jeweled bits. In the photo, the bookmarks peered out from a stack of tattered old hardbacks, and the photo itself exuded vintage charm. I'd never made bookmarks like that, but I was sure I could. "So, you want some of these for the store?"

Nichole's head bobbed up and down. "If you can make them and they're not too labor intensive. Or expensive."

They would be easy to make, and they'd also help me use up some of those single charms and baubles that were always left over from projects. "Let me whip up a few and see what kind of time it takes, then I'll quote you a price, and we'll go from there."

"Perfect." Nichole crossed her arms. "And hey, can I wrap up the rest of these cookies for you two?"

"No, thanks," I said as Carleen came out with a "Yes."

Carleen batted her eyelashes. "What? No use pretending I wouldn't love to have them, because I would."

While Nichole headed behind the café counter and packaged the cookies, Carleen seemed smitten by the idea of the fancy bookmarks.

"Would you consider making some of those with sterling charms?"

"Sure. Why not?"

"Occasionally, I buy these random lots of old silver jewelry that have odds and ends like charms. I've never found just the right way to display them, so a bookmark would be a great idea. Could you make the charm detachable?"

I considered that. "If you don't mind a lobster-claw clasp being attached."

"After you get some made for Nichole, come see me, and we'll talk." Carleen took another sip of coffee. "I bought a batch of silver jewelry from a man who came to the store just this morning. And lucky for me, he offered them for a fantastic price. He struck me as a little arrogant, to be honest with you. Said he has a new girlfriend and hopes to move in with her soon, and he wants to unload a few old family odds and ends first."

Something in my brain pinged. "You don't happen to remember his name, do you?"

"Mm-hmm. You might have heard of him, since he's an artist—Tyler Montgomery. Why?"

I closed my eyes and groaned. "Gus Townsend has a thing for him, and I've even seen them out together just this week, but I found out last night that he's also been seeing Caitlyn Hill."

"Gus doesn't know?"

"Apparently not. I hear his artwork is great, and Justin was even thinking of joining forces with him and a few others, including Gus, to stage their own shows. But now..."

"Now you're worried that this Romeo may be leading the fair ladies astray?"

Carleen was so old-fashioned, but her observation was spot-on. "Exactly. Caitlyn was at the Turkey Toss today and mentioned she's got a lot going on at home these days. I'm wondering if maybe that was a reference to Tyler moving in."

Nichole returned with the cookies, and Carleen thanked her before she headed off and greeted a customer. We stood, and Carleen finished the last of her coffee and tossed the cup into the trash can.

I shook my head. "I hope Gus isn't too upset when she learns about this." Tyler's romantic shenanigans were putting a damper on my day.

"Ah, the o'erfraught heart," Carleen said as we parted.

Indeed.

Chapter Twenty-One

J en and Todd got to my house early for the cookout. While Todd caught the tail end of a basketball game on the TV in the living room, Jen joined me in the kitchen. As soon as Jen and I were alone, I hit her up.

"So, what did he say? Does he think you ought to accept the promotion?"

Jen squeezed my arm. "No, and I couldn't be happier. I didn't want to move, anyway, and he came back even more excited about his new website plans because of the seminar he attended."

Hugely relieved, I gave her a hug and had just returned to the counter when I got a text alert. Justin said he was running late but would be there soon with the ribs he'd marinated for us to grill.

I had finished washing and drying the Haviland cream soup bowls I'd bought earlier, then Jen rolled her eyes as I pulled out rolls of paper and prepared to wrap Carleen's gift. "I can't believe you're already wrapping Christmas presents. Ugh. I don't even want to think about buying gifts until December."

I wagged a finger in her face. "No, no, no. That's not the way to have a merry Christmas, now, is it?"

She laughed. "No, but people like you always make me feel guilty. I like shopping in December. How can you possibly know in early November what cute stuff will be in the stores two weeks before Christmas?"

I scoffed. "Let's just say it's a risk that some of us are willing to take. For me, it's a matter of saving time and making sure I'm not stressed out at Christmas. This year, I've already got open houses and craft fairs scheduled for every Saturday from now through mid-December. And since I'm planning to meet up with Mom and Dad in Pensacola the week of Christmas, I've simply got to stay on top of things here."

Jen wiggled her eyebrows. "Tell me again why your folks are in Pensacola. I thought they were going across the country in their RV."

I stopped wrapping gifts long enough to explain. "In good weather, they are. In winter, they've decided they enjoy being snowbirds. So this year, I'm going to their house—or their RV, rather. I'm looking forward to it, too, because Pensacola's a great town with a lot to do."

"Meaning good antique stores and junkin'?"

"Exactly." Cutting my eyes at Jen, I said, "Now, would you mind putting your finger on this ribbon for me?" She did as requested, and I tied a perfect red satin bow around the box containing the Haviland china. I wasn't sure when Carleen and I would get together to celebrate, but I planned to give her the china before Thanksgiving in case she wanted to use it for her holiday entertaining.

Jen lent a hand—or a finger—while I tied bows around a few other newly wrapped gifts as well. As payment for her assistance, I promised her a sample of the easy but scrumptious pumpkin spice shortbread baking in the oven.

Once the wrapping paper, tape, and bows were out of the way, I took the first pan of cookies out and offered her some. "Want regular cocoa"—I held up the familiar packet of cocoa mix—"or their new caramel cream flavor?"

"Caramel?" Jen wrinkled her nose. "Do we have to tinker with everything?"

I grinned. "Good. I wanted the caramel anyway, and I only had one left. Came in my exhibitor gift bag at the bazaar, and this stuff is to die for."

Jen sucked in a breath, and I realized what I'd said.

"Sorry. I didn't mean that literally, of course."

Jen nodded. "I know, but wow. This town has gone nuts over the murder of Miranda Hargrove. Or Horgrave or whatever her name was."

Standing by the electric teakettle to make our mugs of cocoa, I snapped my head around to look at Jen. "What are you talking about?"

The doorbell rang, and I held up a finger. "Hold that thought." I assumed Justin was there, so I made a beeline for the front door, and after I saw a familiar head of blond hair, I opened it. "Hello again."

Justin gave me a quick peck on the cheek, his arms laden with grocery bags.

"Please tell me that isn't four bags of marinated ribs."

He laughed. "I got a little carried away at the grocery store when I stopped by this afternoon. I wasn't sure what variety of potato salad everyone liked, so I got three different kinds. And some coleslaw too."

Jen and Todd helped carry in the bags, then she and I went outside with the guys to get the meat on the grill. Todd and Justin promptly decided to pull up lawn chairs so that they could continue watching the ballgame on Todd's iPad Pro.

Once Jen and I were back in the kitchen, I reminded Jen that we had unfinished business. "Hargrove, Horgrave. What were you saying about that?"

"I guess I didn't mention it. One of the reporters checked out Miranda's hometown newspaper to see if he could get more info for our story. According to the reports he found, her name was Horgrave, not Hargrove."

I told her I'd learned that same thing earlier in the week—skipping the part about how I found out—and asked what she and the news staff thought about it.

"Not much, actually. But it did surprise me to find out she didn't go to college. These days, it turns out plenty of smart people never went to college, but considering who's on the board of Happy Hometown, I'm surprised they hired someone without a degree."

My mind whirled. "But Miranda did have a college degree. It was hanging on the wall of the Happy Hometown office when I was there yesterday morning to help Caitlyn clean up. It was from some small community college."

Jen tapped something into her cell phone.

"What are you doing?"

"Asking one of the reporters to send me that info from his notes." I watched her tap Send then look up at me. "What?"

I shook my head. "Just marveling at your ability to command the troops at any time from anywhere, including my kitchen table."

She laughed. "Multitasking is my superpower."

I pulled the second pan of pumpkin spice shortbread out of the oven, thinking it would suffice for a bite of something sweet after our barbecue dinner. I scooped the pumpkin-shaped cookies off the pan and onto a plate, and Jen snatched one and took a bite before I could stop her.

"This stuff is heavenly. You know how I love me some cookies."

I tapped her arm. "Just be sure to save room for some ribs."

Jen's phone pinged. "Ah. Here we go." She tapped the message, peered at it, and scrolled.

"Well?"

"Just like I thought. Her hometown obit says she was a graduate of Reederton High School, and that's it. No mention of a college."

"Hmm." I grabbed my phone, tapped a number, and held the phone to my ear.

"Who are you calling?"

I held up a finger as I waited for an answer. "Hi, Caitlyn. It's Emma. Sorry to interrupt you on your busy weekend with your parents, but I need to ask you about something I saw in your office yesterday. I noticed that whoever vandalized the office broke the framed diploma that Miranda had hanging on the wall. The one from...?"

"Reederton Community College?"

I stepped to the counter and scribbled the name on a sheet of notepaper. "Yeah, that's the one. Anyway, I wondered if you'd like me to bring by a new piece of glass. I'm assuming her family or someone will claim her things eventually, and it might be nice to repair that framed diploma before it's picked up."

"That's thoughtful, and yeah, that'd be great. Thanks for thinking of it."

I felt a wee bit guilty for having thought of it only at that moment. "Sure, no problem. I'll drop it off first thing Monday."

After ending the call, I turned to Jen with a smirk. "You're not the only one who knows how to conduct cell phone investigations. Reederton Community College. That's where her degree is from."

Jen frowned, then her thumbs tapped furiously on her phone. "Aha!"

"Yeah?"

"There's no such school."

"What?" I reached for her phone, and she handed it over.

"Check out the search results for yourself. Riverton. Reedley. But there's no Reederton Community College."

"Huh." I drummed my fingers on the Formica-topped table. "Isn't that strange?"

Jen chewed her lip. "Yeah. I mean, if she lied about that, what else did she lie about?"

Todd and Justin came inside to get refills on soft drinks, and I asked if it was getting too cool for them in the backyard.

"Nah, we're good," Justin said. "Thanks, though."

He closed the door, and Jen grinned at me. "If he's anything like Todd, he'd prefer to stay out there even if he's freezing to death."

"Not much danger of that around here," I said.

Our speculations about the not-what-she-seemed Miranda Hargrove-slash-Horgrave soon dried up, and Jen and I gathered bowls and platters for the chips and sides.

Before long, the kitchen door opened, and the delicious aroma of barbecue wafted through the air.

"Mm." I gave Justin a thumbs-up. "Smells as good as I remember from the last time you made that marinade. I'm not ready to eat holiday food yet, so this is perfect. When we were at Michele's open house last night, I couldn't believe how many people said they're already making cranberry sauce or turkey and dressing. I mean, I've still got leftover Halloween candy, for Pete's sake."

Jen nodded. "Us too."

I pointed toward the living room. "The candy corn is next to the TV if you want some after dinner."

"Good to know. Oh, and I saved you all the Goetze's Caramel Creams from our Halloween candy too. They're in my purse."

"No way!" I couldn't believe Jen had remembered how much I liked those.

"Hey, what are friends for?"

We all seemed to have worked up an appetite, and after we loaded our plates, we gathered around the table. Justin said grace, and soon we were chowing down on the ribs.

Jen took a break from her rib eating and leaned back. "So, were many people at that open house at the Feathered Nest? Looked like a lot of buzz downtown when I was leaving the office last night."

"It was packed." Todd pointed at a bowl of chips, and I got his wife to pass him the bowl. "Still kind of odd that so many people get into putting up the tree and cooking and baking so early in the season."

"You know when we put up the tree at my house growing up?"

I had only known Jen since moving to Roseland after college, so I shook my head. "When?"

"Christmas Eve."

"What? Were there even any left?"

"Back then, yeah. It was a tradition. Mom and Dad and all us kids had a ball while driving around town and trying to find that one last tree that wasn't completely pitiful. Then we always went home and watched *It's a Wonderful Life* while we put up the tree, ate popcorn, and drank cocoa."

"Huh." I couldn't believe I'd never heard that story before. "Sounds like a neat tradition, but I think I would have missed enjoying the decorations all through December. I can see why people like to put up their trees by Thanksgiving now." I turned to Justin. "What about your family? Did you have a tradition?"

He wiped his hands on a paper towel. "My mom adored Christmas, so we always had a tree up by Thanksgiving. In recent years, she's even started decorating the day after Halloween."

Jen had a mischievous grin. "You know what they say about putting up a tree too early?"

I stared at her. "No, I don't. What do 'they' say about it?"

"For every Christmas tree that goes up before Thanksgiving"—she laughed, bracing for her own punch line, apparently—"one of Santa's elves drowns a baby reindeer."

"Jen! You're terrible."

Todd, reaching for more potato salad, cracked up.

"Hey, I read it on Facebook, so it must be true." Jen's eyes sparkled.

"I guess we know *somebody* who's going to be on the naughty list this year. Baby reindeer, my foot." I crossed my arms and humphed. "I can't believe you're being so ugly about some of God's most magnificent creatures."

Jen rolled her eyes. "You know I'm kidding. And for your information, once Todd and I get a fence up in the spring, we're hoping to get a Labradoodle that can play in the yard."

My eyes widened. "Shh. Better not let Gerald hear you say that you want anything but a rescue puppy."

"Won't he be happy to hear that we're planning to become pet owners?" Todd asked.

"Not necessarily."

Jen motioned for another paper towel, so I passed the roll down to her.

"He thinks everyone needs at least one rescue animal before they adopt a 'designer' pet, as he puts it."

Justin added his two cents. "I don't mean to be rude, but Gerald can really turn off some people with that kind of pressure. And wouldn't that prevent him from getting the animal shelter built as fast as he wants?"

I swallowed a sip of my sweet tea. "You'd think, but this seems to be the year for pets here in Roseland. The new dog park opened in April, that new Pampered Pets boutique opened downtown in June, and the Humane Society announced the no-kill shelter campaign in July."

Justin did a double take. "You just happen to remember all that?"

I gave him a sheepish smile. "Hey, I'm an animal lover, and personally, I'm thrilled to live in a place that cares about them as much as I do. I think that speaks heaps about this community and sets Roseland apart from other small towns that aren't as pet-friendly."

Todd rose, grabbed a notepad from the counter, and jotted something down.

Jen waited for him to return to his seat. "What prompted that?"

"Look"—Todd glanced around the table—"I'm in the business of selling homes. If being a pet-friendly city is such a great selling point for Roseland, I need to include that in my listings. I had a few thoughts while Emma was talking about the pet lovers in town, and I wanted to write them down while they were fresh on my mind."

"Figures." Jen sounded resigned. "I get excited about breaking news and have to write things down, Emma gets jewelry ideas and has to write them down, and you have to write down new ways to sell a house."

I told Todd that I thought he was on to something by marketing homes in a pet-friendly community. "Why would you not? I mean, anybody who hates the sight of dogs being walked downtown or those people who get cranky at the occasional pet being carried into a store is probably not going to enjoy Roseland. We could be the Southern version of Carmel-by-the-Sea in California."

"Huh?" Jen asked.

"You know, that dog-friendly town on the coast. People come from all over just to visit there with their dogs."

Todd held up a finger. "Those who love dogs will want to hear that Roseland welcomes their pets with outstretched arms. Just another thing to love about this town. That's why it's still so odd to me when a couple comes into the real estate office and they actually want to leave here. Like Caitlyn Hill, that gal who's at the Happy Hometown program until they hire Miranda's replacement."

"You said *couple*, and I know Caitlyn's not married, so who was she with?" I asked.

"Her boyfriend, Tyler Something or Other."

"Your new artist friend?" Justin asked me.

I frowned. "I guess so."

"You're just now telling me this?" Jen demanded.

"What?" Todd shrugged. "Caitlyn said she's got a small house here, but they've decided it might be time to move away from Roseland. Something about having some bad luck here and wanting to leave it all behind."

So Caitlyn was serious about leaving town. *Is she already that serious about Tyler?* She couldn't have known him for very long. I hated knowing that Tyler apparently wasn't interested in Gus after all, although it was beginning to sound like that wasn't a bad thing. And with the news coming only one week after the murder of the Happy Hometown program's executive director, that meant the board and I would soon be looking for yet another replacement ED.

"Earth to Emma!" Jen snapped her fingers in front of my face.

"Sorry. I was thinking back to what little I know about Tyler. I was under the impression he was seeing Gus Townsend." Then I filled them in on my experiences with Caitlyn at the Happy Hometown office.

Justin chimed in, "I know you've been helping out at Caitlyn's office this week, but you didn't know she was seeing him?"

"Nope. She never mentioned it. And it certainly wasn't like she was wearing an engagement ring, or I would have noticed."

Jen scoffed. "Oh, come on. I know you live and breathe jewelry, but even you can't always notice the jewelry people are wearing."

Todd laughed. "Yeah, Emma, that's a little much, even for you."

"Humph." I pursed my lips, stood from the table, and turned my back to them. "In addition to your wedding rings, Todd, you're wearing your college class ring, which has a big sapphire in the middle, on your right hand. You're wearing an Apple watch with a black band, and on that same arm is a yellow rubber bracelet whose words I didn't read, but I imagine it's supporting some local charity. Jen, you're wearing those diamond stud earrings Todd gave you for your first anniversary, the ones set in gold. On your right hand, you're wearing the ruby-and-diamond ring that your parents gave you when you graduated from college, along with a red-and-white bead bracelet and two gold Alex and Ani bangles. One of them has a feather on it, and the other has the initial *J*."

I spun around, gave them both a smug smile, and took a seat.

Justin was first to speak. "That. Was. Awesome."

Jen wasn't impressed. "That was cheating. You gave me that feather bracelet when I got promoted at the *Daily Trib*."

I waved off her comment. "Never mind that. I want to know why Caitlyn is suddenly so serious about Tyler Montgomery. She can't have known him that long."

Todd and Justin didn't seem as fascinated by the town's romantic entanglements as Jen and I were, so I rose and began to clear the table. I got Jen to set out the shortbread and a pumpkin cheesecake I'd picked up at Mavis's, then I made pots of coffee and tea.

It was late into the evening before everyone went home, and I'd had a full but rewarding day. Only one thing about it bothered me: more news confirming that Caitlyn and Tyler were definitely a couple.

For reasons I couldn't quite explain, even to myself, I didn't like that idea. At all.

Chapter Twenty-Two

Sunday began with my personal alarm in the form of Miriam tapping my face, her not-so-subtle signal that I was in danger of sleeping past her breakfast hour. I looked forward to getting to church and hearing what Pastor Steve had to say, so I skipped breakfast, took a quick shower, and filled a to-go cup with coffee that I sipped on the drive.

The pastor continued with his sermon series on preparing our hearts for the holidays, and as luck would have it, I was sitting in the choir loft with my fellow soprano, Shareta, when he spoke on forgiveness.

"You know, friends, we don't forgive others just because they deserve it. We forgive others because of how much Jesus has already forgiven us."

I could practically feel Shareta's eyes on me, so I reached over and patted her hand. No better place than church to say, "We're good, my friend." And the grateful expression on her face was worth it.

After church, I declined Michele's offer to join her family for lunch at a local buffet. I'd eaten so much the past week that I planned to get a power walk in at the park. But first, I had some jewelry to finish in preparation for the week ahead.

Once I got home from church, I checked on Miriam, had a grilled cheese sandwich to silence my by-then-growling stomach, and set out my jewelry-making supplies. I tried not to work on Sundays, but so close to Christmas, Sunday seemed to be one of the few days of the week when I could avoid interruptions. I was deep into experimenting with an elaborate new Christmas design when my phone rang.

I'm not answering you.

I wired another bead.

Who am I kidding? I had to know who it was.

I picked up the phone, clicked on my voicemails, and listened to a message from Caitlyn. "Hey, Emma. It's Caitlyn here. Listen, I'm at the office, and I know it's Sunday afternoon, but I'd be grateful if you could bring that glass up here and help me fix Miranda's diploma. Her parents are stopping by after a while to claim her things, and if I could have that, it would really help a lot. Okay? Let me know if you can come by."

Good grief. That sure wasn't on my list of things to do that afternoon. I debated ignoring the call and kept working. Then a hedge trimmer next door cranked up so loudly that I couldn't focus on my jewelry anymore. Maybe it was a sign. Sighing, I reached for the phone and called Caitlyn back.

She picked up immediately. "Oh, good, you are there."

"Yeah, just wanted to let you know that I'm bringing that glass up, and since it's the weekend and the building isn't usually open, I wanted to be sure you're looking for me."

While I drove downtown, I remembered that she wasn't supposed to be at the office alone anyway. Maybe she wasn't too concerned about being harmed. And it might be the perfect time to tell her about my concern for her safety. It wouldn't hurt for her to be more cautious.

I knocked on the door but didn't get an answer, so I knocked louder. "Caitlyn! Caitlyn, it's me!"

A tall figure appeared from beneath the stairs and walked over to the door. When I saw a familiar paint-splattered denim jacket, I was surprised but glad I didn't have to bang on the door any longer.

"Tyler, I'm glad to see you. Caitlyn just called and—"

Then I saw the knife in his hand, and a chill ran down my spine. "Um, you know, I left something in my car and—"

I spun around, but Tyler grabbed my sweater then jerked my purse from my hand and threw it to the floor.

"Shut up." Tyler jabbed the weapon near my face. "I'm sick of you nosing around. Get up to Caitlyn's office. Now."

My heart beat so fast on the way upstairs that I feared I would have a heart attack before I got there. At the doorjamb, I heard Caitlyn sniffling inside. *Thank you, Lord. At least Caitlyn's okay.*

"I want that folder." Tyler pointed his knife at Caitlyn's left-hand desk drawer. "I know it's in there."

"Wait a minute." I looked between the two of them. "Aren't you two a couple?"

"Ha!" Tyler scoffed. "No offense"—he nodded at Caitlyn—"but I dated her just long enough to get the information I needed before I head out of this two-bit town."

Caitlyn looked shell-shocked. "I've already told you. I don't have the registration forms anymore. Here, I'll show you."

She dove into the drawer, removed an armload of folders, and plopped them onto the desk, wilting as though the effort had exhausted her.

Offering a weak smile, she spoke to Tyler like he was a dim eight-year-old. "See, the labels are right here."

I stared at the edge of Tyler's jacket and its colorful splashes of dried paint. A small spot of something white and fuzzy caught my eye.

Caitlyn rambled on, "Spring Banquet. Summer Sidewalk Sales. Fall Festival. But no Christmas Bazaar folder. The police took that one and haven't returned it." She flapped an arm around inside the deep and now-empty desk drawer. "That's it. Nothing else."

Tyler turned his attention to me, and something in his eyes scared the living daylights out of me. "You know." He stepped closer. "You figured it out, didn't you?"

I didn't until I got close enough to see that the "fuzz" was feathers from Miranda's dress.

"I don't know what you're talking about, Tyler. Why don't you have a seat, and let's get to the bottom of this? We'll take care of whatever's bothering you."

"No!" He held his knife against Caitlyn's cheek.

She gasped while I determined not to look as scared as I felt.

"I need my application for next year's bazaar, and I need it now."

Tyler was right. I had indeed figured things out—if a little late. The tiny white feathers stuck to a dab of dried paint had been there the whole time, seen at who knew how many places around town, so that white "paint" on his jacket wasn't paint at all. I stared at the spot in horrified fascination.

"What?"

I shook my head.

"You know, back before the Christmas bazaar, Miranda insisted my work wasn't fit to be in the show. She was certainly entitled to her opinion." Tyler's eyes seemed to focus on something far away. "And did I hold a grudge? No, I didn't."

You're sure holding one now, buddy.

"So I went to that rinky-dink show just to say hello to everyone and support the home team, you know?"

Since I needed to stall him, I summoned my courage. "That's not true. You went there looking to show up Miranda."

He glared at me. "And what makes you think that?"

"When you saw Savannah at the bazaar, you told her about getting excluded from the show."

"How do you know that?"

"She told me. How else? And I'm betting you didn't stop by the bazaar just to shop, did you?"

He sneered. "Everything would have been just fine. I already knew enough about Miss Perfect to put her in her place long before next year's show, but no, she asked to meet privately with me in the kitchen. 'I don't think it's a good idea for you to be here this year,' she said. 'I've heard that you're unhappy about not being in the show, and I won't have you ruining my event.'"

My heart continued to pound, and Caitlyn's pale face told me she was frightened too.

"Then when I saw her acting so high and mighty to Gerald and all those Humane Society volunteers, something just snapped, you know?"

Speaking of snapped... I looked past Tyler, who was still wielding his knife, and at Caitlyn's messy desk. The piles of paper and folders remained stacked there along with what I recognized as Miranda's old diploma still under broken glass.

"She humiliated me." He mimicked a female voice. "'Work on some better paintings for next year's show, and we'll be glad to consider your art again.'" Tyler's eyes widened, and his voice grew louder. "As if she had the final say about what is and isn't good art!"

I needed to distract him. "How did you manage to get her away from everyone? That was a pretty bold move."

"You think?" Tyler scoffed. "When she kicked the Humane Society out, she brushed past me, and I told her to watch out, that some of the new paint on my jacket might get on her precious little feathers." He glanced down and grinned. "But it turned out to be the other way around."

Absentmindedly, he gazed at the spot of white. He seemed almost proud of it. "But I'd had enough of her and told her so. Then she whirled around and bumped into me, so I had no choice but to defend myself. So I pushed back."

"Are you saying her death was an accident?" I wasn't sure I believed that.

"Of course it was! She slipped in some water that had spilled on the tile floor and banged her head on the corner of that steel table. When I saw she wasn't breathing, I panicked. I picked up the lanyard Gerald had left there and wrapped it around her neck so that it would look like someone had strangled her. Then I got out of there and—"

Caitlyn might have been speechless up to that point, but she couldn't let that comment go by. "Her body was found in Santa's bag, you lying cheat."

You go, girl.

Tyler frowned. "That was just dumb luck. I'd cleaned up the tile and realized I could haul her body off in that bag and hide it in the sleigh. I'd stepped into the supply room for more paper towels when some volunteer schmucks came through the kitchen to take the sleigh backstage, so I slipped through the storage door and snuck out behind the stage. Then I spent the afternoon at the bazaar, just like any other guest. But I didn't kill her. She slipped and fell. That's all."

Tyler's hand twitched, his knife quivering. *Is he nervous?*

"Now find my new application!" Tyler commanded. "I don't want any evidence that I ever had a cross word with Miranda. I know that letter's in here somewhere."

I had to think fast and peered up at Tyler. "You know, Caitlyn told me the other day what a mess this desk was after the vandalism. I'll bet it's still here and hidden under all this stuff."

Caitlyn shook her head. "I don't think I missed any—"

I cut her off. "Let's make sure." I let my eyes bore into her, hopefully conveying the message that she'd better agree with me—and fast.

Tyler lowered his knife, and Caitlyn and I flipped through folder after folder. Tyler walked over to the street side of the room and looked out a window. The folders had gotten mixed up, because as I flipped through a file of businesses that were owed money from the Christmas bazaar, I found Tyler Montgomery's brand-new application—and its menacing message.

"What are you reading?" He marched over and reached for my folder, but I'd already flipped over a few pages.

"I'm sorry, but I can't believe how much they got charged for those bags. I order bags for the Foothills Gallery, and this price is ridiculous. Do you know that—"

"Shut up and keep looking."

Tyler headed to the other side of Caitlyn, reached for a folder, and started flipping through it.

Once he was preoccupied with his own search, I returned to my reading and sucked in a breath. The note stapled to the top of his new application couldn't be clearer: "Don't make the same mistake next year, or you'll definitely regret it."

Not exactly subtle, are you? But at least I knew what he was looking for and why.

I had a tin of pepper spray on my key ring, but the purse and my car keys were downstairs. Then I spotted something that might be my saving grace—if Tyler didn't catch on to me first.

Caitlyn shuffled one stack of folders aside and began looking into another, so I pretended to do the same thing. Under one of the piles was that broken glass containing Miranda's diploma from the college that didn't exist. I grabbed a file folder and pretended to examine some papers inside. "Man, you guys sure have a ton of paper around here, don't you?"

Caitlyn looked confused, but Tyler appeared agitated.

"Um, Tyler, I think I may have found what you're looking for." *Dear God, please let this work.* "Come see if this is it."

I held up the frame, and Tyler crossed the space in a flash. As he neared, I slammed the diploma as hard as I could into the side of his face, and tiny shards of glass rained down on him. He howled as his hands flew to his eyes, and he dropped his knife. Seizing the moment, Caitlyn snatched the stapler off her desk and landed a well-placed blow to the other side of his head.

Caitlyn kicked the knife aside, and I grabbed the scissors, the next weapon I saw, but by that time, Tyler was on the run. "You two have lost your minds!"

As he ran down the stairs, I used the desk phone to call 911. "We need the police at the Happy Hometown office. Tyler Montgomery just threatened to kill me and Caitlyn Hill, and he's running out of the building now. Our address is—"

A shrill whistle sounded from the hallway, and I heard shouts of "Police! Put your hands up."

Caitlyn and I headed out of the office and got there in time to see two officers cuffing Tyler. Detective Shelton stood to the side and tipped his head at us.

Tyler brushed stray bits of glass from his hair and ear, and a small trickle of blood wound its way down to his shoulder on the side where Caitlyn had stapled him.

Detective Shelton asked if either of us needed medical attention, and while definitely shaken, we assured him that we were fine.

"How did you know to come up here?"

The detective blinked then frowned. "We do this little thing called investigating, and when citizens don't get in our way by trying to help, we often manage to nail the bad guy and keep him from hurting anyone else."

So much for catching up on jewelry. My Sunday afternoon was spent on yet another round of giving statements and yet another round of cleaning up the Happy Hometown office, which I hoped I'd seen the last of for a while.

Finally, I got to go home, and the jewelry could wait until Monday.

I hugged Miriam then headed to the park for my walk. Unlike the other days that week, I basked in the knowledge that there was no one I needed to be looking out for.

Chapter Twenty-Three

A knock on my front door came promptly at eight o'clock.
"Ready to go?"

"Yep. Just let me grab my purse."

As we walked to her car, Caitlyn gave me a sheepish look.

"What is it?" I asked.

She hung her head. "I just feel so stupid. I shouldn't have gotten involved with Tyler—"

You'll get no argument here.

"And if I hadn't trusted him, Gerald might not have gotten hurt."

I grimaced. "But on the bright side, I imagine you've learned some things and won't ever make those mistakes again, right? That's how I seem to learn all my lessons—the hard way."

Caitlyn looked more chipper as we fastened our seat belts and headed to Roseland Medical Center. When we walked in, Caitlyn asked whether I thought we should get some flowers from the gift shop.

"Not a bad idea." I glanced inside the small shop, and a cart was filled with gloxinias. I picked up a white one. "How about this? Nothing too girly. Hopefully, it won't die before he gets it home."

Caitlyn winced. "Please don't say die."

I raised an eyebrow. "Sorry."

After paying for the plant, we stopped by the information desk, confirmed Gerald's room number, and asked if it was okay to visit him. A gray-haired man in a pink volunteer jacket pulled up something on a computer. "He's approved for visitors, so you're welcome to go on in."

We got on the elevator, and Caitlyn looked nervous.

"He's going to be fine," I assured her. "Gus spoke to him last night and said he may even get discharged in another day or two."

"Thank goodness."

We got to the room, and I tapped lightly on the door. "Gerald? Are you up?"

"Come in."

We stepped inside, and the scene wasn't what I'd expected. Gus sat in the visitors' chair, and posters, brochures, and folders were spread out all over the bed and on the wheeled tray table hovering over it.

"What on earth is all this?"

A nurse on the other side of Gerald's bed arched an eyebrow. "It's a hot mess, if you ask me. I told Gerald he needs to stay still and rest, but he insisted that if he couldn't work, he was going home. At least we can monitor him here."

Gerald smiled. "Welcome to the satellite office of the Humane Society, ladies."

"Are you being a bad patient?"

The nurse's head bobbed up and down, but Gerald assured me, "Absolutely not."

I turned to Gus. "Care to explain?"

She shrugged out of her velvet-collared denim jacket and stood. "You know how I've been planning to have some of my artwork as a fundraiser to support the new shelter? When I told Gerald that I had the sketches ready, he asked to see them. He figures if all he can do is lie in bed for a day or two, at least he can do something productive for the society."

I shook my head. "Just can't give it a rest, can you?"

Caitlyn stepped up and offered Gerald the plant. "We brought you something from the Happy Hometown office. To wish you a quick recovery."

Gerald pointed at the windowsill, which was already brimming with flowers. "Can you squeeze it in there?"

Caitlyn moved swiftly to the window, regrouped a few of the flowers, and made a spot for the glox. "There."

"I'll leave you folks to it. And Gerald, please behave if you want out of here anytime soon." The nurse waggled a finger in warning as she exited the room.

Gerald slowly sat up straighter and peered at Caitlyn. "I'm just glad you're okay. Things could've really ended up bad, you know."

"I do." Caitlyn sighed. "And again, I'm so sorry you got hurt."

"Stop. You had nothing to do with that maniac, and I don't want you to give it another thought. Our justice system will take care of him, and whether he deliberately killed Miranda or not, we know he deliberately hurt me."

"I appreciate that, but seriously, if there's anything I can do..."

Gerald grinned. "Actually, there is something."

"Yeah?" Caitlyn looked happy for the first time that day.

"Turns out that one of the fringe benefits of my getting attacked is that some folks in town have made gifts to the Humane Society, and we've hit our fundraising goal for the year. We'll break ground on the new shelter sometime next year, and I'd like for the Happy Hometown program to spearhead the drive to help furnish it."

He held up his hands as if imagining a billboard. "Your motto can be Roseland: Home of the Happiest Pets in Georgia."

"Just Georgia?" I observed wryly. "Why not the Southeast? Or the whole country?"

Gerald sniffed. "You really ought to lighten up a little, Emma. But I have a favor to ask you too."

"Oh?"

"We got a new batch of kittens in, and almost all of them got adopted pretty quickly. I was fostering the last one, a sweet little calico named Hattie, and I need someone to take care of her while I re-cuperate."

Hattie? I lifted an eyebrow. "Can't your mom take care of her?"

He shook his head. "My mom's severely allergic to cats."

I sighed. "Do you have an extra house key?"

Gerald was beaming. "I thought you'd never ask." He reached under the array of papers and pulled out an envelope. He handed it over, and it had my name written on it.

"How did you know I'd say yes?"

He laughed. "Just a guess."

Chapter Twenty-Four

The rest of my Monday was an absolute whirl. After leaving the hospital, I'd gone by Gerald's house to pick up Hattie, my new foster kitten, from a grateful if sneezing Mrs. Adams. Then I stopped by the Humane Society office to pick up some pet food, kitty toys, and other supplies that Gerald had waiting for me.

Once home, I settled Hattie in the kitchen and explained to Miriam that the situation was only temporary. She'd looked puzzled to see the new feline in her territory, but when I took Hattie out of her carrier and encouraged her to explore, Miriam seemed merely curious. Soon, she and Hattie were nudging each other like old friends.

With my unexpected pet volunteer job having taken up much of the morning, I was feeling a little panicked when I finally got home. I grabbed my jewelry supply cases, tuned in to some jazz on Pandora, and got an assembly line going. Working diligently, I made eight new Ruby & Doris bracelets, which I dropped off at the Feathered Nest later that afternoon. I also packaged and mailed some of the Christmas tree pins that I'd sold online—but not the Hattie Carnegie one. I'd decided that taking care of a new kitten named Hattie, even temporarily, was a sign that the pin should remain a part of my own vintage jewelry collection.

The arts council was meeting weekly before taking a break for the holidays, and I had a feeling I knew what at least one of the topics at that night's meeting would be. I still couldn't believe that Tyler had fooled us all for so long, and I was curious to hear what the others had to say about him.

At five, I closed down the jewelry production for the day, freshened my makeup, and microwaved some minestrone for a quick supper. I didn't have any new jewelry to share, but I did have the new prints of my work, and I needed help deciding which ones to send to the Jewelry Artisans of the Southeast for their official printed program. I had my favorites, but my friends on the arts council were savvy about things like that and might have tips on which photos would appeal to customers.

Arriving early for a change, I entered the library meeting room and found Trish and Shareta poring over a magazine article. They motioned me over.

"Check this out." Trish pointed at a two-page spread. "Shareta's baskets are written up in *Georgia Trend* this month."

"Seriously? We've never been able to break in there before. How'd you do it?"

"Pure luck." Shareta grinned. "Remember when you sold all those baskets to that tour group from Gatlinburg last week? One of those tourists was the mother of a *Georgia Trend* editor. She saw her mom's basket and actually took time to read the tiny tag tucked inside. That editor had just had a writer drop the ball on a feature at the last minute, so she got a piece on Shareta in literally hours before going to press."

My eyes widened. "I'm sure you're glad you include those tags."

"Mm-hmm. And you can bet I'm gonna keep doing them."

Voices in the hallway caught our attention, and Gus walked in, followed by Savannah, Bob, and Martha. Gus was carrying a big box of doughnuts from the Cupcake Café and invited each of us to have one.

I stared at her, puzzled. "But you're not a fan of sugar and always go for the salty snacks. What gives?"

Gus reached for a bubblegum-pink doughnut with colorful jimmies on top. "Comfort food." She shrugged. "You'd need a little sugar, too, if you realized you'd been going out with a murderer."

"Hear! Hear!" Savannah reached for an iced chocolate doughnut. "And they say he'll be charged with manslaughter and not murder anyway. So technically, you were just dating a manslaughter-er."

"Oh, that helps a lot, sis." Gus dumped her tapestry tote bag into a chair then grabbed a bottled water that she'd plopped next to her doughnut.

"We're early, guys, but let's cut to the chase," Trish said. "For obvious reasons, I'm withdrawing that suggestion I emailed all of you asking that we consider Tyler Montgomery for a spot on the arts council board. Can I assume there's no opposition to that?"

"Hardly!" Gus closed her eyes and shivered. "Thank goodness we never actually voted to have him on here."

Shareta stopped eating her lemon-filled powdered doughnut, her hand poised in midair. "I've been dying to ask—were you as floored as the rest of us when we found out he's the one who killed Miranda?"

Gus sighed. "I must have asked myself that question a hundred times in the past twenty-four hours. I knew Tyler talked about Miranda and asked about the investigation a lot, but at the time, I didn't think he was that much more curious than the rest of us."

"How did you hear about his arrest?" I asked.

She nodded at Savannah. "Little goes on in this town without my sister hearing about it. One of her friends saw the commotion uptown yesterday afternoon and called to tell her."

Savannah grinned. "And one of Paul's friends has a son on the force, so he made a few calls and found out what happened. Turns out they knew all along that Miranda wasn't actually strangled, and when some paint showed up on the feathers of her costume, that helped them narrow down the suspects."

Trish's head bobbed up and down. "And Tyler was in Erin's photos from the bazaar, but of course I had no reason to ever imagine that he was a suspect."

I shook my head. "Only an idiot would think they could get away with anything in a town like Roseland." I sat back in my seat and crossed my arms. "But Tyler seemed like such a nice guy. And when I finally saw his art, I thought he was really good."

"Well, he'll have to be painting in his jail cell from now on." Martha, who was polishing off one of Mavis's coveted bacon-sprinkled, maple-glazed doughnuts, wrinkled her nose. "He's brought shame on this town and the bazaar, and I hope he gets the sentence he deserves, even if the victim *was* somebody like Miranda."

Bob added his two cents. "Jimmy says he's just glad the whole thing's over with. He said complaints about Miranda kept landing on his desk, and he's learned the hard way to do a background check on the next person he hires."

Shareta made eye contact with me, and we shared grins.

"Why didn't he do one this time?" she asked Bob.

"This goes no further than this room"—Bob looked around the table—"but Jimmy was busy with his reelection campaign back then and got one of the interns to do it. Later found out his daughter's boyfriend didn't exactly do a thorough job."

No wonder the mayor seemed embarrassed about the whole sorry episode.

Trish cleared her throat. "Now that the unpleasantness is out of the way, let's talk about next year's plans. Savannah, I believe you're working on a special piece for your parents' fiftieth anniversary. Want to tell us about it?"

Savannah grinned. "I'm doing watercolors of historic locations around town, and they're going in a book that will be printed and sold in their honor—with proceeds benefiting the arts council for years to come."

Excited chatter filled the table.

"What will it look like?"

"How many paintings will be in it?"

"How much will it cost to print it?"

Savannah held up a hand. "Gus is spearheading most of the production, and all I have to worry about are the paintings. Oh, and Emma?"

"Yes?"

"We want to commission a special piece of jewelry to be presented to our mom the night of the celebration. Would you be interested? We'll need it finished fairly soon after New Year's."

I had Christmas to get through, a prestigious regional jewelry show to prepare for, new pieces to design, and oh yes, a new foster kitten to care for.

But who could turn down a job like that? Besides, surely everything would calm down in Roseland after Christmas.

I smiled and said, "I'd be honored."

Pumpkin Spice Shortbread

1/2 cup softened butter (no substitutions)

1/4 cup packed brown sugar

1 cup + 2 tablespoons all-purpose flour

1 teaspoon pumpkin pie spice

Preheat oven to 300 degrees. Cream butter and sugar using an electric mixer. Gradually stir in flour and spice. When blended, turn out onto a lightly floured surface and knead till smooth, about 3 minutes. I like to use a rolling pin that flattens the dough into a perfect 3/8-inch thickness before cutting out the cookies with various cookie cutters. Place cookies 1 inch apart on ungreased cookie sheet, prick with a fork, and bake for 25 minutes, just until bottoms are beginning to brown. Yields about 20 (2- to 3-inch) cookies.

Indian Butter Chicken

2 pounds boneless, skinless chicken breasts or thighs (I've used fresh as well as frozen)

1 small onion, sliced

6 garlic cloves, chopped

3 teaspoons cardamom

2 teaspoons curry

1-1/4 teaspoons coriander

1 teaspoon cumin

1/2 teaspoon black pepper

1/2 teaspoon cayenne pepper

1/2 teaspoon ground ginger

1/4 teaspoon cloves

1/4 teaspoon cinnamon

1/4 teaspoon nutmeg

4 tablespoons butter

1 (6-ounce) can tomato paste

2 tablespoons lemon juice

1 can coconut milk (light is okay)

1 cup plain yogurt (I use fat-free Greek yogurt)

Place chicken in five-quart slow cooker and add onion, garlic, and spices. Add the butter and tomato paste, then add lemon juice and coconut milk. Place cover on slow cooker and cook on high for 4 hours or low for 8 hours. Fifteen minutes before serving, add yogurt. Chicken will be very tender and can be shredded easily with a fork. Serve over rice with wedges of naan, a flatbread, on the side. Yields 8-10 servings.

Acknowledgments

My husband, Alex McRae, remains my greatest fan, and I can't imagine what it would be like to write without the love and support of a husband who is also a writer. I am blessed!

My friend Joy Breedlove is also my beta reader, and I take her kind and thoughtful advice to heart because I know it comes from the heart of a fellow cozy mystery lover.

Much gratitude goes to my editors at Red Adept Publishing, Sara Gardiner and Susie Driver, whose fine efforts improved this book at every step along the way. These two ladies entertained all my odd, picky, and just plain curious questions with grace, and I am fortunate to have been able to work with them.

Some folks would give you the shirts off their backs, but Lori Bloss gave me the pendant off her neck, which I have worn and enjoyed ever since, so it was fun to feature it in this book. Similarly, my college pal Nancy Tucker remembered me admiring her gorgeous hobo bag one day and, when she tired of it, shipped it to me. The thoughtful Ann Hendrix gave me some gorgeous vintage clip-on earrings at Sunday school one morning, so those appear in my story as well. Girlfriends, please note: You don't need to clutch your jewelry and purses in my presence. I just seem to know a lot of generous women!

A dear friend I met through my Tea With Friends blog, Ginger Cato, shared my all-time-favorite slow cooker recipe with me years ago, and I happily share it with you in this book. Another blog-reader friend, Sandy Maniscalco, shared a favorite shortbread recipe that I also make with pumpkin pie spice—with great results.

And yes, in case you wondered, Ruby Webster Powell and Doris Lee Howell were my grandmothers, though they would have been the great-grandmothers of Emma, who is inspired by my oldest niece, Madison Horton. Although Madison was a baby when she met the real-life Ruby and Doris, she did indeed have the privilege of meeting these two amazing women.

WONDERING WHAT ALL of Emma's great finds look like? Don't know a Hattie Carnegie Christmas tree pin from an Eisenberg Ice one? Check out my Pinterest board for *Rubies and Revenge* by visiting https://www.pinterest.com/angelawmcrae/rubies-and-re-venge-by-angela-mcrae/

About the Author

Angela McRae began her writing career as a newspaper reporter, initially covering the police beat and then moving on to features. In a small local bookstore, Angela came across Laura Childs's *Death by Darjeeling*, a tea shop mystery set in Charleston, SC. As a longtime tea lover, she had to try it, and she's been hooked on cozy mysteries ever since.

Angela currently lives with her husband in Georgia. When she's not writing, she enjoys traveling, cooking, going to afternoon tea with family and friends, and "junkin'" at flea markets and antique malls, where she often finds inspiring artifacts that wind up in her stories. She also writes a monthly cooking column for a local publication, the *Coweta Shopper*, and enjoys connecting with readers who love to cook.

Read more at https://angelamcrae.com.

About the Publisher

Dear Reader,

We hope you enjoyed this book. Please consider leaving a review on your favorite book site.

Visit https://RedAdeptPublishing.com to see our entire catalogue.

Don't forget to subscribe to our monthly newsletter to be notified of future releases and special sales.

Made in the USA
Middletown, DE
06 November 2021

51749989R00146